"Look," Alex said, "I hear you about not wanting to stir things up with your friends. So if you tell me to leave you alone, I will. But I don't wanna play games with you, Dana. I like you a lot. I think you are, like, *really* pretty. And I'd like to hang out with you more."

"Alex—" I broke off, huffing a bit, but I was smiling. I couldn't help it. I could feel the electrons vibrating in the air between us, like they were buzzing loud enough to make a sound, like I could hear them over the music. "I'm sorry," was the best I could come up with.

I looked at him one more time before I walked away.

Also by Katie Cotugno

How to Love

99 Days

Top Ten

9 Days and 9 Nights

Fireworks

Katie Cotugno

BALZER + BRAY
An Imprint of HarperCollins*Publishers*

Balzer + Bray is an imprint of HarperCollins Publishers.

Produced by Alloy Entertainment
30 Hudson Yards, New York, NY 10001
www.alloyentertainment.com

Library of Congress Control Number: 2016938959
ISBN 978-0-06-296393-2

Typography by Liz Dresner
20 21 22 23 PC/LSCH 10 9 8 7 6 5 4 3 2 1
❖
Revised paperback edition, 2020

For one J. Taylor Hanson, who taught me a good amount about love and about music, and for one R. Sierra Rooney, who probably didn't think I would follow through

ONE

Jonah Royce threw a rager in the field behind his stepdad's house the night after high school graduation, which is why Olivia and I were both so unbelievably hungover on the afternoon everything changed.

"Just kill me," Olivia said, leaning back in her ancient beanbag chair so her long dark hair brushed the carpet. "Seriously, just bludgeon me to death with the phone book and get it over with."

I grinned. "I would love to do that for you, truly, but then I'd have to move." We were sprawled in her rec room, chugging water and watching *Live More! With Junia Jerricksen*, this low-budget, long-airing talk show both of us had been obsessed with since we were twelve. It had a weird, tinkling theme song that we found hilarious, half eighties hair band and half cha-cha; in ninth grade we'd made up a dance to it that we still did sometimes if we were feeling particularly ridiculous. We'd done it last night in Olivia's front yard, both of us stinking of wine coolers, giggling so hard we fell down right on the grass and had woken up this morning with bright green stains on our knees.

Thinking of the wine coolers turned my stomach, even though it was after four in the afternoon and we'd been sitting in these exact spots for most of the day, both of us still in our pajamas. The party had been a big one, the first in what promised to be a long summer full of them—everybody in our graduating class wanting to say good-bye to one another as many times as possible, never mind the fact that nobody was really even leaving town come fall.

Well. Almost nobody. I glanced over at Olivia, then back at the TV.

"Are you girls going to hide out in this cave all day?" Mrs. Maxwell called from the top of the short staircase that led up to the kitchen. Olivia's house was a split-level, somebody always just up or down; the walls in the basement were all covered in fake wood paneling, which Mrs. Maxwell complained about constantly but which I'd always kind of liked.

"That's the plan!" Olivia called back. "It's too hot to go outside."

"Well, you're not wrong about that," Mrs. Maxwell said. Mrs. Maxwell hated the heat in Georgia; she'd grown up in the Northeast and her accent still tended that way, all hard consonants and a general air of impatience. "Olivia," she continued, "get your laundry out of the dining room before your father comes home, at least. I folded it for you, because I'm nice. And then you need to tell me if you're going to do that Orlando thing or what."

With some effort, I pried my head off the beanbag. "What Orlando thing?"

"Oh!" Olivia said. "I meant to tell you about this last night, but then I got so"—she glanced at her mom, who was peering down at us dubiously—"*distracted* that I forgot. Please hold." She heaved herself off the beanbag and up the stairs, moving more than either of us had moved all day.

Mrs. Maxwell was unconvinced, but she didn't press it, crossing her arms and leaning against the paneling. She was wearing one of the sleeveless collared blouses she had in a dozen different patterns—bright pink flowers today; Olivia always joked that she bought them in bulk at Moms "R" Us.

"You staying for dinner?" Mrs. Maxwell asked me now.

"Yes, ma'am," I said. "Thank you."

Mrs. Maxwell nodded. We went through this every night, or most of them; I spent so much time at Olivia's house that in ninth grade her mom had finally just dropped the pretense entirely and put another twin bed in Olivia's room for me. I appreciated the way she never assumed about dinner, though, both of us keeping up our nightly charade that my mom might actually be cooking something I'd want to go home and eat.

Olivia returned a moment later holding a newspaper, which she parachuted down onto the carpet as her mom headed back upstairs to the kitchen. "Voilà!" she said, waving her arms grandly, all dorky talent-show dramatics. "I give you the Orlando thing."

I leaned halfway off the beanbag and braced one palm flat on the carpet, scanning the page: Guy Monroe, the superproducer behind super*star* Tulsa MacCreadie, was looking for teenage performers to join a new girl group. He was holding auditions in New York, California, and Dallas—plus a round in Florida, four hours south of where we lived. I looked back at Olivia, wrinkling my nose. "You're going to be a pop star?" I asked.

"I mean, I'm gonna audition." She mimicked my skeptical face, then turned it into an exaggerated grimace, the kind of overblown expression that would have read from the back row of a theater. "Maybe. Why, do you think that's dumb?"

"No," I said immediately. "I mean, sure, yes, a little, but you should still do it." Olivia had been performing as long as I'd known her, voice lessons and dance recitals and regional theater out of Atlanta. I spent basically our entire childhood making her entertain me on car rides and during long afternoons in the hammock in her backyard: *Olivia, sing "Cherish" again. Sing that Carole King song. Sing "Like a Prayer."* "I actually think it's kind of a great idea."

Olivia looked at the paper again, then back at me. "Yeah?" she asked, suddenly sounding unsure.

"Absolutely," I promised, ready to cheerlead. I glanced over in her direction; she was wearing the CLASS OF '97 T-shirt we'd all gotten during senior week, the neck cut out so it showed off her sharp collarbones—*almost too sharp*, I noticed with a frown. I pushed the thought away and gazed back at the TV, where Junia was encouraging a woman whose husband had cheated on her with his own stepsister to get back at him with a sexy makeover and learn to love herself again. "Why not, right?"

"Right." Olivia sat back in her own beanbag, considering. "Do you have plans for this weekend?" she asked me. Then, without waiting for an answer: "Will you come with?"

"What, to Orlando? I can't." I shook my head. "I have to get job applications this weekend." Until two days ago I'd waited tables at Taquitos, a fake-Mexican restaurant that left me smelling like red onions and fry grease at the end of every shift, but back in the spring four people had gotten food poisoning from the chimichangas, and earlier this week, my manager, Virginia, had announced that we were closing, effective immediately.

"Get them next week," Olivia suggested, like a person who didn't rely on a paycheck to pay for things like bus fare and tampons. When she grinned, it was all optimism. "Come on, it'll be fun. We'll stay in a hotel, swim in the pool.

Plus, maybe Tulsa will be there and he'll fall madly in love with you, and then you won't need a job at all."

I snorted. "Seems like a solid plan. Definitely something to bank on."

"I'm serious," she wheedled. "I mean, not about the Tulsa part. Well, maybe about the Tulsa part! But mostly about needing your best-friend services."

I hesitated. It was tempting, if only for the chance to spend some extra time with her. Olivia was headed to Georgia Southern University come the middle of August, while I'd stay here, living at my mom's and working whatever job I could get. It was fine—it wasn't like I'd ever harbored any delusions about going to college, and I knew Olivia and I would still be friends. It would just be . . . different. "I wish," I said finally. "We'll do a road trip later this summer or something, once I find another job."

Olivia sighed theatrically. "You're very boring," she said, but there was no heat behind it. She always got why I had to work.

"I am," I agreed, leaning all the way back the same way she had earlier, my long hair pooling on the floor. Olivia had used the crimping iron on it before the party last night, though now it was mostly frizz. I probably ought to have gone up and showered before dinner, but I was comfortable where I was: the basement smell of air-conditioning and deeper down of mildew, the hum of the dehumidifier working away in the corner near the laundry room. The shelves were stuffed with games and toys we hadn't touched since we were little—Connect Four and a bin full of Barbies, plus a Fisher-Price dollhouse we'd played with until we were way too old for it, swearing each other to secrecy. It felt peaceful down here. It felt safe.

"Later this summer," I promised again, as Junia closed out her hour by imploring her studio audience to *Live Life Forward!*, everyone bursting into riotous applause. My hangover was mostly gone, just the faintest pulse behind my eyeballs. "Unless, you know, you're too famous by then."

"Obviously," Olivia said, thrusting her chin into the air with great fanfare. Both of us laughed out loud.

"You want me to drive you home?" she asked after dinner. We'd had pork chops and orange carrots, debated the merits of Whitney Houston versus Madonna as optimal audition material. As we loaded the dishwasher, she was leaning toward Celine Dion.

I shook my head. "I can walk it." It wasn't actually that far at all from Olivia's house to mine, five blocks up and four blocks over; we'd been on the same bus route since kindergarten, which was how we'd become friends to begin with. Still, you'd never have mistaken them for the same neighborhood. On Olivia's street, the houses were small but impeccably tidy, proud flowers lining neatly paved front walks and freshly washed minivans tucked under the carports.

My street was . . . not like that.

The TV was flickering blue when I let myself in through the side door, my mom on the sofa with her bare feet up on the coffee table. The curtains on the windows were pulled tightly shut. "I'm home," I called, but I didn't get an answer. I thought she might be asleep. Something smelled rotten in the kitchen garbage, so I tied the bag off and brought it to the alley outside, glass bottles clinking together inside the plastic. My mom's grubby white terrier, Elvis, sniffed around my feet.

I was putting another trash bag in the bin when my mom came into the kitchen and gasped, grabbing on to the counter for balance. "Jesus Christ, Dana, you scared the shit out of me."

"Sorry," I told her. She was wearing one of my tank tops and a pair of denim cutoffs, her hair scooped into a stubby tail at the crown of her head. Also, she was drunk. "I said hi when I came in."

My mother ignored me. "Do you have any cash on you, baby?" she asked, her gaze the tiniest bit slow to focus. "I want to run out and grab something for dinner."

I shook my head. "Sorry," I said again, cringing at how bitchy I felt, but also sincerely doubting that what she was after was money for food. I didn't have a job anymore, I reminded myself. I couldn't be floating her all the time. "I already ate."

My mom rolled her eyes at that, knowing I'd been at

Olivia's; she'd never liked the Maxwells. She thought they were snobs. "Well," she said, "good for you."

"I'm sorry," I said for the third time in thirty seconds. Then, even though it was barely dark out, the endless start-of-summer twilight still visible out the kitchen window: "I'm gonna go to bed."

I shut the door to my bedroom behind me and sat down on the sagging mattress. I thought about Olivia leaving in the fall. I considered my last paycheck from Taquitos, sixty-five dollars and a handful of change that was all the money I had in the world, and imagined the future stretching out in front of me in a wide, flat expanse of nothing but this. Finally, I got up and went for the phone in the hallway, stretched the cord all the way back to my room.

"Hey," I said when Olivia answered. "You still want me to come?"

TWO

A tropical storm hit central Florida the afternoon of Olivia's audition in Orlando, thunder bellowing and lightning skittering across the horizon like the sky itself was cracking open, like all hell was literally breaking loose.

"I thought it would be fancier," I said, squinting through the torrential rain at the huge stucco building, the wipers on Olivia's scruffy little Toyota barely up to the task of sluicing water off the windshield. Guy Monroe's studios were tucked away at the far side of an industrial park off I-4 and, from the outside at least, resembled an airplane hangar more than any concert venue I'd ever seen. "Didn't you kind of picture it fancier?"

"Honestly, I was trying not to picture it at all," Olivia confessed, both hands still gripping the steering wheel hard enough to rip it out entirely. She'd already put the car in park.

"Uh-oh," I said. I'd figured this might happen—for a person who'd been performing as long as she had, and who loved it so enormously much, Olivia was plagued by crazy bouts of stage fright. She'd practically climbed the curtains before her senior solo in the spring chorus concert a couple of months earlier, leaving me running backstage and threatening to sing the whole thing for her in a Donald Duck voice before she pulled it together and knocked it out of the park. "You nervous?"

"Something like that," Olivia said, staring at her locked white knuckles instead of over at me. "Maybe we should just go home," she suggested, her voice artificially bright. "I don't really need to be doing this. I'm supposed to go to college in September, remember? Education is very important."

I snorted. "Education is very important," I agreed, though as of this summer I was personally done with mine once and for all—and, I reminded myself, glad about it. "But there's no way I'm letting you turn around now. Sorry. We have to go in."

"Why?" Olivia wailed.

"Lots of reasons," I told her. "One, because I have to pee, and two, because I want to see if Tulsa is in there scoping out all the hot young talent. And, you know, three, because of your audition."

"Since when are you interested in Tulsa?" Olivia asked, ignoring that last part, but at least looking over at me now, distracted, which was a good sign.

"I'm not, particularly," I defended myself. "I've just never seen a famous person before."

"Hot Rod Davison," Olivia pointed out, and I laughed. Hot Rod Davison owned half a dozen car dealerships around Jessell and ran low-budget commercials on local TV where you could practically see his toupee flapping in the breeze. He'd come into Taquitos back in the spring, failed to tip, then told me I was a pretty girl and asked me if I wanted to "get out of here" with him.

"Hot Rod Davison is definitely not famous." I shook my head. "Come on," I urged, reaching behind me and digging her makeup bag and sheet music out of the backseat. "We drove all this way."

This was a bluff on my part—honestly, I would have been happy to turn around and head right back to Jessell, if I'd thought that was what Olivia really wanted. This trip had been worth it for the drive alone, as far as I was concerned—the two of us eating green grapes out of a cooler Mrs. Maxwell had packed, the windows rolled down and the Top 40 station blaring. I'd spent a good part of my high school career in this car, my bare feet up on the dashboard. I didn't know how many more drives we'd have.

In any case, I knew that turning around and fleeing wasn't what Olivia was actually after. Freaking out was just part of her process. We went through this every time she had a big performance; it was my job as second-in-command to help her get out of her own way. "You've got this," I promised now, knowing that all I needed to do was get her through the door of the studio, and she'd take care of the rest. "Come on, it's me. I wouldn't let you go in there and look stupid."

Olivia nodded, leaning her head back against the driver's seat. "I know," she said, the rain still hammering on the hood of the car. "I just really want it, you know? A big national gig like this? I've wanted it my whole life."

I did know, actually. I knew it by the way her feet were always covered in gnarly blisters from dancing, and the half dozen original Broadway cast recordings littering the floor of her car at this very moment. Olivia was going someplace; I'd known that about her since we were little. By now, the only question was where.

"Well then," I said, unbuckling my seat belt and opening the door before she had any more time to protest. "Let's go get it for you."

The two of us dashed through the downpour and up a short flight of concrete stairs; my ponytail was sodden by the time we made it through the heavy glass doors at the front of the building, raindrops dripping from my eyelashes and the end of my nose. The studios weren't much nicer inside than out, I thought, breathing hard, taking a moment to get my bearings: concrete floors and high ceilings, the faint reek of old sweat hanging low in the air. A giant framed poster of Tulsa MacCreadie filled one wall, while directly in front of us was a large lobby lined with black leather couches and armchairs occupied by more than a dozen other girls, all of whom had looked up at the commotion we'd made coming inside.

I'd been right about Olivia. Nervous as she was, she strode right up to the front desk and introduced herself to the woman standing behind it—all confidence, just like I'd known she'd be once we made it in here. "Hi," she said as another muffled roll of thunder rumbled outside. "I'm here for the audition."

I ran around the corner to the bathroom while Olivia filled out an attendance sheet; when I got back she was having her Polaroid taken, her hair somehow immaculately smooth in spite of the humidity. My ponytail was a lank, ratty mess. "Have a seat," the assistant told us. She was tall and black and elegant looking, dressed in a starched white button-down. A watch with a brown leather strap hugged her narrow wrist. "I'll call your name when it's your turn."

The waiting room was full of girls around our age—mostly white, mostly beautiful, mostly wearing expensive-looking dance clothes. I felt myself shrink a little, glancing down at my fraying jean shorts and dollar-store flip-flops. I'd seen Olivia in any number of plays and concerts and recitals, flanked by willowy girls in full stage makeup, but it was different to be surrounded by them. It was like accidentally wandering into the middle of a pat of flamingos.

"I know," Olivia said quietly, reading my mind as we walked over. "They're horrible. And you see the same ones at every audition down here. A bunch of fake bitches in

Capezio trying to out-nice one another." As if to illustrate, she pasted a grin on her face. "Lauren!" she cooed, opening her arms to a brunette in a pink velour sweat suit. "Hi!"

I shook my head, smirking to myself. No matter how many times I saw Olivia turn it on like that—pitching her voice a couple of octaves higher, smile going wide like she had Vaseline on her teeth—it never failed to surprise and sort of impress me. Showbiz Olivia, I called her, as if she were a different person entirely. Sometimes she'd do it just to make me laugh.

It was a long, tedious afternoon. The assistant, whose name was Juliet, called name after name off her clipboard; girls headed down the hallway and emerged less than five minutes later looking either pleased or gutted, a dramatic tableau. Some of them hugged their waiting mothers—it was all moms here, I noticed, all of them the same shade of pale and plucked and sanitized, like grocery-store chickens—and others simply stalked out the door. I perched on the arm of a leather sofa and wished Mrs. Maxwell had come with us. At the very least we would have had a snack.

The rain had finally stopped; I was about to ask Olivia if she thought we could go outside for a while when the door to the audition room slammed open and Guy Monroe himself—or at least, a man I assumed was Guy Monroe—strode into the waiting room and surveyed the crowd of hopefuls, looking impatient. "Who's next?" he demanded. "Actually, more to the point, is there anybody here who is not planning to completely waste my time?"

I snorted in disbelief—I couldn't help it. There was something about him that struck me as funny—cartoonish, almost, like he should have been smoking a cigar and wearing a solid gold watch, a walking, talking Looney Tune. In reality, he was just an average-looking guy in his forties with a bit of a paunch around his middle, starting to lose some hair on the top of his head. But he had the bearing of someone much bigger, and so everyone acted as if he were. There was a lesson to be learned there, I thought in the millisecond before I realized that just as I was staring openly at Guy Monroe, sizing him up for my own amusement—he was staring openly back at me.

"Who are you?" he wanted to know.

I froze where I was sitting. For a second I actually forgot how to speak. "Oh," I said once I'd recovered, feeling myself blush and not entirely sure why. "I'm not—I'm just here to—I mean, I'm not auditioning."

"Why not?" Guy shrugged and made a face like, *don't be difficult.* Then, without waiting for me to answer: "Can you sing?"

I hesitated. The short answer was *No, of course not.* The long answer was *Kind of, but only the backup parts.* On the car ride down here—and for as long as I had known her—Olivia had sung the lead. I glanced over at her now, both of us wide-eyed, then back at Guy. "A little?"

"A little," Guy repeated, sounding bored. "What's your

name, girl who can sing a little?"

"Dana Cartwright," I managed after a moment. My tongue felt too big for my mouth.

"Finally, we have a straight answer. Dana Cartwright," he announced to Juliet, who was standing to his side like a lieutenant. "Come with me."

I hesitated. Normally I wasn't the kind of person who was easily intimidated, who let herself be bossed around by noisy, hawkish men she didn't know. On top of which, this was Olivia's thing. But already it felt impossible to argue with Guy, like the force field around him was too strong to be resisted by mere mortals. When I looked at Olivia again, she nodded once.

Guy and Juliet led me down the hall and through a doorway into a big room with shiny hardwood floors and one whole wall lined with mirrors. Two other people sat behind a folding table, pens poised to take notes—a guy in his thirties who introduced himself as Lucas, a voice coach, and a Hispanic woman named Charla dressed in dance clothes. Guy took his seat at the end of the table, looking at me expectantly.

"I didn't bring anything to sing," I explained, unsure why I was having so much trouble communicating the reality of this ridiculous situation. "Like, I really wasn't planning to audition, I just came here for my friend."

"*Like,* sing 'Happy Birthday,'" Guy said, imitating me in a voice that was decidedly unflattering. "I don't care."

That made me mad, the idea that this guy was trying to cow me. Who the hell did Guy Monroe think he was? I wasn't here to impress him, or any of them. He was the one who'd dragged me back here to begin with. I felt my spine get straighter. I pushed my shoulders back. "Fine," I said, hearing more than a trace of attitude in my voice and knowing they could probably hear it, too. *Good*, I thought. *Let 'em hear.* "'Happy Birthday,' then."

It was unremarkable, all things considered. At least I didn't have to worry about forgetting the words. My voice cracked on the third *birthday*, and I couldn't keep myself from wincing, but all four of them just kept on watching impassively, their faces impossible to read.

"Um, okay," I said when I was finally finished. The coaches were still peering at me silently. It was probably the strangest moment of my life. "Thank you."

"Thank you, Dana," Charla said. "We'll let you know."

Yeah, I thought, shaking my head a little. *I'll bet.*

Olivia's eyes were big and bright as UFOs when I came back out into the lobby. She scooted over to make room for me on the leather couch. "I cannot believe that just happened," she whispered.

I was about to reply, but Juliet had followed me out into the lobby, looking right past me as if I were completely anonymous, like the last ten minutes had all been a dream. "Olivia Maxwell," she called, looking at her clipboard. "You're up."

It was pouring again that night as we hunkered down in our hotel room, which boasted HBO and a view of the half-flooded parking lot. There was an indoor pool, according to the girl behind the check-in desk, so in theory we could have gone swimming despite the weather, but Olivia didn't want to. "I hate indoor pools," she said, kicking off her sandals and flinging herself onto the bed. "It's like being inside somebody's mouth."

"You're so weird," I told her, but I humored her anyway, and we sat in the air-conditioning on crisp white sheets, flipping channels. My whole body ached with exhaustion. Juliet had asked us both to stay on through the dance portion of the audition—because they'd known we came together and hadn't wanted to kick me out onto the street, I guessed—and once we were done we'd eaten dinner at a Chili's near the hotel, slurping Diet Cokes and splitting a basket of tortilla chips.

"This was better than job interviews, wasn't it?" Olivia asked me now, leaning her head on my shoulder and peering up at me with a hopeful, shit-eating grin. "Huh? Huuuuh?"

"I mean, yes," I allowed, laughing a little, "but ask me again when I'm destitute."

"You won't be destitute," Olivia said, reaching over and flicking the light off. "You'll be with me."

THREE

Back in Jessell Friday night we headed over to Burger Delight just like we always did, our weekly routine since junior high. Olivia picked me up and we drove together, hot wind ruffling her shiny dark hair as the orange sun disappeared behind the low-slung houses to the west. The bells above the door jangled as we walked in, the sub-zero air-conditioning a chilly relief after the dry, still heat outside.

"You came!" Becky called when she saw us, raising her soda cup in our direction. There they all were, clustered in our usual pair of four-top booths at the back: Keith and Kerry-Ann and Jonah, Tim and Sarah Jane—the same half dozen faces we'd been looking at since kindergarten, the ones we'd been sneaking beers with since we were twelve. "Thought maybe you went off to Hollywood already."

"Not quite," Olivia called with a grin, going up to the

counter to put in our order—chicken fingers and a chocolate milk shake for me, a small basket of fries and a Diet Coke for her—while I slid into the booth next to Sarah Jane, across from Becky and SJ's sometimes-boyfriend, Keith.

"How was the road trip?" SJ asked, pushing her onion rings in my direction. I'd known her even longer than I'd known Olivia; she'd lived around the corner from me since we were little, the sound of her mom's yelling echoing up and down the block. She was tall and blond and heavy, the kind of girl who took up space and didn't care if you liked it or not.

"It was fine," I said carefully, picking a bit of fried batter out of the bottom of the basket and crunching it between my teeth. "Liv did amazing." I didn't tell them what had happened with Guy, about getting picked to audition out of nowhere myself. I wasn't sure exactly why. It would have been a good story, after all; it would have set everybody laughing. But some small secret part of me didn't want to play it for comedy, wanted to keep it for myself. "She did awesome."

"Of course she did," Becky said as Olivia slid into the adjoining booth along with everyone else. "Should we go ahead and get your autograph now, or . . . ?"

"Shut up," Olivia said, but she was laughing. "There were, like, a million other girls there." She glanced over at me, seeming to understand by telepathy that I hadn't said anything about my part in the whole proceedings, and thankfully not calling me out. "So what have you guys been up to?" she asked, turning to the others.

We fell into the easy rhythm of every Friday night, the boys rehashing some drunk fight a couple of football players had gotten into at a party while we were gone, and Sarah Jane filling me in quietly about her latest fight with Keith. "He's being an asshole," she reported when he got up to go to the bathroom, and I made sympathetic noises without entirely hearing what she was saying. The truth was, I felt oddly restless tonight, like I couldn't settle back into how things usually were.

"Thanks, Linda," I said distractedly as the waitress came and put our orders down on the table. She was always absurdly patient, considering how many years we'd been testing the limits of how little they'd let us get away with ordering and how long they'd let us stay. When she'd turned and gone, I looked around at the restaurant for a moment—the red vinyl booths held together with duct tape, the grimy fluorescent lights overhead. Usually they felt comforting, familiar. Tonight, they just made me feel bored.

When Sarah Jane got up to go to the bathroom, Tim slid into the booth beside me, smelling of cologne and, underneath that, of cigarettes. He was wearing an Atlanta Braves cap on backward, a tiny gold cross around his neck. "Hey, stranger," he said, and I resisted the urge to roll my eyes.

"Hey." Tim had been trying to date me since middle school, when he'd slipped an actual paper valentine into my locker, a picture of purple grapes with the caption I LIKE YOU A BUNCH. We'd kissed a few times sophomore year, but I'd never let it get any further than that; still, it seemed to be taking Tim longer than average to get the memo that we weren't about to live happily ever after.

"Any luck finding a job?" he asked, helping himself to one of my chicken fingers. I wasn't finished eating, but it didn't seem worth it to protest.

"Not yet." I shook my head. "I've got a bunch of interviews, though." That was a lie. In reality I hadn't been able to bring myself to look at the applications on my desk since we'd gotten back from Orlando a couple of days ago.

"Could come work with me," Tim joked, throwing a casual arm around the top of the booth, just brushing my shoulders. I fixed him with a look like, *come on, dude*, and he hastily pulled it away.

"Oh yeah?" I asked, like nothing had happened. "You guys need help down at the garage?"

"Well, not fixing *cars*," Tim said, like that much should have been obvious given my gender. "But in the office, maybe."

"Thanks. I'll think about it," I said, glancing around for somebody else to drag into the conversation, but Becky had gotten up to talk to Kerry-Ann and Olivia at the next table, and Keith was, as always, about as useless as a stump. I sighed. It wasn't that I didn't like Tim—not exactly. He was a nice guy; he had pretty brown eyes, and I knew that if anything real ever happened between us, he'd be sweet to me. The problem was that I could picture so clearly what our lives would be like together—a decrepit house not far from my mom's place, a thirty rack of Budweiser cans in the fridge at all times, and three kids by the time I was twenty-five, both of us miserable and silent to varying degrees. It was true that I couldn't see much of a future for myself, not really. But I could see enough to know I didn't want *that.*

Once Sarah Jane came back, I extricated myself and wandered over to Olivia with my milk shake in hand, sliding into the booth beside her and snagging one of her fries, which—I saw with a frown—she'd barely touched. "Thanks for the assist there," I said, bumping her shoulder with my own.

"What, with your future husband?" Olivia teased. "You seemed to be holding your own."

"Mean!" I said, stung, feeling weird and sensitive tonight and not entirely sure what to do about it. It was like leaving town, even just for a couple of days, had unlocked something in me—had shown me a glimpse of this whole other world that left life in Jessell looking depressing and drab. I should have just stayed home and looked for waitressing jobs like I'd planned.

I took another fry, nodding down at her basket. "Are you gonna eat those?" I asked, and Olivia rolled her eyes at me.

"Yes, Mom." She made a face, but she pulled the basket toward her, dipping a fry into the delicately mixed ketchup-mustard concoction she insisted was necessary for any kind of potato consumption.

"Thank you," I said sweetly. I knew it sounded like a scold, but I didn't particularly care. It was part of our tacit agreement, since middle school and possibly even longer. I didn't tell anyone—didn't tell her *mom*—when Olivia wasn't eating. And in return I got to do whatever it took to make sure she was.

"Can I ask you something?" That was Sarah Jane leaning over from the booth behind us, speaking quietly into my ear. "Who exactly is gonna be the food police for her once she gets the hell out of Dodge?"

I turned to look at her, scowling; she held up both hands in surrender, and I shrugged, reaching for my milk shake. Sarah Jane had a point, I admitted to myself as I slurped noisily. After all, it wasn't like I'd never thought of it before. Our arrangement worked as long as Olivia and I were joined at the hip, like we were here in Jessell. I had no idea what would happen once we were apart.

I was tired suddenly. I wanted to go home.

"Hey," Olivia said. She'd been chattering with Becky and Jonah but turned around and looked at me now, urgent, as if somehow she'd read my mind. "You ready to get out of here?"

"Definitely," I said, setting my half-finished milk shake down on the chipping Formica table and sliding out of the sticky booth. "Night, y'all."

“Aw, fallen soldier!” Tim chided, pointing at the milk shake, but I ignored him.

“Bye, guys!” Olivia called, hurrying after me. “You okay?” she asked quietly once we got outside.

“Yeah,” I promised, sounding like I was full of garbage even to my own ears. “I’m great.”

Olivia rolled her eyes. “Okay, not convincing. Try again.”

I sighed, looking out across the parking lot. Burger Delight was way down at the far end of what passed for a main drag in Jessell, across the street from a used-car dealership ringed with chicken wire and an empty lot advertising space for lease. I stared for a moment, watching as a waxy paper cup skittered a few yards in the hot wind before finally getting caught against the chain link. “You don’t really think that, do you?” I finally asked, turning to face Olivia in the neon light from the restaurant sign. “That I’m going to wind up with Tim?”

Olivia’s eyes widened. “What? God, no,” she said, shaking her head at me across the roof of the car. “I was just teasing. Shoot, I’m sorry.”

I shook my head. “No, it’s fine,” I said as she unlocked the car doors and I settled myself in on the passenger side, getting a familiar whiff of vanilla from the little cardboard tree dangling from the rearview. “I know you were. I guess since we got back from the trip I’m just feeling weird.”

“Weird about . . . ?”

"Me staying and you leaving, I guess." I felt stupid and embarrassed admitting it, but Olivia just nodded, no judgment or pity on her face at all.

"I know," she said quietly.

"I mean, it was one thing when you were just going to school down the road like a normal person, but now odds are you're going to do something amazing and be actually famous and I'm just going to stay here and marry some guy with a truck and wind up like my mom—"

"Hey," Olivia said, holding her hands up to cut me off. "Uh-uh." She looked me in the eyes. "First things first: you are never going to be your mom, do you hear me? The fact that you're even worried about being your mom means there's no way you're going to wind up like your mom."

I smirked. "I don't think it works exactly like that."

"I think it does," Olivia said firmly, leaning her head back against the seat. Both of us were quiet for a moment. Through the window of Burger Delight, I could see the rest of our friends still inside, laughing and joking around just like we'd done every Friday since junior high, just like we'd all keep doing for the foreseeable future. That had never felt like a bad thing to me before.

"I'm scared about being apart, too. You know that, right?" Olivia asked softly, tucking one leg underneath her and turning to face me. "I'm *terrified.* I don't even know if I exist without you."

I shook my head. "Of course you do."

"We'll see," she said, looking down at her lap for a moment before raising her head. "But I also know it'll be okay. I'm probably not even going to get that Guy Monroe thing, first of all—it's a total long shot. But no matter where I wind up, obviously you'll come visit me all the time."

She was right, I knew. I couldn't imagine a time when I wouldn't drop everything to be with Olivia, when I wouldn't skip job interviews to keep her company at an audition or spend all night on a Greyhound to see her in a show. We were best friends; we were there for each other. That part of it would never change. Still, I knew it would never be exactly like this again, the two of us on one side and the whole world on the other. It was part of growing up; it wasn't surprising. I just wasn't sure if I was ready to say good-bye.

"You sleeping over?" Olivia asked, turning the key in the ignition. The Toyota gurgled to tenuous life.

"Yup," I replied, so quiet I wasn't sure if she heard me. "Let's go home."

FOUR

I finally started the job-search rounds in Jessell the next morning, dutifully dropping my application at Waffle House and Pizza Planet, a video store, and a place that sold pet supplies. "We'll call you," the skinny, oily-looking manager said unconvincingly, as I tried not to wrinkle my nose against the overwhelming smell of dog pee.

By the time I got back to the empty house, all I wanted to do was sit in front of the TV and not talk to anyone, but I had barely closed the door behind me when the bell rang. I was surprised, first at the sound itself—we didn't exactly have the kind of neighbors who just popped by—and second to find Olivia on the other side of it, her cheeks flushed and dark eyes bright. She hardly ever came over here, especially with no advance warning. If our friendship was a movie, the set was her house, not mine. "Hi," I said, swinging the door open. She was wearing shorts and a pair of sneakers with giant platforms, her shiny dark hair slipping out of a ponytail. "You okay?"

"Why are you not answering the phone?" she asked.

I frowned. "I just walked in," I said slowly. "I was out looking for a job."

"I think I got one," Olivia said, her face glowing bright, "with Guy Monroe."

"What!" My mouth dropped open. "Really?"

"Really." Olivia made a funny face, eyes wide and tongue stuck out on one side of her mouth. "*Really* really."

"What! That's amazing!" I flung my arms around her, disbelieving, a hundred different emotions ricocheting around inside my body. "That's beyond amazing. What's a word for beyond amazing?" I pulled back, scanning her face. "What happens now?"

"I have to go back to Orlando at the beginning of next week," Olivia explained. "They're going to put me up in an apartment with the other girls so we can learn the songs and routines and do media training and stuff. And then we go into a recording studio, I guess? And at the end of the summer is the tour."

"I love how casually you're saying that," I teased her. "The *tour.* Oh, you know, just your national tour with Tulsa-fucking-MacCreadie."

"I don't feel casual," Olivia said. "I do not feel casual at all. Like, what was the biggest thing I did before now,

Cinderella? Like, this is not freaking *Cinderella*."

"*You're* freaking Cinderella," I said, trying to picture it: Olivia cutting an album, Olivia in a music video like the ones we watched after school on MTV. Olivia walking the red carpet at the Grammys, and me back in Jessell, pointing at the screen: *I know that girl*. "I cannot get over this."

"You were my good luck charm," Olivia told me. "Is that lame?"

"It's totally lame," I said, "but who cares? This is amazing!" It *was* amazing; it was incredible, it was unlike anything I'd ever dreamed about. But there was a tiny part of me that was sad, too—after all, this meant she'd be leaving home way before we'd planned, off on adventures I could only ever dream of—the rest of our lives arriving immediately, hers with a bang and mine with a whimper.

"We should celebrate," I said, pushing the thought away. I wanted to be properly excited—I *was* properly excited—but that was harder if I was feeling sorry for myself. "Should we get drunk?"

"It's three-thirty in the afternoon," Olivia pointed out, laughing, and I was about to tell her that famous people boozed at all hours of the day and night when the phone rang.

Grabbing the receiver off the wall in the kitchen, I breathlessly asked, "Hello?"

"Is this Dana Cartwright?" asked an unfamiliar woman's voice.

"Yes," I said slowly, twisting the cord distractedly around one finger. "Who's this?"

"Hi there, Dana," the voice said warmly. "This is Juliet Evanston, Guy Monroe's assistant. I'm calling with some good news."

I was confused. "Are you—are you looking for Olivia?" I asked, looking at her across the kitchen; she peered back at me, brow furrowed. *Who is it?* she mouthed.

"I'm looking for you," Juliet told me. "I'm calling because we'd like you to come join us in Orlando and be a part of Daisy Chain."

For ten full seconds I was silent. I honestly thought I'd heard her wrong. "Dana?" Juliet said, sounding unsure all of a sudden. "Are you there?"

"I'm sorry," I said finally. "Are you sure you have the right—?" I broke off, tried again. "I mean, at the audition I'm the one who sang—?"

"'Happy Birthday,'" Juliet supplied. "We know who you are, Dana."

Olivia was staring at me anxiously now, standing on one foot like a stork—perfectly still, though I could practically see the waves of energy vibrating off her.

"What?" she said, out loud this time. "What?!"

I waved my hand so she'd be quiet, listening as Juliet gave me the same details she must have given Olivia—the apartment, the media training, the tour. "I'm overnighting you a package with all this in writing," she told me. "I know it's a lot to take in."

"I—okay," I said, in a voice that didn't sound anything like normal. "Thank you."

Olivia was practically apoplectic by the time I hung up the phone. "Who was that?" she asked shrilly. "You look like you're about to die."

I hesitated. For a moment I was weirdly worried she'd be mad at me—this was her rodeo, after all, the dream she'd been working toward since she was a toddler in a tutu. I was only ever meant to tag along. I didn't want her to feel like I was trying to take something from her, like I'd stolen it out from underneath her when no one was looking; still, what could I possibly tell her besides the truth?

"They picked me, too," I said.

"I—" Olivia blinked. *"What?"*

"I'm not going to do it," I said immediately. "But—that was Guy's assistant person. They picked me, too."

"And you're not going to *do* it?" Olivia's eyes darkened. "Why the hell not?"

"Because I'm not a pop star!" I said, feeling like that should have been glaringly obvious. "I don't perform. I've never even wanted to do anything like that! This is your deal, not mine. I don't know why they picked me to begin with. It must be some weird mistake."

"Are you kidding me?" Olivia shook her head. "They

saw something in you, that's all. You have to come, I need you. It'll be like if we'd gone to college together, but a million times better."

I let myself imagine it for a moment, adding myself to the images I'd conjured up of Olivia's new life. I didn't fit in there, even in my own imagination. In a lot of ways she was a shape-shifter: able to chameleon herself into Showbiz Olivia, to be whoever the situation demanded. I was just . . . myself.

"I don't know," I said. "I—what is even happening right now? No."

Olivia looked at me like I was speaking Chinese. "What are you going to do if you don't do this?" she asked. "I mean it. I'm sincerely asking. Are you just gonna stay here forever?"

It was a blunt truth, the kind of thing only Olivia could have said out loud to me. It was a slap in the face meant to bring me to my senses, and it worked. I looked around at the kitchen in my mom's house—the linoleum peeling up by the refrigerator, the curtains above the sink that had gone yellowish from cigarette smoke. The empty vodka bottle poking out of the trash can, the one that hadn't been there last night.

I ran my hands through my messy hair, yanking at the tangles. I tried to be calm and rational and smart. Olivia had wanted this her whole life, but she didn't truly *need* it. In a very real way, I did. Random and potentially disastrous as it was, this was the universe throwing me a life preserver. I'd have to be an idiot not to take it.

I took a deep breath. "Okay, then," I said. "Looks like we're going to Orlando."

Olivia let out a loud, delighted squawk, then dashed across the room and flung her arms around me—all long limbs and strawberry shampoo hair—both of us laughing our heads off. I should have known she wouldn't be upset. That wasn't how our friendship worked.

"I can't believe this," she said, twirling me around the kitchen. "It's perfect. It's the best thing."

I smiled and let her spin me, the dingy kitchen blurring before my eyes. Already I knew nothing was going to come of this. I had no training, no real talent. That I'd auditioned at all was a freaking mistake. But I couldn't shake the feeling of warm possibility that was unpacking its suitcase inside me, the idea that maybe there was something out there for me after all.

FIVE

The address on the paperwork Guy's assistant had sent us was for an apartment complex not far from the studios where we'd auditioned, a cluster of two-story stucco buildings arranged in a square with an in-ground swimming pool of questionable cleanliness at the center. The sun was already setting by the time Olivia pulled into the parking lot, the cast of pink and gold more forgiving than I suspected broad daylight might be. "Tulsa lives here?" I asked with no small amount of skepticism, peering from the buzzing neon sign identifying the complex as THE COCONUT PALMS to the low-rent strip mall across the boulevard.

"Well, he used to," Olivia said, in the clipped, efficient tone she used when she was nervous. "Not anymore, obviously. Which apartment is it, again?" Then, pulling a sheaf of papers out of her purse before I could answer: "Wait, never mind. I have it."

A good thing, too, since I actually had no idea what I'd done with my copy of the information Juliet had sent us. I thought I'd packed it, but my stuff was all in a jumble—I didn't have a suitcase big enough to fit everything I needed for the trip down here, so I'd shoved the overflow into a beach tote, plus a couple of grocery bags. The plastic handles cut into my wrists now as we climbed the metal steps to the outdoor walkway that ran along the second story of the building, Olivia knocking a cheerful little tattoo on the front door of apartment 208.

"You're here!" trilled the blond girl who opened it, flinging her arms up in a cheerleader's V like she'd just stuck a landing. She was tall and pretty, dressed in expensive-looking jeans and a T-shirt that showed off a jewel in her belly button, her hair so thick and straight and shiny you could have used it to sell prenatal vitamins. "Ash and I got set up in one of the bedrooms already. We figured you guys wouldn't mind." Then she shook her head. "Oh my God, I'm sorry. Hi. I'm Kristin Aires. I'm in Daisy Chain with you guys. Clearly."

Something about her—the *clearly*, maybe, or the fact that she said her name as one word, like *millionaires*—irritated me right away, but Olivia flung her arms around Kristin like they were long-lost friends and said, "Hiiii!" I was surprised—usually Olivia hated being touched by anybody who wasn't me or her immediate family—but then again, I reminded myself, as I remembered how she'd acted at the audition, this was Showbiz Olivia. The rules were bound to be a little different here.

There were four of us in Guy Monroe's Daisy Chain, Olivia and me plus Kristin and a tall, pretty girl named Ashley Coombs, who was black and from a suburb outside Chicago that sounded rich. All four of us were staying in this apartment with Charla, the choreographer who'd run the dance audition and who met us in the living room now. "Hey, ladies," she said, smiling warmly; she had an easy-going, big-sister quality to her, the opposite of Juliet's chilly efficiency. She was dressed in leggings and a T-shirt that said HOUSTON BALLET, with a long, flowy cardigan overtop. "Let's get you settled in."

The apartment was bare-bones but huge, with a master bedroom that Charla slept in and then two smaller ones for the four of us, connected by a bathroom with double sinks and tilework in a seasick shade of green. The couch and love-seat were upholstered in plasticky pink fabric that seemed to have been chosen specifically for its stain-repelling qualities; a watery painting of palm trees was hung above the TV. A laminate breakfast bar separated the kitchen from the living space.

Olivia dropped our bags in the bedroom we'd be sharing, which was outfitted with a pair of twin beds and a couple of windows that didn't actually open. The AC whooshed noisily from a vent over the door. Still, it was ours, mine and Olivia's. "This isn't so bad, is it?" she asked, bouncing a bit on one of the mattresses and grinning across the room at me. "I mean, I can live with this."

"Me too," I agreed, smiling back at her. It wasn't until I felt myself relax that I realized I'd been clenching my jaw, my shoulders migrating upward to somewhere in the general vicinity of my ears.

Once we were all unpacked, Charla made popcorn and had us sit in the living room and go around in a circle saying where we were from, our favorite song, and what our hopes were for Daisy Chain. It felt like summer camp, which I'd never actually gone to—like we should have been huddled around a fire instead of a prefurnished college apartment with a noisy highway right outside. Kristin put the soundtrack to the musical *Rent* on a boom box on the shelf. She and Ashley both had performing backgrounds like Olivia's, and I dug into the popcorn as references flew through the air: Bernadette Peters and Tommy Mottola, whose range had how many octaves and who'd auditioned for which directors in New York. I nodded and tried to look interested, hoping nobody would notice that I had exactly zero to add.

"I hope our first album goes platinum," Kristin said earnestly when it was her turn to say what she wanted for Daisy Chain. Ashley hoped for a number one single, and Olivia said that all she really wanted was to make people happy by performing, which I suspected was probably a lie and fully intended to tease her about later. She was using her audition voice again, I noticed, pitched way higher than she normally spoke. I was going to tease her about that, too. I couldn't wait until later, when we could close our bedroom door and compare notes.

"I'm Dana," I said dumbly when it was my turn, although obviously we didn't have to introduce ourselves. "I'm from Jessell, same as Olivia. My favorite song is 'Tangerine,' by Led Zeppelin, which Olivia hates."

"I don't hate it!" Olivia protested from across the circle. "I just think it's, like, a weird, clangy, old-man song about a breakup." Then she tilted her head to the side. "Okay, I kind of hate it."

"Uh-huh." I grinned. "As for what I hope happens with Daisy Chain . . . I don't know, really. I guess I'm kind of just here to have fun and see what happens."

Right away I could tell that was the wrong answer. Kristin's eyebrows crawled toward her hairline. Olivia looked down at the floor. I felt myself blush. Just because I was here on a lark and weird luck didn't mean the rest of them were. "And of course I want the group to be successful," I added lamely.

Charla went to her room not long after that, but the rest of us stayed in the living room, where I ate the rest of the popcorn in its entirety while the three of them chatted, listing their accomplishments, sizing one another up. Kristin had been in a series of Wendy's commercials when she was a toddler. Ashley had been dancing ballet since she was three. My attention had started to wander when Kristin looked at me shrewdly. "What about you, Dana?" she asked, tilting her head to the side in curiosity that might have been genuine. "What shows have you done?"

"Um, not much, really," I admitted. "I'm kind of new to performing."

"Dana's a natural," Olivia said, and I smiled.

Kristin was nodding. "We heard how you weren't even going to audition, that Guy just picked you randomly. Ash and I figured you must be super hot or something."

I shrugged in what I hoped was a self-deprecating kind of way, feeling myself chafe and trying not to show it. "Yeah," I said, holding my hands up. "I don't know what the deal was, either."

"It's weird," Kristin agreed. "Well, I hope you're a fast learner."

I bit my tongue and smiled. "I hope so, too."

"Okay," I said to Olivia as we got ready for bed a little later, digging through the pile of clothes I'd dumped on the floor and unearthing a pair of boxer shorts to sleep in. "Did it seem to you like Kristin's gonna strangle me with a pair of pantyhose if it turns out I'm not as good as you guys?"

"What?" Olivia asked, pulling her T-shirt over her head. All her clothes were already folded neatly in the bureau. "No, why?"

"I dunno," I said, grinning at her across the room. "You find me bashed over the head with a platform sneaker, I wouldn't look too far for the culprit, you know what I'm saying?"

"Oh, stop," Olivia told me. "You're gonna be fine."

There was enough of an edge in her voice this time that I looked at her curiously. "Hey, crabby," I said, twisting a hair elastic around a messy bun to sleep in. "You okay?"

Olivia sighed. "Yeah," she said, sitting down on the mattress. "Sorry. Just nervous, I guess."

I nodded; I got it. After all, this had been her dream as long as either one of us could remember, and it was *real* now, our first rehearsal just hours away. Of course her nerves were kicking in. "You're gonna be fine, too," I promised, climbing into my own bed and pulling the unfamiliar covers up. "This is us, living our lives forward!"

Olivia smiled at that, flicked off the bedside lamp. "Junia would be very proud," she agreed.

A few minutes later, I heard Liv's breath get deep and even across the room. I waited for sleep myself, staring out the hermetically sealed window and watching the moon creep across the unfamiliar sky. But the longer I lay there, the more uneasily I found myself replaying my short conversation with Liv in my head. I didn't have a Plan B if I crashed and burned in Orlando. It didn't matter whether I belonged here, really: I had to make this work or go back home.

Sleep wasn't coming, that much was obvious; my stomach growled, reminding me that all I'd eaten for dinner was a few handfuls of fat-free popcorn. Finally, I got out of bed and pulled on a pair of denim shorts and a T-shirt, then let myself out of the apartment as quietly as I could.

It was after ten now, but still hot and sticky, the sweaty concrete smell that all of Orlando seemed to have hanging heavy in the air. Cars whizzed down the wide, busy street beyond the parking lot; across four lanes of traffic was a strip mall housing a grimy-looking Kmart and a liquor store, plus two empty storefronts like a pair of missing teeth. Most of the people who lived in this complex were college kids, a fact evidenced not only by its cracked facade and the beer cans and cigarette butts floating in the pool, but also by the huge bank of vending machines at the near end of the parking lot.

When I got to the bottom of the steps, I saw there was a blond guy about my age already down there, balancing an armload of Gatorades and chips in the crook of one elbow while he punched the keypad with his opposite thumb. I kept my distance while he finished up, arms crossed warily over my chest. The Coconut Palms didn't seem particularly unsafe to me, on top of which this guy didn't look like a serial killer—cargo shorts and a crisp white T-shirt, immaculate

Adidas shell tops on his feet—but I wasn't an idiot. In the harsh white glare of the parking lot floodlights, his hair was a messy yellow-gold.

I'd planned to wait him out, but he was taking forever, adding a couple of chocolate bars and a package of pretzels to his vending-machine haul. Without entirely meaning to, I sighed. The guy looked up and saw me, his expression turning from surprised to embarrassed, a sheepish grin appearing on his face.

"Oh, gosh, sorry!" he said, stepping aside immediately. He had a nice smile, I could give him that. "I didn't see you there. Me and my roommate, this is how we grocery shop. Here you go. It's all yours."

"Thanks," I said, edging past him and digging a dollar out of my shorts pocket. Up close he was taller than me by nearly a foot. I rubbed my crumpled dollar back and forth against my thigh to flatten it out, then fed it into the machine, which spit it right back out immediately. A pair of grubby, homeless-looking cats eyed me dubiously from the curb.

"That one's tricky," the guy said from behind me. He'd stopped a few feet away, lanky arms still laden with junk food. "You gotta sweet-talk it a little."

"I got it, thanks," I said, sounding harsher than I meant to.

"Sure thing," the guy said, nodding earnestly as I tried again with absolutely zero success to get the machine to take my stupid dollar. I sighed, picking at the corners of the bill to straighten them out, feeling a hot, irrational embarrassment over the crappy condition of my money.

He must have been able to read my mind, or more likely I wasn't being particularly subtle, because he set his stuff down gently on the curb and held one big hand out. A tangle of brightly colored friendship bracelets looped riotously around his wrist. "You mind if I try?" he asked.

Something about his general bearing—like, here was a person who was used to getting what he wanted, who had no reason to expect otherwise—made me want to say no to him, to struggle it out on my own. But it was late, and I was hungry. "Be my guest," I said.

He held either end of the dollar and rubbed it back and forth over the corner of the machine for a minute, then fed it into the slot with almost surgical precision. The hair on his arms was a pale golden blond. Of course the dumb vending machine took it right away this time, beeping happily like it was a robotic dog or something and he was its master.

"Thanks," I said, stabbing at the buttons on the keypad until the machine whirred to life and a Twix bar *chunk*ed to the bottom. I bent down and snatched it out.

"No problem," the guy said easily, scooping up his vending-machine groceries. The back of his shirt rode up a tiny bit, revealing a strip of tan, smooth skin. "You live here?" he asked.

I raised my eyebrows. "You're a stranger," I pointed out.

"Sorry," he said immediately, that same dopily sheepish expression crossing his pretty face. "You're right, that was invasive. I didn't mean it. I'm Alex. I live up in two-two-eight."

I nodded, tearing into my Twix bar and taking a huge bite, swallowing without hardly bothering to chew. "Dana," I allowed, after a moment of consideration.

Alex smiled then. "Dana," he said, like he was committing it to memory. "Nice to meet you."

I smiled back; I couldn't help it. "Nice to meet you, too."

Alex nodded. "Okay," he said. "So I don't know if you live here, or if maybe this is just your querulous vending machine of choice. But if you *do* live here . . ." Alex tilted his head, shrugged a little. "Maybe I'll see you around."

"Maybe," I agreed. I could smell him—boy-who-just-took-a-shower smell, the zing of antibacterial soap. I felt myself blushing, my whole body warm.

"G'night, then."

"Good night."

Alex jogged across the parking lot and up the concrete steps to what I saw now was unit 228, on the same level but on the other side of the parking lot from ours. He looked over his shoulder, caught me watching. He grinned and waved before he went inside.

SIX

The alarm went off at six-thirty the next morning, our first day of Daisy Chain rehearsal. The paperwork from Juliet had told us to pack clothes we could move in, so I pulled on a pair of shorts and my Jessell Jaguars gym shirt, scooped my hair up into a messy bun. "So hey," I said to Olivia when she came out of the bathroom. "The weirdest thing happened last night." I was about to tell her about the guy by the vending machines when I realized she was looking at me funny. "What?"

"Is that what you're wearing?" she replied.

I raised my eyebrows. "I mean, not with that tone in your voice, I'm not."

Olivia grinned, shook her head. "Here," she said, pulling her drawers open again and handing me an expensive-feeling pair of stretch pants and a tank top that, when I pulled it on, showed a pale strip of my stomach. I'd hardly ever seen her in these kinds of clothes before, let alone worn them myself.

"I feel like an aerobics instructor," I told her, looking at myself in the mirror. "Or, you know, a very athletic prostitute."

"Oh, shut up," Olivia said, but she was laughing.

As soon as we met the others in the living room, I saw that she'd been right: Kristin was wearing a stretchy tank top with a line of rhinestones across the boobs, while Ashley had a fluttery dance skirt over leggings that stopped mid-calf. I would have stuck out even more than I did already in my scruffy gym stuff. At least in Olivia's clothes I looked almost the same as everyone else. *Thanks*, I mouthed as we headed down to the parking lot, and Olivia winked.

The studios were only about a ten-minute drive from the complex; Charla shuttled us all over in her shiny red SUV. I couldn't stop looking around, feeling something like wonder that I'd come back to this place I'd fully expected never to see again—taking in the smell of old sweat and cleaning fluid covered over by a strong vanilla plug-in, the signed tour poster from Tulsa's last trip across the world. It was different to walk through the doors feeling like somebody who actually belonged here—in theory, at least. In practice, I couldn't have felt like more of an outsider.

Charla herded the four of us into the dance room, shiny hardwood and wall-to-wall mirrors; when I looked I could see us all repeating off into infinity, getting smaller and smaller until we finally disappeared. "Drop your stuff in the dressing room," Charla instructed, nodding at a small alcove off to one side. "Shoes and socks off." She hit a button on a boom box in the corner and rhythmic, almost chantlike music filled the room. "We're going to start easy, okay? Just warm-ups."

Charla was good as her word, keeping things simple at first—mostly stretching and a few basic dance steps, all of us getting used to following her lead. Then she had us start putting combinations together. When I'd thought about being a part of Daisy Chain, the dancing was what I'd been most excited about, something I could actually picture myself doing: my mom never had money for dance classes or anything like that, but I'd been making up routines with Olivia for as long as we'd known each other. I understood how to move my body—how to follow the steps in a combination, how to commit it quickly to memory both in my brain and in my limbs. It was actually sort of fun. I was a better dancer than Kristin, I noticed with relief, glancing at her in the long wall of mirrors. Her elbows were constantly jerking around. Ashley was really good, though, and Olivia was downright pristine: forever precise and calculated in her movements, never a step out of place.

It was hard work, physical and demanding; by the time we broke for lunch, my stomach was actually growling. Juliet had run out for sandwiches, which we ate at a picnic table set up on a swath of scratchy crabgrass in the middle of the parking lot. The studio was set back in an industrial park, next to a shipping facility and a paint-your-own-pottery place that looked long shuttered. A couple of guys in delivery uniforms looked over at us curiously as they loaded boxes onto their trucks.

"It's too hot to eat," Kristin said, and the others nodded in agreement, though I personally was not finding that to be the case whatsoever. Olivia picked at her sandwich, pulling the tomatoes off the bread and nibbling around their limp pink edges.

"You're not hungry?" I asked casually, and Olivia shook her head.

I was trying to figure out what I could say to that in front of the others when a black van pulled into the far side of the parking lot and a group of guys piled out of it, slamming doors and laughing and generally making noise. "Um," I said, not wanting to sound like an idiot and knowing I was going to. "Hey. There are boys here."

"Oh yeah, that's Hurricane State," Kristin said, glancing over her shoulder like it was no big deal. "They're living at the complex, too, I think."

Olivia's eyes widened, craning her neck to look. "Hurricane State is here?"

"What's Hurricane State?" I asked.

"The group Guy put together last year," Ashley informed me, in a voice that implied this was something I should have known already. "They're touring, too."

"With us? I mean, with Tulsa?"

Ashley smirked. "That's the idea."

The boys noticed us a moment later and ambled over in our direction in a shaggy, sneakered pack. "Hey, ladies!" one of them called. There were five of them, around our age or maybe a little older, but as far as I was concerned there was only one worth looking at: he had wavy blond hair and high, sharp cheekbones, a dozen brightly colored friendship bracelets looped around his elegant wrist. Alex.

He noticed me at the exact same moment, head tipped to one side and a slow grin spreading across his face. I looked away, feeling my body get warm down to the arches of my feet inside my sneakers, simultaneously annoyed that he hadn't mentioned he was part of one of Guy's groups and fully aware I'd left that information out, too. My tongue stuck dryly to the roof of my mouth.

Ashley was calling hello back to them—so far none of the rest of us had—when Olivia clambered up from the picnic table and beelined in their direction. "Alex Harrison!" she called.

Alex looked over at her, eyes narrowing for a moment before he smiled. "Hey!" he said, gathering her into a hug and lifting her up onto her toes like they were long-lost comrades from a far-off war. "What are you doing here?"

"It's our first day of rehearsal," she told him, motioning to the rest of us. "Daisy Chain."

I stared at the two of them, totally gobsmacked. Olivia

and I knew all the same people—or at least, I thought we did. Clearly, I'd been wrong. I looked away, squinting into the sunlight; it was like the rubber band tethering me to reality had reached its elastic limit, snapping me back into the way things actually were.

The others all introduced themselves—Austin was the oldest, at twenty; Mario wore a Diamondbacks ball cap tilted slightly to one side. Mikey had curly dark hair and was the closest to goofy-looking of any of them, while Trevor, a light-skinned black kid with a ring of puka shells around his neck, had the friendliest smile I'd ever seen. All of them were uniformly attractive. Standing in a cluster, they looked like an ad for the Gap.

"So," Alex asked, "is this the weirdest day of your life so far, or just second or third weirdest?"

I thought he was addressing us generally; it took me a second to realize he was talking directly to me. "Oh, not even top ten," I said, recovering. "But I'm a weird girl, so."

It came out distinctly unfriendly, which wasn't exactly how I'd meant it; still, I thought that was for the best. Olivia was looking at him expectantly, her dark head tilted to the side. I pushed our random late-night conversation out of my head. Alex was cute. So what? They were all cute. That was literally the entire point.

Alex looked like he was about to say something else to me, when Juliet opened the door to the studio, eyes narrowed.

"Gentlemen!" she called, sounding impatient. "You coming in here, or what?"

"We better go," said one of them—Austin, I thought, the big brother of the group. "See you guys later."

"You should come over one night," Trevor added. "We're neighbors, after all."

Juliet called us in a few minutes later, and as we headed back into the studio I yanked Olivia aside. "Who *was* that?" I asked incredulously. "How do you know him?"

Olivia looked over her shoulder, like Alex might materialize at any moment to hear her. "Do you remember Prince Charming?" she asked me quietly.

"*That's* Prince Charming?" I asked. Olivia used to talk about Prince Charming all the time in middle school, when she was doing a bunch of regional theater out of Atlanta. They'd been in *Cinderella* together when we were thirteen. He had not, in fact, played Prince Charming—he'd played a footman—but she'd had a massive crush on him, so the name had stuck. "Prince Charming is in this boy band?"

"Shh!" Olivia hissed. Then, "What, you think that's lame?"

"No," I said. "I think that's the kind of irony that would make Alanis Morissette really proud."

"I can't believe I threw myself at him like that," she said. "I didn't even think he'd remember me."

"You didn't throw yourself at him," I promised. "And of course he remembered you."

"We were kids."

"It was, like, four years ago!" I snorted. "Did you know they were touring with us?"

Olivia shook her head. "I knew he was in Hurricane State now, but that was it. They're, like, borderline actually famous. They did one of those MTV beach house things over spring break." She was practically glowing. "Doesn't that feel like a crazy coincidence?" she asked. "Both of us just . . . being here?"

"Yeah," I said, bumping her shoulder as we headed into the voice room, trying not to think about the fact that she'd known her crush might be here and hadn't told me. "It's pretty crazy."

Lucas, our voice coach, a trim, sandy-haired guy in his thirties wearing a fitted sky-blue polo shirt, was already waiting behind the piano, a massively irritated expression on his face. "First of all, you're four minutes late to be in here," he said, none of the cheery preamble we'd gotten from Charla. Clearly, he was not interested in knowing our hopes and dreams for Daisy Chain. "So let's not waste any more time. You," he said, nodding to Kristin. "Scales."

I blinked, taken aback. Still, Ashley had told us at lunch that Lucas was supposed to be the best voice coach on the East Coast outside of New York City. He'd trained Tulsa from the time Tulsa was twelve. Maybe this was just how it was done.

Kristin sang her scales, then Olivia and Ashley, Lucas starting at one end of the keyboard and working higher and higher each time. I listened eagerly, trying to suss out everyone's place here in spite of my ignorant ears. Kristin was a gunner. She was here to be the favorite, to stand out. Ash seemed more reserved. And Olivia was somewhere in between—capable and calm under pressure, with a voice that smoothed out the rough places in the harmonies, filling in the cracks.

And me?

I'd never sung scales before, but it didn't seem terribly difficult; I tried to imitate what the others had done, *ahh*-ing along with the runs up and down the piano. Lucas didn't say anything while I was singing, but when I was finished, he took his hands off the keys and placed them in his lap. "Remind me again what kind of training you've had?"

I shook my head. "No training," I admitted.

"Right." He raised his eyebrows. "So you can't sight-read."

I shook my head again.

Lucas sighed. "And you've never sung harmony before?"

"Like I said, I've had no training," I said, more snappishly than I meant to.

He eyed me for a moment. "So you did," he said, his voice quiet, and right away I could tell I'd made an enemy. I glanced over at Olivia for reassurance, but she was looking down at her feet. Kristin and Ashley were watching me, though, and I felt my face flame, red and embarrassed.

Once warm-ups were finished, Lucas handed us all binders full of lyrics for the songs we'd be learning over the next couple of weeks, ran quickly through each of our individual parts, then jumped right into the intro of a purring ballad called "Only for You." I gave it my best effort, but it didn't take more than a few minutes before it was clear to everyone, me especially, that I was by far the worst singer in Daisy Chain.

"Stop," Lucas said, cutting us off mid-chorus. He took his hands off the keyboard entirely, the sudden silence startling and huge. "Stop, stop, stop. Dana, come on, pay attention. You're not hitting your harmonies at *all*."

"I'm not?" I asked.

I was playing dumb, and Lucas knew it. "No," he said, running through my notes on the piano, plinking the keys harder than he really needed to. Kristin and Ash were watching, wide-eyed, while Olivia was studying her binder like it was the Rosetta freaking Stone. "Come on, try again."

I *was* trying, truthfully. I could sing my part alone okay, or when Lucas was singing with me, but as soon as the others jumped in, it was like I couldn't hear the notes in my head anymore. "Try plugging your ears," Lucas suggested. "See if you can do it that way."

I blinked at him. "Seriously?"

"Do I look like I'm kidding?" Lucas asked, sounding peevish. "Come on, give it a try."

It occurred to me all of a sudden that possibly this was a power game—that he was getting some nasty little thrill out of humiliating me, the same way he'd made me answer embarrassing questions that he probably already knew the answers to. *No, I'd never taken voice lessons. No, I couldn't read music.*

Yes, Guy had picked me anyway.

Fine, then. I glanced from Lucas to Ashley and Kristin and finally to Olivia, who looked almost as miserable as I did. I wasn't about to let anyone intimidate me. I clamped my hands over my ears as Lucas started up again on the piano. But by the look on his face—and everyone else's—I could tell it wasn't working. "Sorry," I said. "I'll try again."

Lucas sighed. "Yup," he said, rolling his eyes at me. "From the top."

SEVEN

"I'm dead," I announced that afternoon after rehearsal, flopping onto the fake-leather couch of the apartment and propping my feet on the coffee table. I grabbed the remote off the armchair, flipped over to a Puff Daddy video on MTV. "Seriously. Even my *eyelashes* hurt. Also, I'm starving."

"Aw, I thought it was fun," Olivia said, sitting down beside me. Kristin and Ashley had gone to the grocery store with Charla to get stuff for dinner, so it was just the two of us. "I really liked that second song we did, the doo-wop-sounding one."

"Easy for you to say, teacher's pet." I swung my feet up into her lap. "I was a total garbage fire, in case you somehow didn't notice. Lucas hates me."

Olivia just shrugged. "He doesn't hate you," she said

calmly. "The rest of us have been in coaching for years, is all. Of course you're not going to be as professional."

"I— yeah," I said, feeling weirdly self-conscious in front of her all of a sudden, wanting abruptly to talk about anything but this. "What are they getting for dinner, did they say?"

"Salad stuff, I think? They'll be back any minute."

I frowned. I was *exhausted*, back aching and muscles rubbery like I'd never felt before, not even after working a double at Taquitos on Cinco de Mayo. Still, I was restless: there had been talk of hanging out and watching a movie, but the last thing I wanted to do was sit around the apartment all night eating lettuce and discussing which member of Hurricane State would play what role in Kristin's dream production of *Into the Woods*. "Wanna go exploring?" I asked Olivia hopefully. "Go for a ride, see what's around here?"

"What, tonight?" Olivia frowned. "I don't know."

"Yeah!" I said, sitting upright, suddenly cheered. "I'm not saying I want to, like, go to a club and rage or anything. But it's Friday, isn't it? I mean, I doubt there's anything *quite* so delicious as a Burger Delight around here, but we could see."

Olivia grinned at that. "Okay," she said slowly. "Let's do it. Should we wait and ask Kristin and Ash?"

That was the last thing I wanted, but it wasn't like they'd done anything to me. Maybe I was just being a baby, not wanting to share my best friend. "Sure," I said, faking an enthusiasm I didn't feel. "Absolutely."

Luck was on my side, though, and Kristin and Ashley both begged off.

"Home by eleven," Charla told us before we left the apartment. "Curfew."

"Definitely," I promised.

As soon as we pulled out of the complex, I felt my mood brighten; Olivia twirled the radio dial until she found the Top 40 station, singing along under her breath just like she always did while I chimed in on the chorus. I felt like I was finally coming up for air. The apartment made me claustrophobic—the feeling, however dumb or misguided, of everyone watching my every move: like they were waiting for more evidence of just how much I didn't deserve to be here, what a disappointment I was turning out to be.

It was easy to let that stuff go as Olivia and I cruised down the main drag toward the commercial district, the last dregs of late-afternoon sunlight turning everything toasted and gold. We passed car dealerships and a dozen different chain restaurants, bright stuccoed strip malls filled with drugstores and tanning salons and payday loan parlors. The farther we went, the more it looked like all the buildings had gone up in the last five minutes, everything somehow artificial looking, as if it might fold down at night like a child's pop-up book.

"There?" Olivia motioned to a burger joint off to the side, a riff on an old-fashioned drive-in where you ordered through a speaker and they brought your order out to your car.

I nodded. "Will you eat, too?" I asked pointedly.

"Of course," Olivia said, making a face at me. "The usual?"

I smiled. "You bet."

We ate with our feet up on the dashboard, the radio on and the smell of fry grease and salt thick in the air, the neon colors of the drive-in mixing with the purple twilight outside. "What do you think everybody else is doing right now?" Olivia asked. "At home, I mean."

I shrugged. "Same thing as every Friday, right?"

Olivia smiled, rolling her eyes ruefully. "God, it's such a relief not to be there for a change, isn't it?"

I thought about that for a moment. "Yeah," I said. "I guess it is."

Olivia nodded. "I mean, don't get me wrong, I love those guys, but none of them are ever getting out of Jessell."

That surprised me—not because it wasn't true, or because I hadn't thought it myself before, but because of the way she said it. It was the first time I'd ever heard Olivia make that kind of distinction between herself and the rest of our friends. Sure, her life had always been more structured than the rest of ours, her afternoons and weekends filled with any number of rehearsals and lessons while we sat around in SJ's yard and drank beers. She'd missed a whole summer once, at a quasi-professional performing arts day camp that left her too exhausted in the evenings to do anything but go straight home and sleep. Olivia was different; that much was undeniable. Still, that had never seemed to matter before—to her or to anyone else.

Olivia frowned then, at an expression on my face real or imagined. "I didn't mean—" she began, but I shook my head at her.

"No, of course not," I said quickly. "I know." Still, I thought suddenly of what she'd said the night Juliet called to offer me the spot in Daisy Chain: *What else are you going to do?* Right up until the moment the phone rang, there'd been no way I was getting out of Jessell, either—and if the look on Lucas's face today had been any indication, I might wind up right back there. I didn't know which side of Olivia's line of demarcation I fell on.

"I'm sorry today sucked so much," Olivia said quietly.

I waved my hand, not wanting to make a big deal out of it—not wanting to think about it at all. "Oh, I'll survive."

"I know you will." She smiled. "It's what you do."

"Like a cockroach," I joked.

"That's not *exactly* the metaphor I would have picked."

"I never said I was literary," I pointed out.

"Dork." Olivia made a face at me, but then she smiled. "So," she said, pulling one leg up onto the seat and looking for all the world like a little kid with a secret. "Alex."

"Uh-huh," I said, happy to change the subject. *"Alex."* It had been a long time since Olivia had liked a boy—not since things with her last boyfriend, Stupid Pete Tripp, had crashed and burned at junior prom last year. I bit my lip, remembering how devastated she'd been when he broke up with her for Valerie Burton: I'd watched her like a parole officer for weeks afterward, packing all her favorite foods in my own lunch and doing everything I could think of short of force-feeding her to get her to eat them. It was the first time I'd ever seriously considered getting her mom involved: it wasn't until she almost fainted in gym one morning and I'd actually gone to the pay phone in the lobby and dialed her house phone that Olivia came after me and promised me she'd stop. We'd gone directly to the cafeteria, where I'd watched her eat a turkey sandwich with chips and a fruit salad. It took two full periods; I missed a geometry test and had to take a zero. I sat there until every bite was gone.

That had been more than a year ago, though. Olivia was better now.

"So what's your plan of attack?" I asked, tucking one foot under me as I finished my milk shake. It felt good to be talking to her about non-performance stuff, to be back on more familiar ground.

Olivia shrugged. "I don't know. He's kind of reticent, you know? Shy, like."

"Well, in that case"—I raised my eyebrows—"you could always stand under his apartment window, sing him a love song."

"Shut up." Olivia made a face at me. "I'm serious."

"I know you are," I said. "Just talk to him. Be your fabulous self. He'd be crazy not to fall in love with you."

"Are you pep-talking me?" Olivia asked.

"A little." I grinned. "Is it working?"

"A *little*." She banged her head lightly against the seat. "He's already a *little* famous, you realize. I don't know. He seems like . . . out of my league."

"He is not out of your league," I said immediately, feeling irrationally annoyed at Alex, wherever he was, and not wanting to think about why. "And he's not even that famous! Regionally at best. One MTV spring break show, you said? That hardly even counts."

"Snob." Olivia laughed. He was a big deal around Atlanta, she told me: he did a lot of regional theater, had cut a demo a couple of years earlier that had made it all the way up the ladder at Jupiter Records in Hollywood. He'd toured with the Broadway Across America company of *Oliver!* when he was five. "Either way, he's, like, not the kind of guy they make at home, you know what I mean? He's . . . different."

"Sure," I said. "But he's also kind of a nerd, right? I mean, he seems so *corny*."

Olivia looked at me quizzically. "What makes you say that?" she asked.

"I just—" I broke off, realizing abruptly that I hadn't actually gotten around to telling her about meeting Alex by the vending machines last night. It was a small, stupid thing—but for some reason it felt like it was too late now, that there was no way to say it out loud without making it into something bigger than it was. "All of them are, I mean. Hurricane State. The whole pop star thing."

"You know we're doing the exact same thing as them."

"Uh-huh." I grinned. "And I think it's corny of us, too."

Olivia made a face at that. "All right," she said. "But promise you'll come to my rescue if you see me looking like a total loser."

"Don't I always?" We laughed, and I breathed a secret sigh of relief. "Should we pick up fro-yo to bring back to everyone?" I asked as we crumpled up our waxed paper wrappers. "I think I saw a place on the way."

Olivia nodded. "That sounds awesome." She put the car in drive and turned to look at me before she pulled out of the parking lot. "I'm really glad you're the person I'm here with, you know that?"

That made me smile, something deep inside me settling down. "I'm glad you're the person I'm here with, too."

EIGHT

"Need another?" Trevor asked a few nights later, handing me a Corona from the fridge in one of the dingy apartments on the ground level of the complex. Austin had gotten a cartload of beers at the liquor mart across the street, so the Hurricane State guys had invited us for a party.

"Sure," I said, smiling. Trevor was easy to be around, I was finding, with his casual bearing and relaxed, *isn't this bananas?* attitude about all things pop star. "Thanks."

"Okay, okay, important question!" Mikey called from the living room, voice as loud as a carnival hawker's. "If you were going to have a threesome with two Spice Girls, which two would you pick?"

He was answered by assorted groans and hoots from the group crammed into the living room, all of us crowded onto various surfaces and the smell of body spray and weed pungent in the air. "You're disgusting," Ashley informed him, rolling her eyes from where she was sitting beside me cross-legged on the carpet. We'd spent the afternoon singing scale after scale with Lucas, and my throat felt scratchy and raw.

Mikey shook his head. "Now, don't feel left out of the conversation, ladies," he said magnanimously. He was the self-styled cruise director of the group; it was easy to picture him telling crowds of girls to clap their hands and jump. "You're welcome to answer as well."

"Ignore him," Austin said, passing a joint around the circle with one hand and a bag of Doritos with the other. The apartment was his and Mario's; they called their place the Model UN because Austin was Filipino, Mario was Mexican, and they'd both done catalog work for department stores before they came here. Everybody in the boys' group looked like they'd been genetically engineered for maximum physical attractiveness. "We don't let him out of his cage much."

"Clearly," Kristin said, then shook her head as he offered her the weed. "That stuff is murder on your voice." She looked at the rest of us with authority. "You guys shouldn't do it, either."

"Yes, Mom," Ashley said with a smile, and I laughed. A few days in, I was starting to feel a little less awkward around her and Kristin. Both of them were super into hugging, which didn't really bother me except when we were all sweaty and gross from rehearsal, which was actually a lot of the time.

I finished my beer and got up to pee in the grody bathroom; when I came out, Alex was waiting in the dimly lit hallway, leaning against the wall with his hands shoved deep in the pockets of his baggy khaki shorts. "Hey," he said.

"Hey," I said, stopping abruptly, with a quiet intake of breath I hoped he didn't notice. I'd purposely avoided him since the first day of rehearsals, pushing Olivia forward and melting into the back of the group whenever Hurricane State was around, telling myself whatever flicker of interest I'd felt wasn't worth it. "Having fun?"

Alex nodded. "I am," he said, and there was that slow, sweet smile again, the same one from the night by the vending machines, the one I was working hard not to notice. The girls and I, crowded into the doorway of the studio and probably looking anything but inconspicuous, had caught the very end of Hurricane State's dance rehearsal yesterday. Even just watching for a few minutes, it was obvious that Alex was the most talented one in the group: in my experience, teenage boys mostly look like total boners when they're dancing, but Alex looked natural somehow, like he already knew the steps in his body, so he didn't have to think about it too much. "How about you?"

"Uh, yeah." I glanced over my shoulder toward the living room, where I could see Olivia with her head ducked close to

Kristin's, their matching waterfalls of shiny hair. "I'm good. So. I'll see ya."

Alex nodded, still smiling. "Okay."

"Okay," I repeated like an idiot. "So. Bye."

I told myself to pull it together and met up with the other girls, who had decamped to the apartment's tiny patio, presumably to escape the voice-ruining pot smoke. As I opened the sliding glass door, the damp heat slammed into me like a wall of water, carrying the smell of car exhaust and humidity. Across the parking lot I could see a couple of barely dressed women waiting at the bus stop—probably not, I suspected, for a bus.

"He definitely likes you," Ashley was saying, tipping her Corona in Olivia's direction and stretching her long legs out in front of her, crossing her delicate ankles. She was perched primly on one of the wobbly rubber-and-metal lawn chairs that came with all the apartments. "Dana," she said, "don't you think Alex likes Olivia?"

I tugged the end of Olivia's hair and squeezed into the rickety chair beside her. "I think he's a moron if he doesn't."

"That's what I keep telling her," Ashley said confidently. Ash was seventeen, a year younger than Olivia and me; she had a boyfriend at home in Oak Park and was saving herself for marriage, which didn't stop her from taking a healthy interest in everyone else's sex life. She'd flat-out asked me if I was a virgin the first night we met. "I love this, you guys meeting up again after all this time. It's classic. I think he's just shy, is all. He needs a girl who's gonna make the first move."

Mikey slid the door open just then, the noise from inside suddenly amplified in the hot, quiet air. His shirt had Dr. Evil from *Austin Powers* on the front of it. "What are we gossiping about, ladies?" he asked.

"Nothing you need to know about," Olivia said, her voice turning so chilly that I almost felt bad for him—Mikey seemed harmless enough. She stood up, brushing some imaginary debris off her white denim shorts. "We're going back in."

Inside, the boys were watching old episodes of *SNL* on Comedy Central; Alex grinned at me as we came through the door, scooting over to make room on the couch. Mario plopped down beside him before I could react one way or the other: "You all wanna play Asshole?" he asked. "I got cards."

I settled myself on the floor instead, rubbing idly at a spot on the side of my knee I'd missed when I shaved that morning. I was starting to feel tired and bored. The *Saturday Night Live* rerun ended; Mario wound up Asshole three rounds in a row. Olivia got up for another beer and Kristin followed her, a look on her face like she was about to hatch a plot—and sure enough, on their way back into the living room the two of them started singing that song from the musical *Rent* about lighting the candle, which I knew from earlier this week was one of Kristin's favorites to belt at the top of her lungs whether anyone was listening or not.

I was surprised—for all the parties we'd been to together, I'd never seen Olivia stage an impromptu performance like this—but I understood all at once why she'd done it the moment Kristin dropped out and pulled Alex off the couch, pushing him up toward the TV, where Olivia was standing, as he jumped right in on the boy part, like a star athlete who'd been waiting for the coach to put him in. Their voices sounded right at home together. Olivia wrapped her arm around his waist.

Well, I thought as they got to their big finish, taken off guard by the sharp zing of disappointment behind my rib cage, feeling caught out and embarrassed and not wanting to investigate why.

That's that.

I wanted to dump my Corona in the sink and call it a night, but Trevor followed me down the hallway, and ten minutes later I was sitting on the counter next to the refrigerator, eating Cheetos out of the bag and talking to him about Stephen King movies, which Olivia despised with every fiber of her being but which it turned out he and I both loved. "Ever seen *Cujo*, though?" I was saying, when Alex came in. "*Cujo* is freaking terrifying."

"*Cujo* is scary as shit," Trevor agreed. Then, to Alex, who I was clearly ignoring: "Hey, man."

"Hey," Alex said, leaning against the counter for a minute. He opened the mostly empty fridge and peered inside it. Then he closed it again.

"Looking for something?" I asked him finally, an edge in my voice.

"Looking for you," Alex said.

I snorted, disbelief and a little bit of horror. Alex grinned.

"I gotta go," Trevor announced suddenly, tipping his beer in my direction before he headed back into the living room.

"You shouldn't have said that," I told Alex, once we were alone under the bright fluorescent light. This kitchen had the same dingy countertops and white cabinets as ours did, though it was closed to the living room: for the moment, at least, he and I were alone.

Alex raised his eyebrows. He was wearing a soft-looking gray T-shirt, that tangle of brightly colored friendship bracelets looped around his wrist. "Why not?" he asked.

"Because he's gonna think—" I broke off, waving my hand vaguely. "Whatever. Forget it."

"Trevor's my roommate," Alex told me, like this explained something. "He's a good dude."

I shrugged. "I'm sure he is."

"He is," Alex said, taking a couple of steps closer. His skin was perfectly, immaculately clear, just a couple of tiny freckles near the side of his mouth. It kind of made me want to punch him. "You feel like taking a walk with me?" he asked.

I felt my eyebrows shoot up like I wasn't even controlling them, like they were two independent creatures on the top of my face. "You've got time for a walk?" I couldn't resist saying, even though I knew it was infantile. "You don't have a duet you need to be working on?"

Alex made a face at that, sheepish, like I'd caught him at something embarrassing: painting his nails, maybe, or jerking off. "That was kind of a performance we put on back there, huh?" he asked.

I wiped my Cheeto-y hands on my thighs, leaving a pale film of orange dust on my skin. "It was kind of a performance," I agreed.

"I know," Alex said. He was close enough now that his hip bone was touching my bare knee, his body burning-hot through his T-shirt. "It looked like showing off. I just get real wrapped up in it when people are singing, you know?" he asked, sounding sincere. "It doesn't actually matter who or what. My dad's a minister, and my brothers used to hate sitting there all day on Sundays wearing ties and whatever. But I always kind of liked it, 'cause of the singing."

I didn't know if it was real, this *aw, shucks* thing he did all the time. A minister's son, Jesus Christ. "The music moved you?" I asked dubiously.

That made Alex laugh—this openmouthed rumble that was deeper than his normal voice so that for a moment it felt like I could see how he'd be when he was older, when he'd grown into all his long, elegant limbs. He was going to be a lot more than regionally famous. "Kind of!" he said, shrugging sort of helplessly. He had a little bit of an accent, that southern lilt. "Don't be mad."

"Oh, I'm not mad," I said. I wasn't, either—after all, I had no reason to be. Olivia was my best friend; Olivia liked Alex. As far as I was concerned, I told myself, it was as simple as that.

But Alex wasn't buying. "You sure?" he asked, slipping one bold finger into the belt loop of my shorts and tugging me a little bit closer.

I let myself be pulled for just a second, then sat back on my hands. God, what was I doing? "I'm sure," I said firmly.

"Okay," Alex said. "Then I believe you. But I also think you're probably not taking that walk with me, huh?"

I grinned back at him then—it was impossible not to, his eyelashes and his collarbones, the pull in my stomach and chest. Then I hopped down off the counter. "You're smarter than you look," I told him cheerfully, tugging his belt loop once in retaliation and slipping past him out the kitchen door.

NINE

Olivia's bed was already made when I woke up on Saturday morning, though I could hear voices in the living room; when I got up and went in to investigate, hoping Charla had made something besides oatmeal for breakfast, I found Kristin, Olivia, and Ash all getting ready to leave. "Oh!" Kristin said when she saw me. "You're up!"

"Hey," I said, tightening my sleep-messy ponytail; Olivia's car keys dangled from her hand. "What are you guys doing?"

"We're going to check out the mall here," Ashley said, a little too brightly. "You wanna come?"

I glanced from Olivia to the others and back again, thinking, *Thanks for the invite*, but not wanting to betray myself by saying it out loud. Olivia was looking at something in the neighborhood of my left ear. "Sure," I told them slowly. "Let me just get dressed."

The mall was a twenty-minute drive from the complex, newly built and aggressively air-conditioned, filled with the kinds of high-end stores I'd only ever seen ads for in magazines. We had a mall in Jessell—we weren't *that* much of a backwater—but it was nothing like this. The floors were a shiny white marble; a fountain burbled away in an atrium, giving off a clean, bleachy smell. I felt like somebody was going to accuse me of shoplifting if I breathed wrong.

"I figured it wasn't worth it to wake you," Olivia explained quietly as we trailed across the food court. "I mean, you hate malls."

I nodded. "No, yeah," I said, telling myself it didn't bother me, that I was bringing this strange, unsettled feeling upon myself. "Of course."

Kristin and Ash were in their element, flitting from store to store, trying on that dress and those sandals, shiny gold sunglasses and jeans specially designed to give your butt extra lift. Olivia and I had never really been recreational shoppers—it's *boring*, if you never actually buy anything—but I was surprised how much she knew about different designers, keeping up with Kristin and Ashley as they chattered away happily.

"You know what would be so cute?" Kristin suggested,

doing laps in a boutique where all the clothes were black and white and denim. "We should get matching T-shirts."

"Yes!" Ashley said. "How adorable would that be?"

I thought it sounded kind of like something out of peewee soccer, honestly, but this didn't feel like the time to say that out loud. When I looked at the price tag on the shirt they were talking about, though, my eyeballs almost fell right out of my head.

"Olivia," I said urgently, catching her by the arm and pulling her behind a stack of jeans. "This T-shirt is, like, forty bucks."

Olivia bit her lip. "I can lend you the money," she said.

"No, that's not—" I shook my head. "I'm not asking you to front me, I just think it's ridiculous to spend that much on a T-shirt when—"

"They are really cute, though," she pointed out. "And we're supposed to get our first paychecks this week. We need to look the part, right?"

"Look the part?" I repeated, trying not to laugh. "You sound like Kristin."

"What's up?" Kristin asked, and I shook my head again. The last thing I wanted was for her to know I couldn't afford it, that I could stretch forty bucks into a month of groceries back in Jessell. That it was one more way I didn't belong here.

"Nothing," I said brightly, holding up the T-shirt and smiling. I could always return it later, right? Nobody needed to know. "You're right—these are perfect. What else are you getting?"

A couple of nights later, we'd just gotten back from rehearsal, were still dropping our bags in the bedrooms, when the apartment phone rang. "Dana!" Charla hollered from the kitchen. "Phone's for you."

I was surprised. My mom hadn't called at all since we'd been down here; instead Mrs. Maxwell had phoned for both of us, Olivia and I passing the phone back and forth like sisters at camp. "Mom?" I said when I picked up the receiver. "Everything okay?"

"Dana?" Sarah Jane's voice said. "Is that you? We're in town tonight!"

She turned up twenty minutes later, pulling her beat-up hatchback into the parking lot with Kerry-Ann and Becky in tow. She was wearing cutoffs and a tank top, barefoot on the concrete as they all climbed out of the car. "Look at this!" she crowed, turning a 360 on the concrete. "You guys are *fance*!"

"Your high school friends!" Kristin cooed as we all tromped back up to the apartment, Kerry-Ann exclaiming over the size of the bathroom and Becky bouncing experimentally on the bed. "That's so cute!"

Ashley was more direct. "How long are they staying?" she wanted to know.

"Just the night," Olivia assured her quickly. It was the

first thing Liv had said in a while, actually; when I glanced over at her, she had a funny look on her face.

"You okay?" I murmured.

Olivia nodded. "I just wish they'd called first, you know?"

"They did," I pointed out.

"No, like, *actually* called." She shrugged, dropped her voice to a whisper. "I just worry we're, like, imposing by having them stay here, you know?"

I frowned. "Imposing on who?" I asked. "Kristin and Ash? What do they care?"

"I don't know." Olivia glanced over her shoulder. "But nobody else's home friends have showed up."

"Maybe they don't have any," I suggested, and Olivia laughed. Still, I watched her eyes cut again to Sarah Jane and Becky, and all at once it occurred to me that it wasn't imposing on the others she was worried about. Olivia was *embarrassed*, I realized—of Sarah Jane's shitty car and loudness, of Becky's thick accent and the fact that you could see her purple bra though her top. I bit my lip, looking back and forth uneasily. If our friends—the people we'd grown up with, the place we'd come from—were something to be ashamed of, did that mean I was, too?

"You guys hungry?" I asked.

All of us went out to dinner at Chili's that night, the boys tagging along when they heard we had friends in town. Becky and Trevor paired off almost immediately, the two of them all over each other down at the far end of the table like a pair of climbing vines. I sat between Kerry-Ann and SJ, trying not to notice when Olivia stayed on the other side of the table with Kristin and Ash. *These are our friends*, I wanted to remind her. *Our* real *friends*.

Instead I turned to Sarah Jane, gesturing grandly around the noisy restaurant. "So this is fame," I joked. "All the nachos and quesadillas you can possibly eat."

"I mean, we don't usually go to places like this," Kristin assured her from across the table. She glanced over at Olivia, who'd ordered a salad. "It's almost impossible to stick to a diet here, you know? Even the cheese and whatnot they put on supposedly healthy stuff really adds up."

"Olivia can eat whatever she wants," I said loudly. Then, turning to the waitress, "May I please have extra guac?"

When I glanced back across the table I saw that Alex was looking at me, grinning. I turned away, but not before SJ saw and nudged my leg with hers under the table. "Who's that one?" she asked me quietly.

"That one is Olivia's crush," I informed her, and SJ didn't ask about him again after that.

"Me and Keith broke up," she reported later, when I went outside with her for a smoke break while the boys demolished another plate of nachos and Kristin and Ash debated seriously the best technique for achieving pure vowels while singing. "For good this time. That's why we're going to Miami."

I exhaled, sitting down on a wooden bench near the door of the restaurant. "Oh, SJ, I'm sorry."

Sarah Jane shook her head. "It's fine. I mean, it's not, it sucks, but. Like I've been saying since freshman year, he's an asshole. Anyway." She blew a long plume of smoke into the muggy air. "No reason not to get away for a couple days, right?" She grinned. "You should screw this Popsicle stand, come down with us."

"I wish," I said. It sounded awesome, actually—sitting on the beach with no responsibilities, finding a couple of guys to buy us beers. No rehearsal. No pressure. No niggling interest in a boy who was decidedly off-limits; no feeling of always getting it wrong.

"So is this what it's like all the time?" Sarah Jane asked, flicking her cigarette into a nearby ashtray and sitting down, neither one of us in any hurry to go back inside.

"Going out and stuff?" I shook my head. "Normally we're rehearsing and learning lyrics and dances. Honestly, I'm usually passed out in bed by ten."

"No," Sarah Jane said, smirking a little. "I mean, is this what *they're* like all the time?"

"They're not so bad!" I said, and Sarah Jane laughed.

"You're a terrible liar."

"Fine," I admitted after a moment; then, unable to resist, I told her about the matching forty-dollar T-shirts.

"For a *T-shirt*?" She gaped. "Come the fuck on."

"Thank you!" I said, vindicated. "I thought it was insane, too."

SJ shrugged, stretching her legs out in front of her. "They're a different kind of girl, is all."

"Yeah," I fired back. "Rich."

"Not even that," Sarah Jane said thoughtfully. "I mean, like . . . sheltered. Used to having other people take care of them. You know I love Olivia, but she's that way, too."

I felt my back straighten, involuntary. "No, she isn't."

"She is," SJ said gently, no judgment in her voice at all. "But you're not." She was quiet for a moment; cars pulled in and out of the parking lot, velvety night-blue sky and the smell of a storm coming. "Is everything okay with y'all?" she asked, sounding cautious. "You and Liv?"

"Yeah," I said, too quickly; it sounded like I was lying, but I didn't know how to try to convince her without making it worse. "Why wouldn't it be?"

"I don't know," Sarah Jane said, frowning. "Just asking. Lots of changes."

"Not that many. Come on," I said, standing up and holding out my hand. "Let's get back."

I walked Sarah Jane and the others downstairs the next morning, sun glaring off the concrete and SJ's pink sunglasses shoved onto her face.

"I wish you guys didn't have to go," I said, and I was surprised to realize that it was the truth. Since yesterday, I'd felt happier and more at home than I had since we'd gotten to Orlando. But how could that possibly be true—how could I possibly be lonely here? I had Olivia with me. My actual best friend in the world.

"Let me know if you need anything, okay?" Sarah Jane instructed, rolling down the window to look at me over the top of her sunglasses. "You ever want to be picked up, I can be here in a day to take you home."

"I'm good," I promised her. "But thanks."

I stood in the parking lot, waved good-bye as they pulled out into traffic. I watched the car until it disappeared.

TEN

In Orlando, I was an insomniac. Physically exhausted as I was from our hours of rehearsal, every night it felt like it took me longer and longer to settle down. I'd been sharing rooms with Olivia for more than a decade, her deep, even breaths lulling me like a metronome; now, though, I stared at the ceiling for hours after we turned the lights off, my mind whirring with a strange new anxiety, with harmonies I had yet to properly learn. Ashley suggested hypnosis. Charla plied me with chamomile tea. But nothing worked.

I kicked off the covers and then pulled them on again, shivering in the chilly forced air as Olivia breathed deeply on the other side of the room. Finally I got up, put a bra on underneath my T-shirt, and headed downstairs to the pool. It was late enough that the college kids who were usually down here at night had all passed out, and save for a couple of empty beer bottles rolling back and forth on the concrete, it was quiet. The two cats that always hung out around the complex—Boy Cat and Girl Cat, the guys called them—skulked underneath the lounge chairs, their green eyes glowing in the dark. I sat down on the edge of the deep end, dangling my feet into the cool, still water.

The pool was lined with a couple of sad-looking palm trees and surrounded by rough, cracked cement. I hadn't packed my bathing suit when we came here—I hadn't known there'd be a pool—and it felt stupid to go out and waste money on one now when we hardly had any free time. The lights recessed into the walls of the pool turned the water pink and blue.

"Don't get scared," a quiet voice said, somewhere over my left shoulder. "It's just me."

I gasped and turned around, legs splashing in the water, scraping the side of my knee on the sharp concrete edge of the pool. There was Alex, sitting at one of the metal tables next to a giant freestanding ashtray, face half-dark and half-golden in the yellow glow of the bug-pocked lights.

"Jeez, Alex," I said, louder than I meant to. "What are you, stalking me?"

"I was already down here!" he protested. "Maybe *you're* stalking *me*."

"Yeah, right. *Don't get scared*," I mimicked in a low, creepy voice, rubbing my skinned knee. "How am I not supposed to get scared when you say that?"

"Crap, did you actually hurt yourself?" Alex asked, getting up out of the chair and crouching down on the side of the pool next to me. His white T-shirt looked almost translucent in this light. "Shit, Dana, I'm sorry."

"No, it's fine," I said—it was, too, not even really bleeding, but Alex ducked his head to peer at it anyway, and when I looked up his face was right next to mine. "Hi," I said, feeling like I might laugh.

"Hi," he said back, and then we were just staring at each other, this charged moment passing between us that felt like shoving a fork into an electrical socket, which I had actually done once when I was three but didn't really remember. This jolt I could imagine feeling for a long time.

"I should go," I said, making to get up off the pool deck. "I'll see you around, yeah?"

"Can I ask you something?" Alex looked at me curiously. "Why are you avoiding me?"

I huffed at that, shaking my head a little. *Because I think you're cute and weird and talented*, I didn't tell him. *Because my best friend does, too.* "I'm not avoiding you!" I said instead, trying to sound like I thought he was ridiculous. "I have rehearsal in the morning, is all."

"Yeah. So do I," Alex pointed out, shrugging. "How's that going, anyway?"

"What, rehearsals? Fine," I lied. In reality, Lucas had yelled at me for so long today that I thought it was a minor miracle he hadn't burst a blood vessel in his eye. "How are yours?"

"They're good," Alex said immediately; then he grinned and shook his head. "Actually today was brutal. We had to do that breath control exercise for like an hour—you know, the one where you have to hold a scrap of paper against the wall for an eight count just by blowing on it? Have they made you guys do that? I almost passed out."

"Yeah, so did Ashley," I told him, leaving out the part where my vision got pretty spotty, too. But then I didn't like that, the idea that I was trying to impress him, so I added, kind of abruptly, "I almost barfed."

Alex laughed, but not meanly. "It's so hard, right? I can sing and dance fine, but stuff like that kills me. Me and my brothers used to have these contests at the pool, you know, who could hold their breath underwater the longest? I lost every time."

"How old are your brothers?" I couldn't resist asking. Alex seemed like somebody who came from a house like Olivia's—where everyone was neat and tidy, swing set in the backyard and all of them pressed and combed for church on Sunday. I wondered if he could tell just by looking at me that I'd never been inside a church in my life, and told myself I didn't care.

"Nineteen and twenty," Alex told me. "I'm the youngest. My mom had us all in a row."

"Olivia and I are like sisters," I blurted, desperate to work her into the conversation any way I possibly could. I felt myself blush, but Alex just nodded.

"You guys know each other from home, yeah?"

"She's my best friend," I told him. "She's great. She's the one who wanted to audition in the first place. I mean, you know how talented she is."

"So you're what, just kind of tagging along for the ride?"

That cut a little close to the bone. "I mean, I'm not party crashing," I snapped. "I got picked same as everybody else."

Alex turned ghost-white. "No, no, of course," he said quickly. "I didn't mean—I just meant you kind of give off a different vibe than the other girls, was all."

"And what vibe is *that*?" I demanded.

"No, I mean—" Alex huffed out a breath, then smiled a little. "I'm doing this wrong," he said. "I noticed you, is what I meant. From that first night in the parking lot. You stood out to me." He shrugged, glancing down for a second, then back at me. His eyelashes were as long as a girl's. "In, like, a good way."

"I—Oh." I snorted a laugh of my own, then frowned abruptly: God, this was so, so bad. I started getting to my feet for real now.

"Anyway," Alex said, like he knew I was about to bolt and didn't want me to, like he was trying to keep me talking. "I'm just saying, I don't doubt your pop-star capabilities. A year from now you'll be living in Beverly Hills and driving a Ferrari, just watch."

I smirked. "Of course that's what you want," I said, sitting back down again in spite of myself, kicking my legs through the chilly water. "A Ferrari. Boys always want stupid stuff like that."

"Stupid stuff, huh?" Alex raised his eyebrows. He had a really pretty mouth. "What would *you* want?"

I shook my head, looking down at the frayed hem of my shorts. A door opened up on the second floor of the building, the flick of a lighter as a middle-aged woman lit a cigarette up on her balcony. The smoke curled through the humid air. "Forget it," I said quietly. "It's dumb."

"Come on," Alex said. "I'm just teasing. Tell me."

"You're going to laugh at me."

"I'm not going to laugh at you."

"You are."

"I'm not."

"A minivan."

Alex looked at me full-on then, elegant eyebrows arched and the edges of that pink mouth just barely twitching. "I'm not laughing," he said finally.

"I just like the idea of it, okay?" I said, feeling stupid, glancing up to make sure cigarette lady hadn't overheard. I don't know why it never occurred to me to just lie to Alex about my answer, to say something cooler and more normal. For some reason it didn't seem like an option. "Like one of the fancy ones with a TV in it, like it's this little house that just rolls around and nobody can touch you. Like being in a spaceship."

"A Dodge spaceship," Alex said.

I shook my head again, making a face. "I knew you'd think it was dumb."

"I don't think it's dumb," he said, sliding his hand a tiny bit closer to mine on the concrete in a move I wasn't sure if I was meant to notice or not. The edges of our pinkies brushed. "Hey. Dana. I don't think it's dumb."

I took a deep breath, glanced up at where Olivia was sleeping. Pulled my hand away. "My mom's car," I told him, "the car I learned to drive on? We've had it since before I was born and it just, like, scrapes along the road. Like you can almost feel the highway under your butt. That's all." I shrugged, pretty sure that just from those couple of sentences he'd be able to extrapolate a whole bunch of other undesirable things about me, my family, and where I was from. It made me feel equal parts embarrassed and defensive, worried what he'd think of me and simultaneously telling myself I didn't care. "What do you actually drive, like, a Volvo or something?"

"No!" Alex said, like I'd offended him somehow. Then, though: "A Suburban."

"Oh, *okay*, then." I rolled my eyes. God, his house probably had a white picket fence in front of it. I would have hated him, anywhere else. "Who even *are* you?"

"Who are *you*?" Alex countered. "Hmm? Mysterious Dana Cartwright."

I laughed. "I am not mysterious."

"You are, though," Alex said, and I didn't know what

to say to that, exactly. Upstairs, cigarette lady went back inside. I was getting ready to leave for real when Alex stood up all at once. "I'm gonna swim," he said decisively. "You coming?"

"What?" I said, gawking at him. It had to be almost two in the morning by now. A hot, stuffy wind rustled the fronds of the palm trees overhead. "Right this minute? Absolutely not."

"What are you, scared you're gonna get in trouble?" he teased.

No, I'm afraid I'm going to break my best friend's damn heart. "Okay," I said, standing up to look him in the eye, though even at my full height, my forehead was only about level to his chin. "You of all people are not calling me chickenshit."

"Why me of all people?" Alex asked, taking both my hands this time. I didn't pull away. My heart was a hummingbird inside my chest, a constant shallow thrumming; I smelled concrete and chlorine and boy. "What is it about me in particular that makes it so especially ridiculous?"

"Well, you drive a Suburban, to start."

"This from the girl who aspires to own a mom-mobile."

"Oh, you're a comedian." I let go of his hands to flip him a double bird, but I was smiling. A hot, humid breeze ambled across the back of my neck. "And you're a rule-follower, is why it's ridiculous. I can already tell." He was, too. I wasn't just giving him a hard time for the fun of it. He was the kind of person who'd never had a reason not to be. He probably got straight A's at school and still asked the teacher for extra credit.

Alex tipped his head at that, like, *fair enough*. "Sometimes," he admitted, reaching back behind him and pulling his T-shirt off in one fast, fluid motion. "Not always."

I glanced at him, glanced up at the apartment.

Glanced back.

It wasn't like I'd never seen a guy without his shirt on before—wasn't like I'd never taken a guy's shirt off myself—but something about seeing Alex half-naked unnerved me a little, his flat, smooth stomach and the sharp cut of his hip bones. There was a thin golden trail of hair that started just below his navel and disappeared into the waistband of his shorts. I felt my whole body flush.

"You coming?" Alex asked, and jumped in.

"No!" I said, then: "Damn it." I huffed a noisy breath, then pulled off my T-shirt and hopped over the side of the pool with a quiet splash. When I surfaced he was staring at me.

"Jesus, you're pretty," he said, and I rolled my eyes again. My bra was a screaming neon pink.

"You are," Alex said, taking a step closer. There were flecks of pool water in his eyelashes. "I know you think I'm corny and, like, southern, but, you're the prettiest girl I've ever seen."

"I'm southern, too," I pointed out, ignoring the other part.

"Dana," he said, like I was being dense on purpose.

"Alex," I replied, mimicking his tone exactly. God, I had to go inside.

Alex smiled almost bashfully. "You think I'm full of crap?" he asked.

I thought about that for a moment. "No," I admitted finally.

"Come here," he said, holding his hand out until I took it, pulling me through the cold water until my chest was right up against his.

"Why?" I asked him as I went.

"I want to do something."

"What?" I asked, even though I already knew what, knew exactly, and for the first time all night I wasn't thinking about Olivia at all. I could feel the steam rising off Alex's skin. When he kissed me, it was totally new and like something we'd already done a hundred times before, his soft tongue and the press of his shoulders and his fingers threaded through mine underneath the water, both of us holding on tight tight tight. Up above us, the purple sky stretched out to infinity, too much light from the city to see any stars.

ELEVEN

I woke up the next morning with a pit in my stomach the size of the Grand Canyon, a cold, damp gust of guilt yawning through. I stared at the ceiling for a long time while I waited for Olivia to wake up, trying to think about anything but Alex, about last night in the pool. About the way he'd looked at me like I was so valuable, like I was a rare, precious thing.

It didn't matter, I told myself firmly. It wasn't going to happen again. I didn't want to be the kind of girl who'd kiss the guy her best friend liked. I felt like a piece of crap. I'd tell her first thing this morning, I'd apologize like hell, and then we could move on. That would be that.

Finally, I couldn't wait another second: "Liv," I said softly. "Olivia, wake up. I need to talk to you."

Olivia stirred, her dark hair a curtain across her face. "Hmm?" she mumbled into the pillow, but before she could lift her head, there was Charla's sharp rap at the bedroom door.

"Up and at 'em, ladies! Breakfast in five!"

Olivia's eyes popped open then, one smooth movement as she flung the covers back, stretched, and headed for the bathroom. "Morning!" she called to me over her shoulder. I flopped back onto my pillow, all my momentum lost at once. I'd tell her tonight, then, I promised myself. It wasn't even that big of a deal, after all—just one kiss, a stupid mistake, temporary insanity.

Right?

Lucas was in a particularly crummy mood that day, the frown lines in his face so deep you could have planted a row of corn in them. For once it wasn't just me, either—he yelled at Olivia for the way she was holding her shoulders, snarked at Kristin until she was on the verge of tears.

"Don't worry, teacher's pet," I said to Olivia as we packed up our stuff and headed down the hallway toward the exit. Her mouth had gone thin and pale the way it always did when she was upset; I wanted to cheer her up. "He's on me like that every day, and I'm still here."

"For now," Kristin said behind me, not quite under her breath.

That stopped me. I whirled around to face her, eyes wide. "Whoa." It was the first time she'd said anything like that to me—and sure, I'd assumed she was thinking it, but it was a whole other thing to hear it out loud. Right away I was spoiling for a fight. "I'm sorry?"

Kristin looked like she was about to say something else—and *Good*, I thought, *let's get into it*—but the boys spilled out of their own rehearsal just then, the whole noisy scrum of them, Mikey singing a loud, warbly version of a Sting song: *"Roxanne,"* he wailed, *"you don't have to put on your red dress."*

"It's red light," Trevor corrected, ambling down the hallway after him. "She doesn't have to put out the red light."

"What? That makes no sense," Mikey argued. "It's her red dress, you know, her prostitutin' dress."

"No, it's the red—"

"Ladies," Austin said, interrupting their argument. "How's your day been?"

"Living the dream," Olivia said, all smiles all of a sudden, but I barely heard her. I barely heard any of them, because Alex was looking at me—not a general look, the way one normal person would look at another normal person, but a very specific kind of look, the kind of look that could have given both of us away in half a second. His cheeks were flushed from rehearsing. My face was on fire from what Kristin had said. It was all too much, this whole entire summer was; I had to get out of here.

"Come on," I said, slinging my arm around Olivia and steering her toward the parking lot. "I'm starved."

"Can you believe that?" I asked Olivia when we got back to the apartment, shutting the door to our room and flinging myself onto the mattress. "When have I ever been anything but nice to that girl? To her face, anyway."

Olivia smiled. "She didn't mean it," she said, sitting down on her own bed and pulling her lyrics binder out of her shoulder bag. "It's been a rough day for everybody."

"It's been a rough day for her *face*," I said, grimacing; Olivia laughed for real then, which was what I'd been going for in the first place. "Hey," I said, picking at a loose thread on the bedspread. I'd spent the whole day trying to push Alex out of my mind, but seeing him made it obvious I needed to tell Olivia what had happened. "Can I talk to you a sec?"

"Yeah, of course." Olivia nodded, tucking her bare feet underneath her. The room smelled like hair spray and body mist. "Actually, okay, I wanted to talk to you, too. I was making a list of a bunch of vocal exercises you should try."

I snorted. "Really?"

"Yeah!" Olivia flipped to the front of her binder, pulling a sheet of paper out of the front pocket and handing it to me. "They're stuff my voice coach had me do back at home when I was just getting started. They're really helpful."

"Okay," I said slowly. I scanned the page, which was filled with Olivia's cramped, arthritic-looking cursive. She'd divided them up into categories, each with its own underlined heading: *Breathing, Pitch, Ear Training, Posture.* I felt the anxiety swell up in my chest just looking at the list.

"You think I need all these?"

"Yeah, no, I think you should try them!" Olivia urged. "It'll help. Here, stand up."

I blinked. "What, now?"

"Do you have a better time?"

I put the paper down on the bedspread. "No, but . . ." *But I need to tell you something important, and I'm afraid of what's going to happen when I do.* "I'm kind of tired now, though."

Olivia frowned. "We don't really have time for you to be tired, Dana."

There was an edge in her voice that took me by surprise. "Are you mad at me?" I asked, sitting up and looking at her closely.

Olivia shook her head. "No, of course not. It's just—I know you hate Kristin, but she and I were talking, and we thought—"

My heart dropped. "You talked to *Kristin* about me?"

Right away, I could tell Olivia knew she'd made a mistake. "Don't get defensive," she said.

"Well, then don't pick on me with some girl we just met!"

"I'm not picking on you!" She held her hands up. "But realistically, if we're going to make this group work, we need to do everything we can to make sure everybody's more or less at the same level, you know?"

I felt my cheeks flame. "I know I'm the worst one here, Liv. I don't need you to remind me."

Olivia rolled her eyes. "Don't be a baby," she said. "This is work, is all."

"Don't be a *baby*?" All at once I remembered what Sarah Jane had said about Olivia being the kind of person who was used to being taken care of. I'd never been the person in our relationship who got upset.

"I'm sorry," Liv said, putting the binder aside and coming to sit on the edge of my bed. "I didn't mean that. I know it's been harder for you than we thought since we got here."

I sighed noisily, flopping back onto the pillows. I felt embarrassed and bruised and far from her. "Today sucked," I said.

"Yeah," Olivia said. "It kind of did, huh?" She lay back beside me, nudged me with her shoulder. "I'm sorry," she told me.

"I'm sorry, too," I said to the ceiling. "I know you were trying to help."

We stayed like that for a while, the silence not quite comfortable. I could hear the sound of her breathing, the air conditioner clicking on and off overheard. Suddenly Olivia looked at me, alert. "I'm an asshole," she said. "What did you want to talk to me about?"

I hesitated. What I wanted to talk to her about was Alex, but now I didn't know how. It felt like a weird fissure had opened up between us, and telling her what had happened would only widen it. "Nothing," I promised, shaking my head into the pillows. "It wasn't a big deal at all."

TWELVE

"What are you doing tonight?" Alex asked me on Thursday afternoon at the studio, leaning against the wall beside the water cooler where I was refilling my bottle. He was wearing an old blue T-shirt from the Galveston Children's Theater; he smelled like deodorant and clean sweat.

"Um," I said, straightening up too quickly, splashing water all over my bare feet. I'd been dodging Alex all week, making sure we were never alone in the same place at the same time. "Hmm."

"Yeeeeees?" Alex prompted, the hint of a smile teasing at the edges of his mouth.

I made a face at him. "Well, I've got a binder full of vocal exercises with my name on it," I said. "So, you know. Probably that."

Alex shook his head at that. "That's too bad."

I rolled my eyes. "Too bad, huh?"

"It is too bad."

We looked at each other for a moment. *I like you*, his expression said. *You shouldn't*, is what I was trying to tell him, but I must not have been doing a very good job because Alex smiled for real then, one of those silver-dollar grins that you could use to power a city or send rocket ships to outer space. It felt like hitting the lottery, Alex's smile. It felt like getting picked to join a band. "I should get back," I finally said.

"What you *should* do is come out with us tonight," Alex told me, still leaning against the wall like he had no place in particular to be, even though I knew his rehearsal was going on just down the hall. "That's what I wanted to tell you in the first place. Austin knows some bar near here that doesn't card. We're going to go around nine or so. It'll probably be a total dump, but it might be fun."

"It might be," I agreed; in fact, I liked the idea of spending some time out with Olivia, for us to have a chance to goof around together like we used to back at home. And I liked the idea of seeing Alex, too. "But I don't think the other girls are going to go for it."

"You could come by yourself," Alex suggested, and I snorted.

"Yeah, right." I looked at him for another moment, debating. "I'll float it," I said finally. "Okay?"

Alex smiled again, pushed himself off the wall. "I'll take what I can get."

The bar Austin brought us to was a hot, tiny dive at the edge of a sketchy-looking strip mall twenty minutes from the apartments, with no windows and a big bald bouncer sitting on a stool outside the narrow door. He waved us inside without asking for ID, though, offering the girls and me an appraising leer as we passed. Cigarette smoke was thick in the air, coupled with the smell of old beer and something that seemed to be coming from the bathrooms.

"This is bleak," Ashley announced, peering around the dark, windowless space at the neon bar signs and a huge, smudgy mirror stamped with a whiskey logo. Alan Jackson was clanging away on the jukebox. A couple of greasy-looking guys sprawled on stools at one end of the bar.

"What'd I tell you?" Alex asked me, his mouth tipped so close to my ear that I could feel his warm breath on the back of my neck, making all the tiny hairs there stand straight up. "Kind of fun, right?"

I swallowed hard, then glanced at Olivia, who was flagging down the bartender. I'd been surprised when the other girls had been so willing to come out, knew in the back of my mind it was mostly so that Olivia could hang out with Alex. I felt like the worst kind of traitor.

"Come on," I said now, stepping away from Alex without looking back at him, grabbing Olivia's hand and pulling her toward the jukebox. "Let's dance."

The bar wasn't actually so bad once we switched the

music up; I drank my Bud Light, danced with Olivia and the others to the Spice Girls and Mariah Carey. Even Kristin seemed to be having fun. "I really love you guys," she promised as Austin spun her around and around, her dark hair swirling, the sentiment weird and out of character for her. "I'm sorry I was a bitch to you! We're gonna get so famous, I can feel it."

"What she can *feel* are those rum and Cokes," Olivia muttered, and I laughed. It felt like she'd come back to me, like we could have been at a house party in Jessell, everything the same as it had always been.

The bathrooms were through a back room with a pool table and a couple of dusty old pinball machines, wooden floors creaking like your foot might fall right through at any moment. I was wiping my hands on my jeans as I came through the door—of course there were no paper towels—and almost crashed right into Alex, who was waiting outside.

"Hey," he said. He was wearing jeans and a clean white T-shirt that made him look even more impossibly tan than normal, like someone whose body stored up sunlight.

"Hey," I echoed, tucking my hair behind my ears, suddenly nervous. He was standing so, so close. We stared at each other for a moment; I thought again that it was easy to see why Guy had picked him for Hurricane State, why everybody said he was the star. Alex was the kind of person you wanted to look at. The kind of person you wanted to be near all the time.

The jukebox had changed over to Joe Cocker, a lazy kind of old-school rock and roll that begged for a slow dance. I wished it were something really unromantic, like Ozzy Osbourne. I wished it were a polka from 1935.

If we stood here another second, I was pretty sure he was going to kiss me, so instead I grabbed his wrist roughly and held it up in front of my face, examining the dozen friendship bracelets looped around it—the bright primary colors of the ones that were newer, and the faded blues and greens of the ones he'd obviously been wearing for a long time. The designs were complicated—not just the simple braids I'd learned how to do at recess when I was a kid but intricate knots and patterns, thick diamonds and chevrons. They must have taken forever. "Where did you get all these, huh?" I asked him, brushing my thumb over the hard knot of bone in his wrist before I could stop myself. His skin was very warm.

Alex tilted his head to look at me. "I made 'em," he said.

I snorted. "You did not."

"It's girly, I know." Alex shrugged. "I had this babysitter when I was a kid who taught me how, and I like to. It calms me down."

"Does it?" I said distractedly. I wanted to bite him. God, I needed to get out of here before Olivia saw us talking, or worse. "Okay," I said. "Well. See you out there."

"Do I smell?" Alex asked me.

I blinked. "Pardon me?"

"I just— The way you're running away from me all the time,

I thought maybe I have a hygiene issue I'm not aware of."

I blew out a noisy breath, checking over his shoulder like an instinct to make sure Olivia wasn't watching. "Maybe I'm just not interested."

Alex looked surprised at that, and a little hurt. "Is that true?" he asked, blue eyes narrowing, taking a step back like he was suddenly worried he was crowding me. "If that's true, then my bad, I'll get out of your hair."

I glanced over his shoulder again, crossed my bare arms. "You're not in my hair," I said sulkily. "And you don't smell. Overmuch."

Alex smiled. "Okay," he said, perching on the edge of the pool table, settling in. "So you wanna tell me what the problem is, or should I keep guessing?"

I hesitated. I wasn't going to throw Olivia under the bus, not ever. But I also couldn't bear the idea of Alex thinking I didn't want him around. "One of the other girls here likes you," I told him finally.

"Oh yeah?" Alex's eyebrows went up. "Which one?"

I scowled. "Don't be gross," I said. "If you're gonna be like that, then I'll just go back out there and—"

"I'm sorry." Alex scrambled to his feet so fast it was almost funny. "I'm just teasing, I'm sorry," he said sincerely. "Don't go."

I sighed noisily. "Okay. Well. In addition to the whole not-shitting-where-I-eat thing, which, honestly, would be enough of a reason to stay away from you, I'm not going to go around breaking the girl code the first chance I get."

Alex nodded slowly. "Does it matter who *I* like?" he asked.

"Not particularly," I told him.

"That doesn't seem very fair."

"Life's not fair," I replied. "You're eighteen; you should know that by now."

"I'm a young eighteen," he said, taking a step closer.

I rolled my eyes. "That's a fact."

"Okay." Alex took another step, smirked. Looked at me again. I shivered. I never knew that looking could do that before, that it could feel so obscenely intimate.

"Anyway," I said, clearing my throat. "I didn't, you know, call shotgun fast enough. So."

"Call shotgun?" Alex snorted. "What am I, the front seat of your car?"

"I don't have a car, remember?"

"Yeah, and I'm not claimed or whatever just because somebody else says I am."

"That's not—" I broke off, struggling. The real point was getting lost here, that Olivia was my best friend and worth more to me than some guy I'd barely met, no matter what kind of pull I felt when I looked at him. "I can't do this," I said finally.

"Look," Alex said, "I hear you about not wanting to stir things up with your friends. So if you tell me to leave you alone, I will. But I don't wanna play games with you, Dana.

I like you a lot. I think you are, like, *really* pretty. And I'd like to hang out with you more."

"Alex—" I broke off, huffing a bit, but I was smiling. I couldn't help it. I could feel the electrons vibrating in the air between us, like they were buzzing loud enough to make a sound, like I could hear them over the music. "I'm sorry," was the best I could come up with.

I looked at him one more time before I walked away.

THIRTEEN

I woke up the next morning with a beery headache pulsing behind my eyeballs, my stomach a swamp full of acid and bile. I could barely choke down a slice of toast. No matter how much concealer I smeared under my eyes, my face still looked swollen and puffy. "Are you hung*over*?" Kristin demanded in the bathroom, as I poked at my cheeks with a bronzer brush.

I didn't understand how she *wasn't*, frankly; still, considering the way she was looking at me in the mirror, there was no way I was about to admit that out loud. "What?" I said, trying to look alert and ready. "No, not at all."

"You better not be," she said, scowling. So much for last night's drunken lovefest, I supposed.

"Drink water," Olivia advised quietly, but all it did was

make me nauseated. I could feel sour sweat prickling on my back as we crossed the parking lot to the studio.

"Pull it together, Cartwright," I muttered, pinching my cheeks as we walked into the dance studio. I stopped like I'd been punched in the stomach: sitting in a folding chair in the corner was Guy Monroe himself.

"There they are," he said cheerfully, standing up as we came in. "How you doing, ladies?"

"Guy's here to check out your progress," Juliet explained, crossing her arms over her perfectly starched button-down. "We're going to have you girls put on a little impromptu performance today, show us what you've got so far."

An impromptu *performance*? I gaped at them, a fresh wave of nausea cresting over me. Olivia's lips had all but disappeared.

"I'm looking forward to you wowing me," Guy told us. He smelled like aftershave, something lemony and faint. In the weeks since rehearsals had started, Guy had turned into a kind of storybook character in my mind, like Santa Claus or the Big Bad Wolf—larger than life but also not exactly real, something adults had invented to keep kids in line. Seeing him in the flesh again was kind of a shock. "Charla and Lucas tell me you've been working your asses off."

Olivia was the first to recover, poised and pulled together. "We have been," she assured him. "Definitely."

I nodded in agreement, though I was barely listening,

already running through a mental catalogue of my harmonies, going over and over the moves to our songs in my brain. *Pop, arms, arms, hips, turn, turn, down, right, left—*

Left, right?

Shit.

"All right, ladies," Charla told us, pushing herself off the wall where she was leaning, clapping her hands together once. "I'm thinking 'Only for You,' 'Across the Ocean,' and 'Slam.' Ready to get started?"

"Olivia," I whispered as we took our places. "In 'Only for You,' what order are the elbows?"

Olivia turned and looked at me like I was insane. "In—"

"'Only for You'!" I whispered again, but Charla was already dimming the lights to make it feel more like a real performance. Olivia was still staring at me, wide-eyed. *Calm down*, I told myself. *You've got this.* I hadn't been a tenth this nervous at the audition. Back then, it had all felt like a silly lark, like an adventure. It hadn't felt like anything was actually at stake.

Now, in the split second before the music started, it occurred to me that everything was.

As soon as Lucas's hands hit the keyboard I could feel that I had the rhythm wrong in my body. When I opened my mouth to sing, I couldn't find my note. It was like that dream where you get to school and realize you have a huge test you didn't know about and haven't studied for, only this wasn't a dream—it was actually happening. I felt like I was outside myself, watching; I could see Guy's impassive face in the dim light, his expression impossible to read.

The three songs felt like they went on forever; I wasn't finding my harmonies, wasn't hitting my marks, my limbs feeling awkward and foreign and leaded. I tried not to make eye contact with Guy or any of the coaches, but I could see that Juliet's lips were pursed disapprovingly. Lucas looked like he was going to puke.

"Girls," Juliet said when we were finally finished, her voice as tight and clipped as her expression. Nobody had clapped. "Go change your clothes and get some water. Then come back here ready to listen." Her voice didn't leave any room for argument. My whole body felt hot and prickly with shame.

"Oh my God," I said once we were all in the bathroom, clustered tightly together like hens in the rain. "Oh my God, you guys, that was a disaster."

"It wasn't so bad," Ashley said.

"It was bad," Kristin said, tossing an icy glare in my direction. "Nice of you to care all of a sudden."

"What do you mean, all of a sudden?" I demanded. "I care about this just as much as you."

"Do you?" Kristin asked. "Could have fooled me."

"Enough," Olivia said, grabbing my arm and tugging, her dark eyebrows knitted together. It was the first time she'd spoken since we'd been back here. "Let's go."

Guy was standing in front of the mirrors talking to Juliet when we got back into the rehearsal studio. "Ladies," he said, crossing his arms. He didn't say anything else for a moment, just looked at us with open appraisal, like he could see straight into our souls and wasn't particularly impressed by them. I could feel my heart like a giant ball of phlegm at the back of my throat. The silence seemed to stretch on for ages, just hanging there like some kind of awful set decoration, although in reality it was probably only thirty seconds and made for a nice bit of theater on his part: if it hadn't been obvious already, in that moment it was clear there was a whole new sheriff in town. I could tell Olivia was about to open her mouth and start apologizing when Guy finally spoke.

"Well, I'm not gonna sugarcoat this," he said, settling back into the flimsy folding chair with his hands on his knees. He had a slight New York accent I hadn't noticed before, or otherwise it only came out when he was really annoyed. "That was one hundred percent the opposite of what I was hoping to see."

"Well, okay, the thing is—" Kristin started, but Guy raised one thick eyebrow at her and she shut up like he'd waved a magic wand.

"Tulsa MacCreadie made thirteen million dollars last year," he continued calmly, leaning back and resting his ankle on his opposite knee like he was sitting in a leather armchair in some fancy smoking lounge. "Do you understand that?

Do you have any idea how much money thirteen million dollars is? I do. I've been doing this for a decade. I don't need the money; I have the money. And I can tell you, girls, you're never gonna see it with a crap performance like the one you just made me sit through."

I winced. My head was still throbbing; my skin felt clammy and hot.

"Do you think that was thirteen-million-dollar work we just saw?" Guy asked us. It sounded rhetorical, but after a moment he pressed, "*Do* you?"

"No," we all mumbled.

"No," Guy repeated. "And I'm not here to be the bully and the bad guy, but if you want to have any kind of success in this business, you need to give a thirteen-million-dollar performance every single time. I don't care if you're tired, and I don't care if you just broke up with your boyfriend, and I don't care if you're on your period, or whatever. Amateur hour is over here. You with me?"

A flicker of annoyance sparked in me at his examples, but Guy changed tactics then, expression softening. "Part of this is my fault, because I haven't been here to push you," he told us. "I'll be honest. I've been spread too thin lately, and I haven't been able to give you the attention you need, but that's going to change. You're going to be seeing a lot more of me as we move forward.

"Look, girls," Guy said, "greatness takes sacrifice. It's how I got here; it's how Tulsa got where he is. And it's what

I'm gonna require from all of you if I'm going to keep Daisy Chain together."

If he kept the group together? I felt my stomach flip unpleasantly, cutting my gaze over to Ashley and Kristin, who looked equally cowed. Olivia was staring hard at the floor.

"I know what I'm doing," Guy said, and from the way his voice changed I could tell we were getting close to the end of what he had come here to tell us. He had a quality to him like a politician or preacher, convincing like that. "All you girls are here for a reason—I *picked* all of you for a reason, and I don't make mistakes. All you girls have the capacity to do the kind of work that's required here." He looked at each of us in turn, and I felt myself straighten up like a reflex, suddenly wanting him to know I was paying attention.

"Take the weekend, think about whether you actually want to be here," Guy advised us, standing up and nodding at the coaches, then looking at the four of us one more time. "And come back on Monday ready to work."

FOURTEEN

"Do you care if I borrow your car for a couple of hours?" I asked Olivia the next afternoon, putting one knee up on the bed where she was flipping through the pages of her lyrics binder, a furrow between her brows. "I've got some errands I wanna run."

"Yeah, go ahead," Olivia said, glancing up for the briefest of moments, and I told myself I was imagining the coolness in her tone. We hadn't talked about what had happened at rehearsals yesterday. For the first time in the history of our friendship, it felt like neither one of us knew exactly what to say.

I thanked her and scooped the keys out of the bowl on her dresser. Instead of driving west toward the shopping center or the mall, I turned east and made my way to the studio. I let myself into the cool, dark space, flicked the lights on in the voice room. Took a deep breath and got to work.

I don't know exactly why I hadn't wanted to tell Olivia where I was going. Maybe I was worried that no amount of practice would be enough. I wasn't used to being embarrassed in front of her, to feeling like I was letting her down all the time just because I wasn't as good at something as she was. I'd *never* been as good at this as she was—I'd never had any reason to want to be. That had never mattered, until now. Coming here had felt like my only option for getting out of Jessell. But I worried that it had been a massive mistake.

I warmed up with scales to start with, my voice echoing off the tall beige walls. I took my time, singing phrases over and over, doubling back when they didn't sound right, starting over. It was weird, but I actually liked being in there with nobody listening, nobody to make faces when I didn't hit my notes correctly. Nobody to disappoint. I'd made it all the way through "Only for You" when someone behind me started to clap.

"Jesus *Christ*," I exclaimed, whirling around with no small amount of horror to find Alex standing in the doorway. My heart was pounding, my face flooded hotly with embarrassment—that he'd heard me, that he knew I was struggling, that I was here rehearsing at all. "You gotta stop sneaking up on me, buddy."

"Sorry," Alex said, smiling like a person who wasn't,

really. "Didn't mean to. What are you doing here?" he asked, taking a couple of steps into the studio. He was wearing baggy shorts and a T-shirt, a faded baseball cap pulled down over his golden hair. "It's Saturday."

I shrugged. "You're here," I pointed out.

"Yeah, but I'm an overachiever."

"I bet." I glared at him a moment longer, then sighed. There was something about Alex that made me want to tell him the truth. "I bit it in front of Guy yesterday," I admitted. "Like, full-on crash and burn, couldn't hit my harmonies, screwed up all three songs. And now everybody hates me even more than they did before."

"Ouch," Alex said, wincing. "That bad, huh?"

"Bad," I assured him. "It was *humiliating*, if you want to know. So anyway"—I gestured around—"here I am."

Alex nodded thoughtfully. "Can I hear you again?" he asked.

My eyes narrowed. "What, now?"

"Yeah."

"Why, so you can make fun of me?"

Alex made a face like that was ridiculous. "Maybe I can help."

No way. I wasn't about to spend any more time alone with Alex, if I could help it, on top of which I was too proud to let him hear any more of my suckage than he already had. I shook my head. "Thanks," I said, "but I don't want to keep you from your own practice."

"Well, from the sound of things, you need it more than I do."

"Screw you," I said, but he was smiling at me again, and after a moment I couldn't help but smile back. Still. "That's okay," I told him. "Really."

"If you're going to do this, you're going to have to get used to people hearing you," he pointed out.

"I know that, thank you," I said, irritated. He could be such a know-it-all sometimes. "But it's also easier to let people hear you when you've had, like, a million years of voice training. Which everybody else here has, just FYI."

"Well," Alex replied, sounding unruffled, "you better start playing catch-up, then. You got sheet music?"

"What, you're going to—" I broke off as he sat down on the bench Lucas usually occupied and reached for my binder, flipping through the pages until he found what he was looking for. "You can play piano?"

"Sure," Alex said, shrugging like it was no big deal. "Here"—he tapped "Only for You"—"this is the one you were just singing, right?"

"I—" I sighed. "Yeah."

Alex nodded and set to playing the intro.

So. This was happening, then. There didn't seem to be anything to do but sing—which I did, fumbling my way through the first verse as Alex listened seriously, his sharp face still and thoughtful, not giving anything away. When I was finished, he looked up at me and nodded again.

"Well, first of all, I know this is probably the last thing you want to hear from me, but you're breathing wrong."

I scowled. "I hate you."

"No you don't," Alex said with confidence. "Come on, I'll show you."

Which is how we wound up spending the afternoon working through every Daisy Chain song in my lyrics binder, Alex breaking down the harmonies and going over them as many times as it took. He was a good teacher: knowledgeable and easygoing, exacting and particular, but patient, too. I liked that he never made me feel stupid for not knowing a musician or a vocal term he dropped into conversation—and, though I didn't want to admit it to myself, I liked the glowing smile he shot my way whenever I got things right. When I finally glanced up at the clock on the wall, it was almost dinnertime.

"I'm a jerk, I'm sorry," I told him. "I ate up your whole afternoon."

"Are you kidding me?" Alex asked, shaking his head. "I had a blast. You're talented, Dana," he told me. "Like, sure, you haven't had the training or whatever, but you have whatever that *thing* is that just makes me want to listen to you, you know? Not everybody has that."

I ducked my head, not knowing how to respond, exactly; it was the first time anyone had ever said anything remotely like that to me. "Thanks," I finally said. "For all of it, really. You didn't have to help me like that."

"I wanted to," Alex said stubbornly, then, reaching for my arm as we headed across the parking lot: "Dana." In the late-afternoon sunlight he looked almost shy. "Look, I'm going to ask one more time, and if you say no, then I'll drop it. Will you—"

"Alex." I shook my head. "I can't. I just—it has nothing to do with not wanting to. But I can't."

Alex smiled. "Can't blame a guy for asking, right?" he said. "I'll see you around."

It was nearing dark by the time I got back to the complex; I was tired and starving, a little cranky as I climbed the stairs to our unit. I wanted to collapse into my bed and take a nap. I had just reached the door when I heard Ashley's voice from the living room: "—she's completely screwing up our chances. And even if she manages to somehow pull it together, which is a big if, I just don't understand why she got picked in the *first* place."

"Because she's hot," Kristin fired back, just as I put my key in the lock. "Probably Guy wanted to screw her, so he chose her even though she's got zero talent."

I froze for a moment, stunned and stupid and still somehow completely unsurprised that this was happening: of course it was. I felt my face, my whole body, flame with embarrassment and anger.

If I hadn't already given myself away with the key in the door, I would have walked away right then, back down to the car and straight home to Jessell. As it was, I had to go inside. Ashley, Kristin, and—I realized with a dull thud—*Olivia* were all sitting in the living room, silent as stones and just as motionless, like somehow I'd accidentally cast a spell over them. As I came into the living room, it broke. "Hey!" Olivia said, too brightly, her wide-eyed gaze darting to the other girls, then back to me. "You're home!"

"Hey," I said slowly, putting my bag down on the sofa, not making any actual eye contact. For some reason I hadn't thought she'd be in here with them. For some reason I hadn't imagined that at all. "What are you guys up to?"

"We're going to drive out to the mall and see a movie," Olivia said, speaking for all of them; I couldn't tell if this was a plan they'd actually made or if she was just making stuff up to distract me, compulsively filling the silence like she sometimes did when she was uncomfortable or afraid. Kristin was examining her fingernails. Ashley was looking at the floor. "You wanna come?"

"Nah," I said, swallowing; for a second it felt like I might be about to cry, which was ridiculous. "I'm, um, pretty beat."

I sat on the couch for a long time after the three of them left the apartment, staring blankly at the vacant TV and telling myself I was being dumb. Girls were bitches sometimes, was all, Kristin and Ashley in particular. It *was* weird that Guy had chosen me, frankly. And there was no reason to expect Olivia to defend me at every turn.

Still, our high school had been full of best friends who

weren't really, girls who talked behind each other's backs and secretly schemed against each other, like happiness was a zero-sum game. Olivia and I had never been like that. We'd rooted for each other; we'd cheered each other on.

We'd been here all of three weeks, and already things were changing.

Finally, I got up off the couch and left the apartment. The air was even swampier than usual, thick gray clouds hanging low and suffocating. I stomped downstairs and crossed the parking lot, then climbed the flight to Alex and Trevor's apartment, banging the tiny, useless knocker that decorated all the doors at this place.

Those girls from school made out with each other's boyfriends, too, said a nasty voice at the back of my mind. I made myself push the thought away.

Alex's eyes widened the tiniest bit when he answered the door, wavy hair damp and curling down over his ears. He was wearing a soft-looking gray T-shirt and looking at me like I was Cinder-freaking-ella, never mind that I was still in my sweaty rehearsal clothes, that I hadn't showered or even combed my lanky, tangled hair. Nobody, not one other person, had ever, *ever* looked at me like that. "It's you," he said.

"It's me," I said, feeling my bad mood melt away at the sight of him, like a puddle of ice cream on the hot, steamy sidewalk. It was Saturday night, and we were eighteen. "You wanna get out of here?"

Alex grinned.

FIFTEEN

Alex was appalled that I'd been in Orlando this long and still hadn't made it to Disney, so we did what felt like the obvious thing and drove all the way to the park before realizing that tickets to get in were, like, fifty bucks each. Instead we got King Cones and brought them back to his car in the parking lot as the sun sank behind the dark outlines of the roller coasters inside the gates. "I thought you were regionally famous," I teased, bumping my shoulder with his. "You don't have a personal in with Mickey Mouse?"

"Guy's got us on an allowance," Alex explained, looking sheepish. "I didn't really think this plan through."

"No, it's perfect," I promised him, licking my ice cream to avoid a drip—the inside of the SUV was immaculate, especially considering it belonged to a teenage boy, and I didn't want to make a mess. "I'm teasing, really. I just needed to get away from the apartment for a minute."

"How come?" Alex asked, seemingly oblivious to his own melty cone. "What happened?"

I shook my head, watching the steady trickle of park-goers through the windshield—couples and families, little kids in Mickey Mouse ears and old people in motorized wheelchairs. I didn't want to tell him about Olivia and the others, what a disaster this all had turned into. How sure they all were that the only reason I was here was how I looked.

"Do you ever get nervous?" I asked instead, wanting to change the subject. "When you perform?"

Alex shook his head. "Nah."

"Of course not," I said, which made him smile. The hand that wasn't holding his ice-cream cone was resting on my bare knee, his palm warm and heavy against my skin. It felt like every nerve ending in my body was focused in that one single spot, like iron filings rushing to a magnet.

"Seriously, though, what's there to be nervous about?" Alex asked. It was just twilight, the last of the sunset casting the side of his face in pinks and golds. "You got this, Dana. Guy picked you for a reason."

"He picked me because I'm pretty," I blurted before I could stop myself, then blushed. "I'm not saying that to be conceited, I just—"

"That's not true," Alex said, then hurried to correct himself: "I mean, you *are* pretty. Really pretty. But that's not all."

"It's not, huh?" I raised my eyebrows, not buying it. I wasn't fishing for compliments. The truth was, my looks had gotten me plenty of stuff in my life so far: a C on a test I knew I should have failed in Mr. Lambert's geometry class last winter; a simple warning from the store manager when I'd gotten caught shoplifting lipstick when I was thirteen. Being pretty, I'd learned, was enough to keep you in the competition for a little while. But it was never enough to win.

Alex was shaking his head, sincere. "I meant it, what I said earlier. *You*, you're like—you're the whole package."

That made me blush. I couldn't help it—it all felt like a *lot* all of a sudden, his hand on my knee and the close quarters of the front seat, the cold ice cream in my throat. "I already made out with you once," I managed finally. "You don't have to flatter me. When I actually stop and think about it for five seconds, I know there's no way this is going to be an actual real thing that happens. It's a nice diversion, being down here. That's all."

Alex wasn't buying it. "So why even bother practicing?" he asked pointedly.

"Because I don't want to humiliate myself every day if I can help it." I shrugged. "But I'm not—I'm not the kind of person stuff like this happens to. Do you understand that?"

"Stuff like what?"

"Like being a pop star!"

"You are, though," Alex argued. "The fact that you're here at all means you are. You can have this if you really want it, there's literally no doubt in my mind. You've got, like, that indefinable *thing.* The know-it-when-you-see-it thing."

I was still blushing. I wasn't used to the kinds of compliments Alex threw around like handfuls of confetti, didn't know if he meant them for real or if this was just how he was. Either way, I wondered how you got to be that confident—in yourself or in anyone else. "I don't know about *that,*" I said.

Alex nodded. "Trust me," he said, and in spite of myself, I did.

He sat back in his seat then, eating the rest of his ice cream in three big bites like he'd suddenly remembered he had it. My skin buzzed hotly where his hand had been. "Can I ask you something? You said you didn't even really mean to audition, right?" He tilted his head to the side, and I nodded. "So why did you decide you wanted to be in the group?"

I hesitated, looking around the Suburban. This SUV alone probably cost more than my entire house. Nobody here knew anything about where I came from except for Olivia. Maybe it was stupid, but I wanted to tell Alex. "It just felt kind of like a last-minute escape plan, I guess," I said slowly. "It felt like a chance to get away."

"To get away?" Alex asked, forehead wrinkling. "From what?"

I took a breath. "The rest of my life? I don't know." Alex was quiet, leaving space, and after a moment I continued. "I don't—we don't have any money, first of all. And my mom . . . drinks a lot. Like, a *lot*. And I graduated last month, and my job ended, and I—" I broke off. "It's not like I had anything better to do, you know? I literally had nothing to lose."

"Really?" Alex asked, looking at me curiously—and maybe with a little bit of doubt. "That's how you wound up here?"

"Oh, yeah." I nodded. "This was Olivia's dream, always. Not mine."

"What would you do if you weren't doing this?"

"Be a waitress," I said immediately.

"Okay," Alex said. "But, like, if you could be anything in the world."

I snorted. "Oh my gosh, please don't try to talk to me about, like, my hopes and dreams."

Alex's brow furrowed. "Why not?" he asked, sounding sort of offended.

"Because it's so corny!"

That made him smile. "I'm literally in a boy band, Dana. You think I care about being corny?"

"Clearly not."

"Come on," he pressed, nudging my knee with his across the seats. "Tell me."

"I don't know." I thought about it for a moment. "I guess when I was, like, really, really little, I wanted to be a doctor. I got it into my head that my dad was one? Which is ridiculous for a lot of reasons, one being that I don't know my dad and two being that whoever he was, he was definitely not the doctor type. I must have seen it on TV or something." I paused, embarrassed for my past self, by how dumb it sounded now. "Anyway, that's what I used to tell people. That I wanted to be a doctor."

Alex nodded seriously. "Do you still want it?"

"No!" I laughed. "God, no."

"Because that is, like, a perfectly attainable dream."

"See, that's exactly the kind of thing a person like you would say."

"A person like me?"

I huffed a little. "I don't need you to unlock my secret potential, Alex. I know what my potential is. I barely graduated high school. I'm not going to magically go to Harvard and become a brain surgeon. Like, it never even occurred to anyone who knows me that college was a thing that would ever happen."

"So?" Alex shrugged. "I'd bet good money that it didn't occur to them that this was a thing that would ever happen, either."

"I bet you would," I fired back. "Because money is probably something you've never had to worry about."

I sat back in my seat, exhausted all of a sudden. I hadn't talked that much about myself in maybe ever. My ice cream was getting everywhere by this point, and I ate the rest of it without looking up at Alex, who was silent. I didn't want to see the expression on his face. It was one thing to make out in a pool after midnight. It was another to tell him the truth.

"Okay," I said finally, wiping my sticky hands on my shorts. It was fully dark now, the sky a deep, velvety blue. "Sorry, did I freak you out with my trailer-trashiness?" I looked up at him then, shoulders squared and jaw set. "It's fine, if I did. I get it."

I was trying to make it sound like a joke, kind of, but Alex gazed back at me, calm and even. "No," he said. "I'm not freaked out."

"Don't feel sorry for me, either."

"I don't feel sorry for you."

I took a breath, feeling on the edge of tears all of a sudden and not wanting to cry. "Prove it," I said.

"Come here."

I shook my head, remembering all the reasons it was a bad idea for me to be here. "I can't."

"You keep saying that. Come here," he said again, and this time I did, scooting toward him in my seat until our knees were touching. Alex put both hands on my face. "Come here," he said one more time, so quietly, and when he kissed me it wasn't any more careful than it had been the other night in the pool.

"Trust me?" he asked, pulling back and looking at me urgently.

I nodded. "Yeah," I said. "I—" I was about to say something else when a huge rumbling *boom* sounded out overhead.

Alex's face suddenly lit up in reds and purples and golds. I looked out the windshield and laughed.

"Fireworks," I said, shaking my head as another blast exploded overhead, this one a dazzling white. I could feel the sound of it vibrate through my jaw. "Very nice touch."

"Wha—I didn't plan that!" Alex protested.

"Mm-hmm." I was grinning. "Sure you didn't."

"I mean, unless you think it's romantic," he said thoughtfully. "Then I totally planned it."

"It's a little romantic," I admitted, and leaned in to kiss him again. Kissing Alex made me feel like an electrical fire had broken out inside my body, the blaze everyplace he touched me. I wanted to get as close as I possibly could. "Hey," I said after a while, sounding breathless, grabbing his hand and tugging him into the back of the SUV, where there was more room for us to move around.

Alex grinned as I climbed into his lap. "This is the real reason you want to buy a minivan, isn't it?" Alex said, but I was too distracted to answer because he had taken my hand and was kissing the very tips of my fingers, sucking a little, his tongue warm and soft against my skin.

"You taste like King Cone," he said.

I snorted. "You hungry?"

"I'm eighteen," he said. "I'm hungry all the time."

I laughed and tugged him closer. I closed my eyes and kissed him again.

SIXTEEN

The next day was Sunday. Olivia's bed was already made when I woke up, and I frowned at the perfectly fluffed pillows. We hadn't talked much when I got back last night, just two terse *good nights* before she turned off the light and rolled over, and part of me wanted to stay in bed and hide out from her and everyone else for the rest of the day.

It was close to noon, though, and finally I pulled on a pair of shorts and a T-shirt, tossing my hair up into a bun. Olivia was eating a banana on the couch in the living room, breaking off tiny pieces and chewing them slowly. On MTV, somebody was hosting a beach party, a bunch of college kids dancing on a pier, and I wondered if it was the one Hurricane State had performed at. "Morning," I said, heading for the kitchen to get a bowl of cereal.

"There you are!" Olivia smiled.

"Here I am," I said, surprised by how glad she sounded to see me. *Zero talent*, I heard at the back of my head, remembering her expression when I'd walked in the door of the apartment last night. *Completely screwing up*. "Where is everybody?"

"Charla's running errands," she said, swallowing. "Kristin and Ash went shopping."

"You didn't go with?" I asked, sitting down beside her on the sofa.

Olivia nudged me with one bare foot. "Was waiting for you, actually."

"You were?" I asked, sounding dumbly pleased and feeling a little embarrassed about it. "You wanna go down to the pool for a bit?"

I wanted to spend some time with her, talk things out, but Olivia shook her head. "I thought we could go into the studio today," she said. "I know you really weren't into those vocal exercises we were talking about, but . . ."

I put my cereal bowl down on the coffee table, untouched. "So we're just not going to talk about last night, then?"

To her credit, Olivia didn't try to act like she didn't know what I meant. "Look," she said, "I don't know what you thought we were talking about when you came in, but—"

"I rehearsed all day yesterday, actually," I informed her, "which you'd know if you'd talked to me at all instead of just bitching about how bad I am with Ashley and Kristin."

"I wasn't bitching about you," Olivia said hotly.

"I heard you guys!" I said. "Do you know how shitty that felt?"

Olivia sagged at that, dropping her banana peel on the table and running her hands through her hair. "I'm sorry," she said when she looked at me again. "You're right. You're right, it *was* shitty, and that's why I want to help you now. It's just that Kristin and Ashley are worried—"

"Kristin and Ashley are a couple of nasty little wannabe pop stars," I snapped.

Olivia scowled. "If you made any effort to get to know them—"

"They don't want to get to know me," I argued. "I get that they're your new best friends and all, but—"

"Hey," Olivia said, catching me by the arm and tugging me to face her. "That's not what I'm saying. Stop it, okay? You're my best friend. Nothing that goes on here is going to change that."

Just like that, I wanted to burst into tears, all the fight going out of me at once. God, I hated arguing with her. "You told me to come here," I pointed out, trying to keep my voice even. I'd been thinking it more and more lately, remembering how my first and deepest instinct had been to step aside and hers had been not to let me. *I need you*, she'd told me, and I'd believed her. "I was going to stay home, remember? I was going to stay in Jessell. I only came here because of you."

Olivia looked at me for a moment, and I thought I saw

the faintest tinge of what might have been regret flicker across her face. "I know I did," she said finally. "I know."

"Look," I said, "I'm sorry, okay? Let's go to the studio. We can get coffee on the way or something, you can teach me whatever you want me to learn, I'll learn it. It'll be fun."

But Olivia shook her head. "No," she said. "You're right; it's Sunday." She sighed. "But let's try and be on the same team from now on, okay?"

I nodded. I wanted that so, so much. "Of course we're on the same team," I promised. "Always."

I went down to the pool anyway, though all the fun was sort of bleached out of the idea at this point. I just wanted to be by myself. It wasn't until I was halfway to the gate that I realized all five members of Hurricane State were already in the water, playing keep-away with an inflatable beach ball.

"Danaaaaa," Mikey called when he saw me, drawing my name out like a catcall. His skinny white chest gleamed in the sun. "Come on in!"

That was the last thing I wanted to do, actually, but now there was no way for me to do an about-face and leave again without looking like a total weirdo. *God, I should have just stayed upstairs.* "I'm good, thanks," I called back, but Alex had already turned in the pool and seen me, his face spreading into a wide, slow grin. He left the game and swam over to the side of the pool, crossing his long, tan arms on the edge.

"Hi," he said, casual as anything, this look on his face like he had a secret only I would ever be able to figure out. "How's your weekend been?"

"Oh, you know," I said, feeling my lips twist in spite of myself. "Can't complain."

"Any fireworks?" he asked seriously, and I rolled my eyes.

"Some."

"Alex!" Trevor hollered from the other side of the pool. "You playing, or what?"

"Be right there!" Alex called back.

"I'm gonna go back upstairs," I told him, glancing at the others uneasily.

"Why?" Alex asked. "You just got here."

"I know, but—" I broke off. I didn't know how to explain, exactly. It didn't feel right to be down here with them when Olivia was upstairs in the apartment—when maybe I *should* be rehearsing, should be doing what I'd allegedly come here to do. Maybe Olivia was right: she'd just been trying to help me. And here I was—*again*—with the guy she liked. The guy I'd kissed more than once now, who I wanted to keep kissing.

"I'll see you later," I mumbled, turning abruptly and heading for the gate. I had just made it around the corner to the side of the building where the vending machines were, when I heard Alex's bare footsteps behind me. "Hey," he said, a little breathlessly, catching me by the arm so I'd turn around. His hair was wet with pool water; he smelled like Coppertone and chlorine. He also wasn't wearing a shirt, and it was impossible for me to act like I didn't notice. I wanted to press my palm against his heart. "Talk to me. What's up?"

"Somebody's going to see us," I said, pulling my arm away.

Alex waved his arm at the empty parking lot. "There's nobody here."

"Somebody could walk by," I said, knowing I sounded slightly hysterical. "I'm screwing up enough right now, you know? There's no reason to antagonize everybody." I took a deep breath, tried to pull myself together. "I don't belong here" was what came out.

"I don't think that's true," Alex said. He took my hand again, more gently this time. He tilted his head to kiss me, but I ducked away.

"We have to stop this," I said, meaning it this time. "It's not a good idea."

"Just tell Olivia what's going on," Alex suggested. "Or I could, if you wanted."

"What? *No,*" I said immediately, before I realized I'd given myself away. "How do you know it's even Olivia who likes you?" I asked.

Alex made a face. "Because I'm not dumb, Dana," he

told me. "And I think she's great, I think she's awesome, but I don't—I want *you*."

I banged my head softly backward against the exterior wall of the apartment. "Don't say anything to her," I said finally. "I'll handle it, but just—don't."

"I won't," Alex promised. "You're the boss." Then, looking at me a little closer: "You okay?"

"Yeah." I hooked my index finger in a couple of his friendship bracelets, tugging gently. "Maybe I should start making these," I told him, turning my hand and running my fingertips lightly across the sensitive underside of his wrist. "If they're so soothing."

Alex looked at me sideways. "I wouldn't say I'm feeling particularly *soothed* right now."

"No?" I asked, gazing at him from underneath my eyelashes. "How do you feel, then?"

"I don't know," Alex said, with a hitch in his breath that pleased me. I tilted my head up, pressed a kiss against his mouth.

"Five more minutes," I said, pulling back to look at him. This close up, his blue eyes had tiny flecks of brown in them. "Five more minutes, then I'll go inside and rehearse."

"Five more minutes," Alex agreed.

It was more like ten, truthfully, before I squeezed his hand and headed around the corner, feeling calmer than I had all day. Olivia was alone upstairs, after all; I could talk to her one-on-one, for real this time, try and set things right once and for all.

I turned toward the staircase and stopped in my tracks: there was Kristin, holding a pair of paper shopping bags, an inscrutable half smile on her face. "What are you doing?" I blurted out.

She shrugged, shiny blond hair and an opaque expression. "Oh," she said breezily, turning toward the staircase, "just headed upstairs."

SEVENTEEN

Rehearsals were totally miserable that week. It seemed like what happened with Guy should have galvanized us, made us a stronger team resolved to sink or swim together, but instead it just turned everyone cranky and short-tempered. Lucas was even more peevish than usual, carping every time I hit a bum note. Even Charla, who I could usually count on for some positive reinforcement, seemed frayed around the edges—making us spin until we were dizzy, then yelling at us because we didn't spot. I hurt all over, my arms and stomach aching from our workouts; it felt like my leg muscles ought to peel right off my bones.

"Ice baths," Kristin advised as we picked up our lunches—whole wheat wraps today, which seemed to be mostly full of spinach. I was starting to get the feeling that all four of us were on diets, even though nobody had said it out loud. I wanted to ask Olivia about it, but I was afraid it might upset her. "Fill a garbage bag down at the ice machine and dump it in the tub."

"Seriously?" I gaped at her. "We're not training for the Olympics."

Kristin just raised her eyebrows. "Aren't we?" she asked, and turned back to her lyrics sheet before I could answer.

"This makes me want to die," I complained to Alex as we settled ourselves on the concrete steps around the corner where nobody could see us, midday sun beating down on the pavement even while the sky to the west took on a creepy gray-green tinge. In Orlando in the summertime, a thunderstorm was never more than fifteen minutes away.

"Aw, it's not so bad," Alex said, unwrapping his sandwich—the boys got ham and cheese, which bugged me—and offering me a bite, which I took.

"Not so bad?" I asked once I'd swallowed. "Kristin just suggested I submerge my naked body in a vat of ice, but it's not so bad?"

Alex raised his eyebrows with interest at the word *naked*, but then he shrugged. "I don't know," he said, taking a bite. "It's kind of what I always wanted, singing all day. I'm into it."

That made me smile, and also feel like kind of a jerk. "You are, huh?" I asked. I couldn't imagine what it was like to love something as much as Alex clearly loved this.

"Yeah," he said, his cheeks pinking up a bit, either from the heat out here or from the idea that I might make fun of him. "My brain just gets kind of quiet when I'm singing. You ever feel that way?"

"My brain's quiet all the time," I joked. Across the parking lot, Mikey was juggling three clementines like he was considering joining the circus if all this didn't work out. Thunder rumbled in the distance, the darkness crawling its way across the sky and that creosote smell getting stronger in the air. "Just ask Lucas."

"You know what I mean," Alex said, bumping my arm with his warm, slightly sticky one. "When I'm singing, or dancing, or whatever, it's like all the sharp edges get filed down. Everything kind of makes sense to me that way." He shrugged again, that bashful quality that I found so stupidly winning. "I used to get in trouble at school because I'd sing to myself, real quiet-like, during my math tests."

I snorted. "You did not."

"I did!" Alex said, laughing. "For a long time it was the only way I could do my times tables, was if I sang 'em. My mom had to come in and have a meeting with the teacher 'cause I was disrupting the other kids."

"Well," I said quietly, skimming my fingernail up the back of his calf. "You *are* very disruptive."

Alex shivered. "Quit it," he said, smiling, in a voice that did not in fact mean *quit it* at all. "I gotta get up and walk around in a sec."

That got my attention. "Oh yeah?" I asked, teasing. "And why wouldn't you be able to do that, exactly?"

"Shut up," Alex said, reaching down and lacing his fingers through mine. Thunder rumbled again, closer this time; I rested my chin on his shoulder.

"Sorry, sorry," I said, nudging my nose at his jawbone. He smelled like summer, like this place. "Tell me more about singing."

Alex smiled. "It's the only thing I've ever wanted to do," he said, and now it was my turn to raise my eyebrows. "Well, not the *only* thing," he amended, and I laughed, loud and rowdy. The thunder crashed over our heads.

The girls went for frozen yogurt after rehearsal that afternoon, dashing through the fat Florida raindrops and piling into Kristin's shiny white Volkswagen. "You should come," Olivia told me, and it seemed like she meant it, but I found myself shaking my head. I still felt weird around all three of them together, like they blamed me for what had happened with Guy even if they weren't saying it. Like I was dragging them all down.

Olivia left me her car and I meant to head home and get in the bathtub, maybe see if Alex was around, but I dawdled as I packed up my dance gear, and soon the whole studio was quiet and empty, my footsteps echoing on the shiny floors. I liked it like this, I realized, peering at myself in the wall-to-wall mirrors. Everything felt very calm.

On a whim, I started working through some of the dances Charla had had us learning earlier that day, turning pirouettes and popping my hips even though there was no music to guide me. I felt stupid at first, but it was easier to get into the groove of things when nobody was watching, and as I started the routine over again from the top I realized I was kind of enjoying myself. More than that, I saw as I watched myself in the mirror—I actually looked really *good.* Maybe Alex was right, that I could possibly belong here. Maybe he was right that I could have what it took.

I don't know how many times I went through our dances that afternoon—I stopped counting the minutes, lost in my own body and the rhythm of the steps. I would have kept on indefinitely, might have danced straight through dinner, but the next time I glanced in the mirror there was Charla standing in the doorway, watching me wordlessly with an expression I couldn't read on her face.

I froze cold, then hot, feeling my whole body flush not with exertion but with intense, bottomless embarrassment. I felt like an idiot. I felt *caught.* The last thing I wanted was to make myself vulnerable to her like that, for her to have the chance to find me lacking in a moment when I was actually giving it everything I had. "Uh, hey," I said, pushing my hair out of my face and trying not to breathe too heavily. None of this was real, I reminded myself. "I was just—" I broke off.

Charla nodded, and now I did understand the look in her eyes, or at least I thought I did. She looked *excited,* I thought as I stared back at her, cheeks still flaming. She looked . . . pleased.

"Lock up when you leave" was all she said.

EIGHTEEN

"Is this our training montage?" I asked one afternoon as we headed out to the grassy patch of parking lot where we usually ate our lunches—Subway sandwiches today, turkey with lettuce, tomato, and light mayo that tasted weird and fake. "It's like freaking 'Eye of the Tiger' should be playing every time I walk down the hallway."

Olivia grinned, put her fists up. "Feels that way."

We were rehearsing a song called "Higher and Higher" today, which I'd been dreading—I had a solo in the bridge section, and whenever we practiced it always turned into a three-hour odyssey, during which Lucas felt it was his duty to promulgate a long and comprehensive list of everything I was doing wrong both in performance and in life, including the way I stood on the floor and breathed oxygen.

That section was one I'd been going over a lot in my

spare time, though, working on it with Alex's help, and today it wasn't as bad as I was expecting—in fact, Lucas didn't stop me at all. I made it through the rest of the song in skittish anticipation, waiting for him to realize he'd missed his chance to embarrass me, but he was quiet until the end of rehearsal, content to correct Ashley's vowel pronunciation and leave me out of it.

"'Unreal' tomorrow," he called as we were leaving, which was Kristin's solo. Then, almost as an afterthought: "Nice work today, Dana."

"Dana?" Olivia repeated, sounding surprised, as my head whipped around in disbelief.

"Me?"

"You," Lucas said, sounding immediately annoyed again, which was how I knew he'd meant it. It was the first thing resembling praise he'd had for me since I got to Orlando, and I felt my face warm with pride. It didn't mean anything, I told myself, trying to tamp down the big dumb grin I could feel spreading across my face. I was still unequivocally the worst one in this whole group. But for the first time, it felt like maybe I really was making progress. For the first time, I didn't feel like I had no hope at all.

I couldn't sleep again that night, lying in bed watching the shadows cast across the ceiling by the yellow lights outside the window. I was still having trouble like this a few times a week, my nerves too jangly, my brain too busy to rest. I thought about heading over to Alex's apartment to see if he was still awake, but I didn't know how I'd explain that away if Olivia woke up and caught me gone. Finally, I got out of bed anyway, easing the door open and heading into the kitchen for a glass of water.

I felt like I'd been lying in bed for a long time already, but Charla was still up, sitting on the couch in her Houston Ballet T-shirt and watching the TV on mute, clutching a mug of what smelled like ginger tea in one hand. "Did I wake you?" she asked, when she saw me come out.

I shook my head. The sight of her there in the half-light made me unexpectedly homesick: my mom had never been particularly strict about bedtimes, and I'd spent probably hundreds of nights curled beside her as she watched *90210* and *Melrose Place*, soaps giving way to the news giving way to the late shows. Sometimes she'd get up and make us a snack, Ritz crackers with peanut butter or a sleeve of off-brand chocolate chip cookies. I'd barely called her at all since I'd been here. I promised myself that I would tomorrow. "I was already up," I told Charla softly. "Besides, you're not making any noise."

Charla smiled at that. "I like to make up my own stories sometimes," she told me, motioning to the screen. "My mom always watched in Spanish when I was a kid, so I got in the habit."

I nodded. It was weird, but sometimes I actually forgot that Charla was somebody with a family, the same way I'd forget that Kristin had three sisters or how sometimes I'd go all day without thinking of my mom. It was like all of us existed in some weird vacuum in Orlando, like the rest of the world was in faded, muted watercolors and what was going on here stood out in sharp relief. It had taken a surprisingly short amount of time before it was hard to imagine a life outside this one.

"Can't sleep?" Charla asked now, scooting over on the sofa to make room for me. I sat down beside her, a little cautiously. She and I hadn't spent a lot of time alone together, but I liked her, I thought—she was only about ten years older than us, and sometimes felt more like a big sister than an actual adult. In rehearsal, she was the opposite of Lucas, big on praise and thumbs-ups.

"Nah," I said. "I'm, like, an insomniac since I got here. It's weird."

Charla nodded seriously, like she was giving more weight to that throwaway comment than I'd meant for her to, and right away I wished I could take it back. "How you doing, Dana?" she asked, turning and pulling one long leg up onto the sofa, looking at me straight on. She'd washed her face for bed already, her hair spilling down over her angular shoulders. "You having fun here?"

"Of course," I said too eagerly, nodding fast like a puppet on a string. "I'm great."

"You *looked* good the other day," Charla said. "When I saw you in the dance room. You've got real talent, you know that? When you're on like that, you're incredible to watch."

I shook my head even as I felt myself flush with pleasure—embarrassed by the memory, that feeling of having been caught with my guard down like that. Still, it wasn't lost on me that the compliment was similar to ones I'd gotten from Alex, all his talk about watchability and the X-factor. Maybe he wasn't talking completely out of his butt. Still. "I was just screwing around," I muttered. "It wasn't a big deal."

"You shouldn't do that," Charla said gently. "Diminish what you're doing here, or make it seem like it doesn't matter. The others certainly aren't."

It was making me kind of uncomfortable to be the focus of all her attention. "How'd you start working with Guy?" I asked.

Charla sat back against the cushions, took a long, quiet sip of her tea. "I had a couple bad stress injuries when I was still touring," she explained, looking at me over the lip of her mug. "So I took some time off, started teaching at a studio in New York, working on some theater. And I had a friend who knew Juliet."

I nodded, picturing it—a life that had turned out differently, maybe, than Charla had expected. "Do you miss performing?"

"Sometimes." She shrugged. "Not as much as I would have thought. I didn't have that special thing, you know? I blend in up there; I don't stand out. Not everybody's cut out to be a great performer."

I wasn't sure if she was trying to tell me something or not, if I stood out to her or I didn't. If she would have said this exact thing to Olivia or Ashley, if they'd wandered out of their rooms. Over the white-noise drone of the air-conditioning, I could hear cars whooshing by on the highway outside.

"What about you?" Charla asked. "What would you want to be doing if you weren't doing this?"

I shrugged a little, shifted in my seat. "Everybody keeps asking me that lately."

"It's a valid question."

"Because I definitely shouldn't quit my day job?"

It was the closest I could get to asking what she was really trying to say to me here, but Charla rolled her eyes. "Because I care about you," she said.

The idea popped into my head again: *I used to think I'd be a doctor.* It was kind of the same as choreography, I thought—learning a series of steps and performing them in the exact right order. But Alex had been wrong, that night in the car. *That* idea *was* even dumber and more far-out than the idea of touring with Tulsa MacCreadie. It was completely and utterly absurd. "I don't know," I lied finally, looking at the TV and not at Charla. "I guess I can really only picture myself doing this."

NINETEEN

The following weekend, we were all invited to a pool party at Guy's house on the other side of Orlando. Kristin started getting ready bright and early that morning, slinging an L.L.Bean tote full of self-tanner and Sun-In up onto the vanity in the bathroom and getting to work. "I'm going to crap my pants," she announced when I came in to brush my teeth, the fact that normally she didn't have two words to say to me apparently forgotten in the face of this momentous occasion. "I'm going to barf all over him. I'm going to crap my pants; *then* I'm going to barf all over him."

"What?" I blinked. Guy was rich, sure, but I didn't see what there was to get so worked up about. "Who?"

Kristin looked at me like I was insane. "Tulsa!" she replied. "Obviously."

"Relax," Ashley said, dipping her finger into a tin of

shiny pink lip gloss. "We're going to be on the same level as him soon."

"We are *not* on the same level as him now," I pointed out, then felt stupid about it. I didn't like to think of myself as the kind of person to fall all over herself in front of a celebrity.

Kristin wasn't concerned about coolness, apparently. "I waxed my bikini line last night," she announced, lining her arsenal of products up on the vanity. "Just in case."

"Just in case Tulsa MacCreadie wants to have sex with you?" I snorted.

"I can hear you!" Charla called from the other room.

"Dana's too cool to get excited about Tulsa," Olivia said as she brushed on waterproof mascara, plucking at a clump and flicking it away. "It's not her style."

In reality, there was only one person I was really excited to see at Guy's party, but I tried to keep my voice nonchalant. "Well," I conceded, bumping her hip with mine, familiar. "I mean. He's no Hot Rod Davison."

Olivia laughed.

Guy lived in a gated community on the outskirts of Orlando, in a white stuccoed house with big fake Greek columns in the front of it. A fountain burbled away in the front yard. A housekeeper in an actual uniform answered the door, like something out of *Jane Eyre*, which I'd half read in English back in Jessell earlier that spring. "So nice to see you all," she said brightly. "Follow me."

She led us through a living room outfitted with a shiny grand piano and into a sleek white kitchen, then down a short flight of stairs to a rec room with a massive pool table, plus a Pac-Man machine and a jukebox that lit up red and green and gold. "He lives here by himself?" I asked quietly, as we trailed her through the cavernous hallways. Ashley shrugged.

"They're out in the yard," the housekeeper said, motioning at the sliding glass doors that led there. "If there's anything you need, just ask."

In the back was a massive pool landscaped a million times nicer than the one at the complex, complete with a waterslide and a fake grotto like the one I'd seen on a late-night special about the Playboy Mansion. A stainless-steel grill was built into a low stone wall on one side of the yard.

I hardly registered any of that, though, because Tulsa MacCreadie was standing at the glass-topped patio table, wearing sunglasses and drinking a beer. I looked fast, not wanting to be caught staring. Then I looked again. In person he was shorter than I'd thought he'd be, but just as handsome, perfectly curly hair and eyebrows like two dark, expressive punctuation marks across the top of his summer-tanned face. "Hey, Charla," he said, kissing her on the cheek. "How you been?"

"Tulsa," Guy said. He was wearing red shorts and a brightly patterned Hawaiian shirt like the dad in an eighties movie, big dark sunglasses on his face. "This is Daisy Chain."

Tulsa tipped his beer in our direction. "Ladies," he said, though for one weird moment it seemed like he was actually only looking at me. "Nice to meet you."

"Nice to meet *you*," Olivia said.

"Hi!" Ashley bubbled. For all her big talk earlier, Kristin was struck silent, her mouth just slightly agape.

I frowned. It irked me, how Guy had introduced us all together like that, like we weren't distinct people. "I'm Dana," I blurted. "This is Ashley, Kristin, and Olivia."

Tulsa nodded without comment, taking a swig of his beer. I felt like an idiot.

Olivia grabbed my arm and steered me toward the pool. "Be cool," she muttered.

"I was being cool!" I protested, feeling my face flame. "I just don't like being part of some machine."

The boys turned up a little later, with Lucas in Juliet's van. I could hear their noise before I saw them, felt my chest kick up the way it hadn't even at the sight of Tulsa. *Alex is here.* He was wearing his swim trunks and a white V-neck T-shirt, his cheeks a bit pink from the heat. I was so relieved to see him that I wanted to bolt across the yard and catch him in a full-body tackle; instead, I held back, pulling a bit at the bathing suit Olivia had loaned me, feeling naked. "Hey," I said, trying to keep it casual in case anyone was watching.

"You look really, really pretty," Alex murmured, and I grinned.

The boys had been to Guy's a bunch of times before, and

within ten minutes they were playing a noisy game of tag like it was just another day at the complex pool. Kristin sunned herself like a lizard on a rock. Her bikini was so small that I thought it was probably good she'd waxed every last hair off her body.

For lunch, Guy's chef grilled turkey burgers and hot dogs, plus steaks for the adults and vegetables for Tulsa. I stayed far away from Alex, not wanting anyone to get any ideas. "This isn't so weird to you?" I asked Olivia, rubbing my bare feet through the rough Florida crabgrass—even Guy's gardeners were no match for that.

She shrugged. "We gotta get used to this kind of thing, I think."

I smirked. "If I'm ever used to a thing like this, you can throw me in the fancy pool."

I finished my burger and Diet Coke, then went inside to pee, blinking at the darkness of the house as my eyes adjusted. In the bathroom everything was made of marble with gold faucets—the sink, the huge sunken bathtub, and what looked like a second toilet, only without a seat. I stared at it for a minute, then washed my hands and went and got Olivia and Ash.

"Come look at something with me?" I asked, leading them back to the bathroom. "What is this?"

Ashley laughed.

"It's a bidet," Olivia informed me.

"A what?"

"It's for washing your butt after you poop," Ashley

explained. "It's European."

"Wait," I said, shaking my head. "Like, instead of toilet paper? That's disgusting."

"You are such a yokel sometimes," Ashley said, but she was laughing.

"I'd rather be a yokel than a European who doesn't use toilet paper," I said. I reached out and pressed the gold button on it experimentally. The thing made a *fssshhhh* sound and a stream of water arched out, like a water fountain, and I was done. I doubled over laughing, and that set off Olivia and Ashley, and then all three of us were just cackling like maniacs, like we'd totally lost our minds. For the rest of the day, all either one of them had to do was mouth *fssshhhhhhh* and I had to excuse myself.

I was standing by the enormous fruit boat later that afternoon, picking all the strawberries out of the hollowed-out watermelon, when I looked up and suddenly Tulsa was *right there* beside me. "Hey, Polka Dots," he said, gesturing to my bathing suit.

"Um, hey," I said, feeling embarrassed for some reason. Tulsa had that quality about him—the ability to make you feel lame just for being alive, by virtue of the fact that he was also alive and doing it so much better than everyone else. "What's up?"

Tulsa shrugged carelessly. "Having fun?" he asked.

I swallowed. *Be cool*, I reminded myself. "Yeah," I said. "It's good."

"Tell me your name one more time, Polka Dots?"

"Dana," I said, swallowing, glancing across the yard to see if anyone was looking. Everybody else was splashing around in the pool. "Dana Cartwright."

"Dana Cartwright," Tulsa repeated thoughtfully. "I've heard about you," he said.

"About me?" I blinked. "What'd you hear?"

"That you're the only one here worth watching."

I gaped. "Who said *that*?"

Tulsa shrugged again, looking at me over the mouth of his beer bottle. "I have my sources."

I wasn't buying. "You're thinking of Olivia," I said, but Tulsa shook his head.

"I know about Olivia," he said. "I'm talking about you." He tipped his beer in my direction just like he had earlier. "Have fun, Polka Dots."

"I will," I managed. "Thanks."

Tulsa strolled inside Guy's house like he owned it. Everybody else was still splashing around in the pool. Trevor grabbed my ankle and tugged on it when I wandered over, making like he was going to pull me into the water and winking when I shrieked in spite of myself.

"Get in already, Cartwright!" he chided cheerfully. "What are you, too good for such humble accommodations?"

I snorted. "Better get out of the way," I warned him, and cannonballed right into the deep end.

“What’d Tulsa want?” Olivia asked later, once we’d climbed out of the pool and were wrapping Guy’s immaculately white towels around our waists. “I saw you guys talking before.”

I smiled, scooping my wet hair up into a ponytail; as soon as you got out of the water it was unbearably hot again, like being fired from above in a giant kiln. “Oh, you know. Sweeping me off to his private villa. Making me his trophy bride.”

Olivia laughed. “Obviously,” she said as we sat down on the low wall that surrounded the pool deck. “Really, though.”

“He said—” I stopped for a moment, afraid of sounding ridiculous: like I was bragging or, worse, completely deluded. But it was only Olivia, wasn’t it? I could tell Olivia anything. “Don’t laugh, okay? But he told me he heard I’m the one here worth watching.”

“He *did*?” Olivia raised her eyebrows, surprise painted all over her face. “Really?”

“I know,” I said, laughing a little myself. The boys were still horsing around in the pool. “I told him he was probably confusing me with one of you, but—”

“Was he, like, hitting on you?”

“What? No,” I said, stung. “I mean—I don’t think so?” I frowned. *Had* Tulsa been hitting on me and I just hadn’t realized? I thought of what Kristin had said back at the beginning: *I figured you must be super hot.*

"Listen." Olivia grinned at me then, nudged me in the ribs. "If there's any room at that villa . . ."

"Of course," I promised, smiling back at her. "I'll get you a set of keys."

The four of us crowded onto the sofa when we got home that night, eating corn chips from the vending machine and watching one *Fresh Prince* rerun after another. The faint smell of chlorine hung in the air. "Can I play with your hair?" Kristin asked Ashley, reaching over and tugging on the ends of it to get her attention.

Ashley rolled her eyes like somebody who got asked this question a lot. "Why?" she asked. "Because—"

"Here," Olivia intervened, sliding off the couch and settling on the carpet in front of Kristin. "Play with mine instead." Then, peering up at her with a crooked smile, "I'm really sorry Tulsa didn't get the chance to appreciate your wax job."

"His loss," Kristin and I said at exactly the same time, and Kristin grinned.

We hung out for a while longer, Kristin twisting Olivia's hair into a complicated-looking braid crown, then turning and offering to do mine. "Sure," I said, surprised and kind of flattered. "That'd be nice."

"Let's make cookies," Ashley said when Kristin was finished, tucking the last of the bobby pins into place.

"I don't think there's anything in this whole apartment

to make cookies with," I pointed out. "There's, like, protein powder and filtered water and that's it."

"We'll improvise," Ash decided, which is how we wound up making the world's most disgusting cookies with flour, Equal, Egg Beaters, and two packs of vending-machine M&M's. We listened to a TLC CD on Charla's boom box while they baked, making up a stupid dance to go along with it.

"Until, like, last year I thought this song was about a guy named Jason Waterfalls," I admitted, and Ashley laughed so hard she started wheezing and Olivia had to run into the bedroom and grab her inhaler. When Charla opened her bedroom door, I thought she was going to yell at us to pipe down and go to bed, but after watching us for a minute, she stretched her arms a little, like she was warming up. "Can I get in on this?" she asked, raising her eyebrows.

"You wanna learn this dance?" I asked.

Charla nodded. "Is that okay?"

"Yeah," I said, a slow grin spreading over my face. The timer on the oven dinged: the cookies were finished. "Of course."

It was fun as hell, being in charge of Charla for a change, turning the tables as she gamely let us boss her through the steps we'd already come up with. "Sharp movements!" I called out in a singsong voice, hands on my hips. "Remember to smile!"

That stopped her, the dark arches of her eyebrows going

up. "I'm sorry," she said, lips pursed. "Are you impersonating me right now?"

Ashley snorted; Olivia looked innocently away. ". . . No?" I said, but Charla only laughed.

"Show me the turn one more time," she said, and I did.

It was after two in the morning by the time we called it a night, still giggling. I'd had fun today, I realized—not just with Olivia, but with everyone, Kristin and Ashley included. Maybe this was how it was supposed to be all along. I rinsed out the mixing bowl we'd used for the cookies, changed into my pajamas. I pushed open the bathroom door, and gasped—there was Olivia on the floor in front of the toilet, one hand holding her hair back as she puked.

"Shit," I said, taking a step back. "Sorry. Are you sick?"

She shook her head. "I'm fine," she told me, wiping her mouth.

I blinked, my sleepy brain slow to put things together. Then it clicked. "Oh, *Olivia*, no."

"It's nothing," she said immediately, sitting back against the wall next to the toilet paper holder. Her eyes were watery and bloodshot, her face flushed. "I'm not—stop, it's not a big deal."

"Liv." I felt my eyes fill with tears—I couldn't help it. She'd never done this before, that I knew about; I wondered what else I didn't know. I swallowed, pulled myself together. "Come on."

Olivia shook her head again. She looked more like herself

now—or rather, she looked like Showbiz Olivia, putting up that cool facade. "It's really fine. It's just a one-time thing. I seriously think it's just nerves or something."

I studied her, skeptical. There had been signs she was struggling, I admitted to myself now. The way she'd been picking at her food since we got here. The way her cheekbones had begun to jut. I'd told myself she was just stressed. I'd told myself we all had a lot of adjusting to do. "Are you sure it's just one time?" I asked. "Like, I didn't think it worked like that."

"Well, *I* work like that," she said briskly. Then she softened. "Dana, I'm fine. I promise you this isn't anything to freak out about. And I'd really appreciate you not telling anybody, okay?"

Really appreciate? That was a Showbiz Olivia turn of phrase if ever I'd heard one. I hesitated. I wasn't exactly sure how to play this—I didn't want to scare her, or make her feel attacked or like I was going to rat on her. But I also wanted to make sure she was okay. It felt like I should be doing more than just making sure Olivia ate her dinner. Like maybe our arrangement wasn't working after all. "Okay," I said finally. "But Liv—"

"You know what I was thinking about at Guy's today?" Olivia asked me then, leaning her head back against the green-tiled wall. "Mel Dunbar's birthday party."

"Oh my God," I said, cackling and then clapping a hand over my mouth, not wanting Kristin or Ashley to overhear us. Mel Dunbar had been the most popular girl in our seventh-grade class a hundred years ago. Her thirteenth birthday was a town over at her dad and stepmom's house, which boasted an aboveground pool that looked constantly on the verge of collapse. I'd been eating my weight in barbecue potato chips when I'd spotted Olivia signaling me wildly from an upstairs window: she'd gotten her period for the first time ever, and neither one of us was prepared. We went on a reconnaissance mission into Mrs. Dunbar's vanity, where we found no tampons but enough prescription painkillers to take down a large animal. Eventually we'd improvised with a wad of toilet paper, but Olivia was convinced everyone was going to find out, so I created a diversion by falling into the pool and faking a charley horse until her mom could come pick us up. "That was truly my finest best-friend hour, it's true." I looked at her now. I wasn't ready to just let this go. "I wish you'd told me," I said finally.

"Dana." She shrugged, tracing the pattern in the floor tile with one finger. "I'm saying, there's nothing to tell."

"Okay," I said, not quite believing her. "But, like, if there was. It's just me. I'm not going to give you a hard time, or judge you, or whatever. I didn't even know what a bidet was, remember?"

Olivia laughed at that, looking me in the face for the first time since I'd come in here, and the sound of it was reassuring. *"Fsssshhhh,"* she said goofily, and after a moment, I laughed, too.

TWENTY

"Okay, okay, okay," I said to Alex on Thursday; we were sprawled on the sofa in the apartment he shared with Trevor, the hum of the air-conditioning and one of my old mixtapes on the boom box, Alex's mouth pressed warm and wet against the hollow of my throat. "That's good, that's good, but I want to talk for a second, though."

"You do, huh?" Alex asked, pulling back and smiling, his cheeks flushed pink and the baby hairs around his face frizzing up in the humidity. I could feel his heart tapping eagerly away under my palms. "Whatcha wanna talk about?"

"I don't know," I said, leaning back against the arm of the couch. "Anything." I meant it, too: I wanted to know everything there was to know about him, wanted to hear every single one of his stories and learn all his memories well enough that they became my memories, too, until there'd never been a time when we didn't know each other.

"Anything?" Alex asked, making for my neck again.

I laughed, pushed him gently away. "Anything," I said, rubbing my thumb over his collarbone, like I was polishing a worry stone. "Or, okay, tell me about your family. Are your brothers singers like you?"

"Kyle and Eric?" Alex smirked like I'd said something funny. "Nah. They think I'm a total freak. But, you know, a lovable one."

"Obviously," I echoed, smiling at him. "When I was really little I always wanted brothers or sisters. Then I met Olivia, though, and it's kind of the same."

Alex smiled. "You guys are really close, huh?"

"Yeah," I said, crossing my ankles in his lap, shivering as his fingertips brushed gently over my calves. "There are two kinds of friends in life, I figure. There are the ones who you have fun and party with, right? And those friends are great and all. But then there's the other kind—like, people you can go to the bathroom in front of and who tell you if your shirt is giving you a uniboob, and who have heard your parents fight and don't care." *And who'll keep all your secrets*, I thought uneasily, remembering the other night.

Alex tilted his head to the side. "You go to the bathroom in front of Olivia?" he asked.

I kicked him in the ribs. "You're missing the point."

"I'm not," Alex promised. "I'm just teasing, I swear.

That's awesome, that you guys have that."

I felt a hollow twist in my stomach. I was dying to tell Olivia about Alex. It finally felt like things were back to normal between us, and I hated keeping this huge secret from her. Still, every time I opened my mouth to confess I thought of finding her on the bathroom floor, hunched over the toilet, and just like that I couldn't make myself do it. I was terrified of hurting her.

I looked up at Alex. "Anyway, I don't expect you to get it," I teased him. "You probably had a zillion best friends growing up. You were probably the most popular person in your grade."

Alex scoffed. "I wasn't the most popular person in my grade," he protested, but from the way his voice got a little higher I could tell he was lying.

"You were!" I accused, sitting up straight again.

"I was not," Alex said. "Do you not remember that story I told you about singing to myself during math tests?"

But I wasn't buying. "Uh-huh. And now you're the hot singer kid everybody's obsessed with. I'm dating, like, the Conrad Birdie of Galveston High."

"Conrad Birdie didn't go to their high school," Alex informed me. "He was the visiting celebrity."

"Which you'd know, because you were probably in the revival of *Bye Bye Birdie* on Broadway or something." I rolled my eyes, then kissed him to show I was teasing. "What about your parents?" I asked. "What are they like?"

Alex shrugged. "They're nice," he said. "Just regular parents. Kind of worried about me doing all this."

"How come?" I asked; then, remembering his dad was a minister: "Like, the sin and degradation of it?"

"Yeah, kind of." Alex looked embarrassed. "They'd like you, though."

I snorted. "Doubtful."

"Why?"

"Parents never like me," I explained. "I give off a vibe."

"What vibe is that, exactly?" Alex asked, tipping his face close to mine.

"A shame and degradation vibe," I shot back.

Alex leaned back then, frowning, looking me right in the eyes. "Can you do something for me?" he asked. "Can you allow for the possibility that you're more special than you give yourself credit for?"

"I like this motivational speech you're giving me," I teased. "It's very charming."

"It's not a motivational speech," Alex said, sounding hurt. "It's what I think." His accent got a little thicker when he was passionate about something, *ah* instead of *I*, that Texas lilt. I could tell he was being sincere, and I felt like a jerk about it. It wasn't Alex's fault we came from completely different universes. I could picture him at home with his family, all of them gathered for an after-church meal around a table with a lace cloth, a golden retriever snoozing in the corner for good measure. For a moment I wondered what would have happened if we'd met back in Jessell, if we'd have had anything to say to each other.

But we never would have met back in Jessell, I reminded myself. Our paths would never have crossed.

Alex didn't seem concerned about that, though. "I am, like, really into you," he told me urgently. "And it's not 'cause of how you look, and it's not 'cause I think I can get something from you. It's 'cause I'm into *you*." He wrinkled up his nose a little, like he was waiting for me to make fun of him. "Is that corny?"

"Really corny," I said, and smiled. I kissed him to show I didn't mind. Still, I couldn't shake the creeping notion that what Alex and I had was specific to us being here in this place together, that it might not survive a change of time or venue. It made things feel fragile and important. It made me want to hold on tight.

We stayed on the couch like that for a while, talking and kissing both; it had thunderstormed that afternoon and the sky outside the window still hung dark and heavy, a greenish tinge to the air. On the tape deck, my mix switched over to "Tangerine," the Led Zeppelin song that was my favorite. "Listen to this," I told Alex, lacing my fingers through his.

"Well, Olivia is right about one thing," he said after a moment, tipping his chin up thoughtfully. "This is, in fact, a sad, clangy, old-man song about a breakup."

"I didn't tell you that so you could use it against me!" I

said, swatting him in the bicep. "You're supposed to be on my side."

"Of course I'm on your side," Alex told me. "Just, maybe, you know, not about this particular wailer."

"Jerk," I said, both of us quiet for a moment as I listened along with him. "I don't think it's about a breakup," I said slowly. "Or maybe it is, but it's *actually* about, like, one perfect moment."

"One perfect moment, huh?" Alex asked, leaning in to kiss me again, his mouth soft and surprisingly tentative. "I like the sound of that."

His warm hands slid up the back of my shirt, and I breathed in, my whole body buzzing like my bones were full of neon. I'd made out with guys before—I'd done more than that—but I'd never really understood what the big deal was, what made people write songs and wage wars and generally act like idiots. I'd seen my mom get bogged down and tangled up by her own emotions, and I'd always sworn I'd never let that happen to me.

But with Alex, I got it.

He touched my hair now, my cheek, running his thumb along my jaw before sliding off the couch and lifting his blond head to face me, kneeling on the floor between my knees. "Can I?" he asked, one finger at the zipper on my shorts, looking shyer than I would have thought possible. "I mean—"

"What, like—?" I blinked as it registered what he was after. "On *me*?"

Alex grinned at that, like I was being funny on purpose. "Yeah, Dana. On you."

I hesitated. "Is that gross?" I asked uncertainly. I wasn't used to feeling inexperienced around him, but it wasn't anything I knew about, not really. "I mean—"

"It's not gross." Alex's eyes were wide, shaking his head at me. "It's . . . yeah. I promise it's not gross."

I nodded slowly, thinking about it. "If you want," I said finally.

Alex laughed. "Do *you* want?"

"I—yeah," I said. "Okay."

I wriggled out of my shorts and sat back on the sofa, my heart doing a kicky bit of choreography inside my chest. All the muscles in my thighs were rubber-band tense.

"It's me," Alex said after a moment, pressing a kiss against the inside of my knee. "Hey. It's just me."

I relaxed some after that—enough to enjoy it a little and, after a few minutes, to enjoy it a *lot*. I gasped and ran my fingers through his hair, my whole body shaking. The feeling of it rolled over me in waves.

"Um," I said after, sitting up a little, tugging at Alex's T-shirt until he looked up at my face. "Okay. Wow."

Alex laughed. "You like that?" he asked, sounding pleased with himself.

"I—yeah," I said. "Yeah, I liked it."

"Good," he said. "I liked it, too."

I grabbed Alex's shoulder and yanked until he crawled

up the couch to be next to me, the two of us smashed side by side on the cushions in a flushed, sweaty mess. I pressed my cheek against the flat expanse of his chest, rubbing my nose against the cotton and feeling calm and wrung out and safe somehow, just the two of us, far away from Guy and the coaches and the world outside. The light was changing in the apartment as the sun sank behind the complex—everything getting purpler, shadows appearing where there hadn't been any before.

I turned my face to look up at him, felt his heart thudding under my hand. "We don't have to go anywhere yet, do we?" I asked hopefully. "Nobody's going to catch us?"

Alex shook his head, smoothed my hair down. "We can stay here for a while," he promised. "We're good."

I got back to the apartment that night and found Olivia sitting bolt upright on top of her bed, fully dressed, like she'd been waiting. "Where were you?" she asked, before hello or anything else.

I took a deep breath, but before I could say anything: "Were you with Alex?" she asked.

My heart dropped thirty stories at once. "Olivia," I said. "I—"

"You were," she said, eyes narrowing. "I knew it. I knew there was something going on between you guys, Kristin tried to tell me she saw you together—"

"Yeah," I said honestly. "I was. I'm sorry. I'm so sorry, I

want to talk to you about it. I've been wanting to talk to you about it—"

"Oh, *now* you want to talk to me about it, now that I freaking caught you—"

"I'm sorry," I said again, coming toward her, perching on the edge of her mattress. "It was fucked up of me. It just kind of happened, I never meant to steal him or anything like—"

"Of course you didn't," Olivia said, crossing her arms over her chest. "You never mean to steal anything."

My eyes narrowed. "What does *that* mean?"

"I don't even care about Alex anymore. You get that, right? I had a crush on him a million years ago, we've talked like three times since I got here, it's fine. Frankly, I think he's kind of stupid-looking now. What I *care* about is that you were too chickenshit to tell me about it."

"I *tried*," I said, struck by the unfairness of it. "I've been trying for weeks and weeks to have a conversation with you, but—"

"When?"

"The very first day anything happened, first of all," I said. "I told you I needed to talk to you and you totally blew me off."

"Whatever," Olivia said. "That was one time. We *live* together. I'm pretty sure you could have carved out two seconds to mention you're boning my middle-school crush." She shook her head. "At least I finally understand why you're still here."

"I want this just as much as you do," I said hotly. "Just because my whole life hasn't been about some regional production of *Cinderella* that I did when I was twelve, that doesn't mean—"

Olivia snorted. "Okay, Dana. Do whatever you want, keep on *Single White Female*–ing me. For your next trick you'll probably murder me in my bed so you can just take over my life entirely, how about that?"

"Now you're being ridiculous."

"That's what Ash and Kristin think, you know that, right? That you're obsessed with me?"

"You're acting insane." I was crying now, not bothering to try to hide it. "Why is it so hard to believe I might want something for once in my life?"

"It's not hard at all," Olivia shot back. "Clearly when you want something, you go right ahead and take it, never mind who it actually belongs to."

"This doesn't belong to you!" I shouted. "Alex didn't belong to you; Daisy Chain doesn't belong to you! You don't have blanket ownership over the whole world, Olivia."

Olivia looked at me with an expression I'd never seen on her face before. "You should have just stayed in Jessell where you belong."

I felt like she'd slapped me. I *wished* she'd slap me; I wanted to hit her back, to hurt her as much as I possibly could—to pull hair and leave scratches, to have this out once and for all. Then I wanted to storm out of the bedroom—out of the apartment, out of the complex, out of Orlando entirely—but one, it wasn't like I had anywhere to go, and two, that was exactly what she wanted, wasn't it? For me to go back to Jessell with my tail between my legs, to let her take her place in the spotlight? No, I thought spitefully, flouncing onto my bed and raising my eyebrows in a challenge. *She* could go if she wanted. I was going to stick it out.

Olivia glared at me, shook her head again, and threw herself into her own bed so hard the springs groaned. Both of us lay there, breathing angrily, neither of us getting up to change into pajamas or brush our teeth, refusing to cede even an inch of space to the other. My whole body ached like a bruise.

TWENTY-ONE

Olivia was already gone by the time I woke up the next morning, the comforter on her bed neatly smoothed, pillow plumped and lying against the headboard. If I hadn't known better, I'd have thought she hadn't slept in it at all. It annoyed me, how meticulous she was, how tidy. Everything about her annoyed me right now.

I wasn't late, but the rest of them were already downstairs waiting in the car, sitting three in a row in the backseat like birds on a telephone wire. Olivia didn't say anything when I opened the door of Charla's SUV, staring out the window with her arms crossed. Kristin and Ash oozed silent contempt from the backseat. *Perfect,* I thought, buckling my seat belt with more force than was probably necessary, my stomach twisting unpleasantly as I imagined what she must have told them about our fight and how it had started. Now they could add backstabbing slut to the long list of reasons they hated my guts.

Charla followed me down the steps into the parking lot, hair tightly secured in a long braid over her shoulder and her car keys jingling in her hand. "Everything okay?" she asked, eyes cutting from me to the rest of them.

"Yup," I said, too loudly. "Everything's great."

Guy sat in on our rehearsal again that day, leaning back in a folding chair in the corner and looking at us critically, his arms folded across the bulk of his barrel chest. "Okay, ladies," he said once we were finished with our warm-ups. "Here I am. Better than last time, right? I want you to amaze me."

I wasn't feeling much like I could amaze anybody on this particular morning, my black mood like a woolen cape out of a fairy tale, but I took a deep breath and tried to focus. I wanted to let the anger fuel me, to use it as motivation to do better than I ever had before—to prove, once and for all, that I deserved to be here just as much as anyone else did. When I glanced over at Olivia she was scowling in my direction; I rolled my eyes and looked away. Let her think I was only here to steal from her, to take what she saw as rightfully hers. Let them all think whatever they wanted. I'd show everyone the truth.

I closed my eyes briefly as Lucas started us on an up-tempo dance number called "Hey," the electronic drumbeat coming from his keyboard matching the thump of my own anxious heart. Ashley was the tiniest bit early on her cue, but the rest of us hit our first poses exactly, crouching down and then exploding upward, elbows popping and fingers spread wide.

We looked and sounded way better than we had the last time Guy had watched us, I knew that much was undeniable. The extra rehearsing we'd been doing—that *I'd* been doing—was paying off. But the tension radiating from us was palpable, like stink lines in a Saturday morning cartoon: when I glanced over at Ashley, her smile had taken on a manic, slightly deranged quality, like she'd been lobotomized. Kristin was straight-up grimacing as she ground her way through the routine. And Olivia's voice was way louder than usual, her volume making it difficult for me to find the harmonies I'd been working so ridiculously hard on, that by now I could usually hit problem-free. Was she purposely trying to out-sing me? I couldn't tell for sure.

"Stop," Guy said suddenly, standing up and waving his hand until Lucas took his fingers off the keyboard; the silence was startling, almost obscene. "Stop, stop, stop." He looked around the room at us, frowning. "This isn't working."

All of us froze where we were for a moment, the color draining out of everyone's faces. *What wasn't working?* I wondered, but none of us dared to say a word. Ash crossed her arms, hugging herself like she was suddenly freezing. Olivia's lips were a pale, thin line.

"Your whole brand is supposed to be carefree fun," Guy

reminded us. "It's summertime, school's out, everybody's enjoying themselves. The four of you look like you're having root canals up there. It's fucking miserable to look at."

Fucking miserable, seriously? It felt like a balloon had popped inside my chest. All the work I'd been putting in lately, and for what? Here I was, in the same place we'd been weeks ago, never measuring up.

Guy shook his head. "Don't get me wrong," he went on, as if he knew what I was thinking. "Technically, you're better than you were. I can see you're trying. But it's a personality thing. The four of you should have gelled by now, and you just haven't. Quite honestly, you're boring to watch. Maybe four is the wrong number here, I don't know." He rubbed a hand over his face. "Look," he said, "the thing about these groups is that there's one star. You get that, right? The Jackson Five had Michael; the Supremes had Diana Ross. All four of you in a line like this, vying for attention—it doesn't work. It's hard on the eye."

Guy was quiet for a moment, his words hanging in the air as if you could reach out and grab them, a handful of broken glass. "So," he said, looking at each of us in turn, "which one of you is the star?"

That took me aback—took all of us aback, our eyes widening, the question sucking all the air out of the room. Nobody said anything; the four of us looked at one another uneasily. After a moment Guy sighed, impatient. "This isn't some cute rhetorical exercise, ladies. I'm looking for an answer."

Silence. Olivia stared at her fingernails. Kristin looked at the ground. Ashley and I caught eyes for a minute, both of us glancing immediately away. Until now we'd been able to keep up the facade that we were all in this together, a team—albeit a messed-up one—working toward a common goal. Asking us to pick among ourselves felt taboo, as if Guy had demanded to know which one of us was ugliest or deserved to be dropped off a bridge. It felt like he was trying to get us to violate some kind of implicit code.

Finally, he shook his head, clearly disgusted. "We're done for the day," he said. "I have to figure out what to do with you. Go away."

"I mean, it's you, clearly," Alex said that night. We were sitting face-to-face on the sofa in the apartment he shared with Trevor, knees bent and bare feet brushing. Dinner with Charla and the girls had been a miserable, silent affair, the tension in the kitchen as thick and starchy as the vegetarian chili Charla had made. I'd dashed out the front door as soon as I could, telling myself I didn't care about the nasty looks the rest of them were undoubtedly shooting me behind my back. "You're the star."

I waved my hand like his words could be batted away. "You have to say that."

"I don't, actually," Alex pointed out. He wrapped one big hand around my ankle and tugged until I scooted down closer to him; he pressed his thumb against my bare instep, and I shivered.

"That feels nice."

"It's supposed to," Alex said, running his palm up over my calf and squeezing. "I'm distracting you."

"You're not, actually, but I appreciate the effort." I sighed, but let him kiss me, closing my eyes and tilting my chin up, breathing in his clean boy smell. It occurred to me again that our relationship would probably only last as long as we were in this place together—that if I got cut from Daisy Chain, the odds were that Alex and I would never see each other again. After all, we'd barely known each other a month. It had been an intense month, sure—we'd seen each other every day, and he knew more about me than arguably anyone else on the planet besides Olivia—but still. It scared me, how much I cared about him. It felt dangerous, like I was asking to get hurt.

"What about now?" Alex murmured after a moment, as my knee came up to hug the side of his body. "Am I distracting you now?"

I swallowed hard. "That's a little better," I allowed.

Alex smiled against my jawline. "It's going to be fine," he promised. "I know it."

I sat up then, gently pushing him off me. "Can you stop saying that?" I asked. "That everything is going to be fine? I mean, I appreciate that you're trying to help me, but you have no reason to think that's true."

"How talented you are is the reason," Alex said, frowning. "How much I like watching you when you're onstage."

I laughed at that, the edge in my voice betraying a frustration I hadn't even realized I was feeling. It seemed like nothing ever went wrong for Alex. So of course he had no reason to think anything ever would. "We're fooling around, Alex! Of course you like looking at me when I'm onstage."

Alex's eyes narrowed. "And you said yourself Tulsa basically told you you're the star of Daisy Chain," he reminded me. "So don't throw some false modesty around like—"

"That's not what he told me," I countered. "And it's not false modesty! I don't get to be sure of myself because one dude gave me a compliment, Alex, even if it was Tulsa MacCreadie. I haven't spent my entire life being a golden child and having everybody tell me I'm God's gift to the performing arts."

Right away, I knew I'd gone too far; Alex looked like I'd slapped him in his face. "Is that what you think of me?" he asked. "That people just hand me stuff and tell me how great I am all day long?"

"No," I said, "that's not—" I broke off, shrugged a little. Told the truth. "I think your life is easier than most people's lives, yes."

"Okay," Alex said, standing up. "You know what—"

"It's true!" I protested. "I'm not saying it as a value judgment, I'm just . . . saying it."

"You *are* saying it as a value judgment, actually."

I huffed a breath out. "I'm sorry," I said. "I don't want to fight."

Alex made a face. "Don't you?"

I didn't know how to answer that. Until now, I'd mostly been able to ignore how different Alex and I were—like the fact that we were here in this bubble together meant it didn't matter that we came from completely opposite places, had completely opposite experiences of the world. But the thing about bubbles was that, inevitably, they popped. I didn't know if what we had when we were together was any match for who each of us was on our own.

"I should go," I told him finally. "You're right, I'm sorry. I'm tired. I'm being a jerk."

Alex looked at me, his expression hurt and baffled. I felt my stomach clench. "Okay," he said. "I'll see you tomorrow."

"Okay," I echoed quietly. I headed out into the twilight toward home.

TWENTY-TWO

"Well, ladies," Guy said the next morning, sitting behind the desk in his cramped, windowless office, "we tried this. And I'm sorry to say it didn't work."

Here it was. I crossed my arms in front of my chest, struggling to keep my gaze steady as I planted my feet far apart and pushed my shoulders back: I wanted to take up space. *I'm not afraid of you*, I wanted to tell him, although obviously that was a giant lie. Guy held my entire future in his pocket, the same way he'd carry a handkerchief or a pack of gum.

"It wasn't just that abysmal performance a couple of weeks ago," Guy continued, "although—make no mistake—it was abysmal. Still, I've seen worse. We could have fixed that if the four of you had developed any kind of chemistry as a group. Dance moves we can teach. Voices I can remix. But that special thing, that lightning in a bottle, you all just—you don't have it." Guy shook his head. "So in the interest of getting this over with as quickly as possible and not leaving you hanging in suspense, I'm just going to lay it out for you girls. You're leaving me no choice. I'm disbanding Daisy Chain. Ashley, Kristin," he said, "you're out."

What? Ashley and Kristin? For a moment I honestly thought I'd heard him wrong. Next to me, Olivia let out a sound that wasn't quite a whimper, but other than that nobody said anything; the four of us stared at him, shocked and cowlike.

"I mean it," Guy said, sounding puzzled by our stunned reaction, addressing Ash and Kristin directly now. "Go talk to Juliet. She's going to book your flights home. You're both lovely young ladies, and it's been a pleasure for me to get to know you, but you've had your opportunity, and now it's over."

"Are you kidding me?" Kristin demanded, puncturing the silence. She looked furious and simultaneously like she'd been gut punched. "You're cutting *us*?" Ashley had begun crying openly, tears rolling down her face. Kristin turned around to gesture at me incredulously. "And she's what, she's staying? You're keeping her over us?"

"Girls," Guy said calmly, "I'm not fucking around here. I mean it. Thank you very much."

"This is a joke," Kristin said, shoving her chair back so hard it squealed against the tiles; Ashley jumped out of the way. "Seriously, this whole thing is bullshit." She yanked the door open so hard I was half afraid she was going to rip it off its hinges, her ponytail swishing wildly. After a moment, Ashley followed her out.

Olivia and I made frantic eye contact, our fight momentarily forgotten. *What the fuck*, I mouthed.

"Now, you two," Guy said, sitting back in his seat once Ash and Kristin had gone, the door shutting with a finality that made me think I'd never see them again. He crossed his arms, looked at us shrewdly. "You two, I'll be honest, I haven't quite figured out what the hell to do with. You're not going to be a duo, that's for sure. Sit down, Dana, you look like you're about to run out the door."

I sat just like he told me to, taking the chair Kristin had vacated, the plastic still warm with her body heat.

"I could keep you both as solo acts," Guy said thoughtfully, "but it feels like shooting myself in the foot to be pushing two products in direct competition with each other at the exact same time. It's bad business." *Products?* Was that how he saw us? Was that what we were? "But that's the problem," he continued, like we weren't even sitting in the room with him. "Which one of you do I keep?"

"Keep me," Olivia said immediately, and I whipped my head around to stare at her. She didn't look at me once as she continued, "I've got more training, I've got the better voice, I'm more reliable onstage. Keep me."

Guy smiled at that, looking genuinely fond of her. "Well, somebody learned something yesterday, huh? Very nice,

Olivia. You're right, that how much you want it is going to be a big part of this. But it's not gonna be quite that easy." Guy sighed. "I think what I'm going to do is keep you both on for now. You'll rehearse separately. We'll try you out as solo artists. And we'll see which one of you earns a spot on the tour."

I gawked at him openly, my brain slow to make sense of what he was telling us here. "So, what?" I asked, unable to help myself. Twenty-four hours ago, the tour had been a sure thing for Daisy Chain, the light at the end of a tunnel lined with hard work and dedication. Now, suddenly, it was the prize in some kind of twisted popularity contest between me and Olivia? Just like that, all the rules had changed. "You're just pitting us against each other?"

"I wouldn't look at it like that," Guy said. "But a little healthy competition never hurt anyone, I don't think. My guess is that it'll make you both better, sharper performers."

Yeah, at what price? I thought of how excited I'd been to come down here at the beginning of the summer, how it felt like this gift Olivia and I had been given, a way to keep us together even as the universe was conspiring to split us apart. Coming here was supposed to mean I didn't have to lose her. But when I glanced in her direction, she didn't look like anyone I knew.

"I'll show you what I can do," she promised, now leaning forward eagerly, like Guy was a coach in some corny sports movie and not what he actually was: a businessman who looked at us and saw dollar signs and nothing more.

"Me too," I heard myself say, then felt immediately embarrassed. It didn't sound like me at all. But I did want to show him, I realized suddenly. In spite of everything, I wanted to prove myself now more than ever. "I'll show you, too."

"I'm sure you will. In the meantime, take the rest of the day," Guy told us. "Come back tomorrow ready to work."

Kristin and Ashley were gone by the time we made it out into the hallway; the studio was quiet and abandoned. Olivia and I stood at the top of the concrete stairs that led to the parking lot, waiting for Charla. It was raining, the pavement giving off a wet, smoky smell. Drops collected on our shoulders and in our hair, but neither one of us moved.

"Tulsa was part of a group at the beginning," Olivia said finally, staring straight ahead at the parking lot and not at me. It was the first thing she'd said to me directly in days. "I forgot that until just now. There were five of them, like there are in Hurricane State, but Tulsa was the only one Guy kept."

"What happened to the rest of them?" I couldn't resist asking.

Olivia shrugged. "I have no idea."

I didn't know what to say to that, so I didn't say anything. Olivia crossed her arms. We stood there for a long time, not talking, waiting for Charla to come and take us home.

TWENTY-THREE

We rode back to the apartment in silence, fast-food joints and nail salons blurring by outside the window. The sky was low with dreary, polluted-looking clouds. As soon as we got upstairs, Olivia stalked into our bedroom and slammed the door behind her, leaving Charla and me alone in the living room. We stared at each other for a moment. I felt like I'd fallen down a flight of steps.

"So," Charla said finally, clapping her hands together, "want some lunch?"

She was kidding, trying to make a joke out of this whole absurd, horrifying situation, and I cackled one insane-sounding laugh before the shock wore off all at once and I realized how totally, enormously angry I was. I was livid—at Olivia, at Guy, at Charla maybe most of all. She'd spent the last month painting herself as our ally, as basically one of us:

fixing our snacks, listening to our secrets, learning our stupid sleepover dances. But apparently she'd been double-agenting for Guy all along.

"Where are Ash and Kristin?" I asked, looking around the apartment with my arms crossed. "Already hitchhiking home, or what?"

Charla rolled her eyes at me. "Juliet's going to bring them back to pack up in a bit," she told me. "They're signing some papers, getting their travel home sorted." Then, more gently, "This is a business, Dana. People get cut. It happens."

"Oh yeah?" I asked. "How long did you know it was going to *happen*?"

Charla exhaled and sat down on the sofa, motioned for me to sit down with her. I stayed exactly where I was. "I knew—" she began, then stopped abruptly as music came blasting from the stereo in our room, where Olivia had turned the volume on her Mariah Carey tape up as high as it would go. The doors and walls were wafer-thin in this apartment, and I thought Charla was going to tell Olivia to pipe down, but instead she just ignored the noise. "I knew he'd been thinking about it," she told me, raising her voice a bit so I could hear her over the music. "But we just got the final word last night."

"And you didn't *tell* us?"

"What was the point?" Charla asked. "What could you have done? And there was always the chance that he'd change his mind. Guy's mercurial that way. He might have woken up this morning and decided he wanted to keep everyone after all."

"This is fucked up." I glanced at Olivia's shut door, figured there was no way she could hear me over the music. "In case you haven't noticed, things are bad enough between me and her already."

"Oh, I've noticed," Charla said.

I made a face. "So you think the solution is to make us fight it out like *Lord of the* freaking *Flies*?"

"I know this is hard for you to believe, Dana, but there's more at stake here than just your feelings. We're talking about a lot of money, first of all. We're talking about people's jobs."

"Like yours?" I asked snottily.

Charla ignored me. "Look, it was obviously not working the way it was," she pointed out. "Can we agree on that much, at least?"

I shrugged. It wasn't like I had any great love for Ash and Kristin, and it certainly wasn't like they had any great love for me; still, the idea that they were so disposable—that we *all* were—made my skin crawl. "Isn't it Guy's job to *make* it work?" I countered.

"Yeah," Charla said, nodding. "And part of what's made Guy so successful in this business is that he can recognize when making it work means he needs to cut his losses." She made a face, like, *what are you going to do?* "For you girls, I know it's love—it's love for me, too, believe me, or I wouldn't be here. But for him it's money, at the end of the day. That's all."

"That's disgusting," I said.

"Is it?" Charla asked.

"Yes," I said, flopping onto the couch with my arms crossed. "All that talk about being a product? Who would want to be a part of that?"

"Plenty of people want to be a part of it," Charla fired back. "And frankly, I'd be careful who I said that in front of, if I were you. Because I'll tell you, Dana, that's a thing that's come up more than once among the other coaches and me. Whether you're actually willing to put the work in. If you actually want this or not."

"Or if I'm just here to steal it from *her*?" I asked angrily, jerking my head toward the door to my and Olivia's bedroom. All of a sudden, I felt like I was going to cry, and I grimaced: I hadn't been a crier before I came here. It was like the last few weeks had stripped away all my protective layers so that everything left was the new skin under a scab, too vulnerable; the feeling of constantly being looked at, the feeling of never once measuring up. I stared hard at the ceiling, willing myself to keep it together.

"Hey," Charla said, reaching over and laying a hand on my elbow; I jerked it away, and she sighed. "Nobody thinks you're here to steal anything from anybody, Dana. Okay? Let's be clear about that. But it's demanding, what we're doing here. It's not a secret that you didn't grow up wanting this. The others have been rehearsing and performing their whole lives. They understand the sacrifices. *Olivia* understands the sacrifices. That's all I'm trying to say."

"Well," I said, raising my chin and swallowing down the crack in my voice, feeling my spine straighten with steel and resolve. If they wanted commitment, I'd give it to them. If this was a contest, I'd win. "I'll just have to prove myself, won't I?"

Charla nodded seriously. "Yeah, Dana," she said as the song ended, a few seconds of blissful silence before the next one started up. "You will."

"I'm an asshole," I said, standing at the door of Alex's apartment that evening. "And I'm staying. I'm an asshole who's staying."

Alex's lips twitched, tilting his head at me in the doorway. His hair was wet from the shower; he smelled like soap and shampoo. "Which part of that would you like me to respond to first?" he asked.

I wrinkled my nose at him, shoved my hands in my pockets. "Whichever you'd like."

"Okay." Alex nodded. "I know this is important to you in a whole different way than it's important to me," he said, leaning against the doorjamb. "I think maybe I didn't entirely get that before, but I get it now, and I'm sorry. But it's still not fair to get freaked out and pissed off and pick a fight with me, okay?"

"You're right," I said. "I'm sorry."

Alex shrugged. "I'm pulling for you, okay? I think you're amazing."

"I know," I said, blushing, reaching down and grazing the tips of his fingers with my own. "I'm pulling for you, too."

"I'm gonna respond to the other part now." Alex's whole face broke open in a grin then; he scooped me clear off the floor. "Yes!" he exclaimed. "I knew it. Of course he's keeping you. He'd have to be an idiot not to. And Guy is a lot of things, but an idiot isn't one of them."

I laughed at that, enjoying the feeling of his warm arms around me. "I'm not a sure thing yet," I told him. "I have to beat Olivia for a spot on the tour."

Alex shook his head. "That's tomorrow's problem. Tonight we should celebrate. Do we have beers?" he called to Trevor, who was back in the kitchen.

"We have, like, one possibly skunky Corona," Trevor called back.

"Sounds like a party to me."

The three of us sat out on the tiny balcony and split it, toasting with coffee mugs as the sun dropped behind the palm trees to the west. It felt nice, being out here with the two of them; for the first time I let myself enjoy it a little, the fact that I'd made it this far. Still, I couldn't help but think that the person I really wanted to talk to about everything was Olivia. I wasn't used to combing through my emotions without her around to help me get the tangles out.

"Solo star, huh?" Alex said, curly smile and his blue eyes sparkling with the promise of it. "Dana Cartwright."

"Yup," I said, watching the last of the twilight. "Just me on my own."

TWENTY-FOUR

Walking into my first rehearsal as a solo act was like jumping into a shark tank with an open wound. The coaches had flipped my schedule so that it was the opposite of Olivia's, voice in the morning now, and even the studio felt different to me: bigger and more cavernous, quieter somehow, even though the boys were rehearsing right next door just like always. "You got this," Alex had promised last night down by the vending machines. I wasn't so sure.

"Here's our star," Guy said when I came into the voice room. He was standing at the piano with Lucas, a half-unwrapped granola bar clutched in one beefy hand. "You ready for everything to change?"

"It already has changed, hasn't it?" I asked. Kristin and Ash had left first thing yesterday morning, Juliet driving them both to the airport before it was even light out.

I'd gotten up early to say good-bye, for all the good it had done me. Ash was concentrating so hard on not crying that she could barely string together a sentence. Kristin slammed the van door so hard it almost took my fingers clean off. I'd glanced over at Olivia a couple of times, searching for some trace of the person I knew behind her sharp, stony expression. She hadn't looked back at me once.

Now Guy nodded approvingly. "You're right," he said, finishing his granola bar in one big, hungry bite and crumpling up the wrapper inside his hand. "Let's get to work."

By the time I got back to the apartment that night, Olivia had moved all her stuff into Ashley and Kristin's old room, her mattress and dresser naked and unsettling, her arty black-and-white posters pulled down off the walls. The message was as clear as if she'd written FUCK YOU in red lipstick on the mirror. "Fine, Olivia," I muttered, pulling off my sneakers and chucking them on top of her old bed like a five-year-old, the springs squealing as they bounced right back off again. "Be like that."

We ate dinner in silence, went back to our rooms without a word; Charla was making a point of ignoring us, flipping through a magazine on the sofa, but it felt like the tension was actually pushing at the walls of the apartment, like the space ought to expand to compensate. Even the potted plants seemed to wilt.

I sprawled on the bed and flipped through my lyrics

binder, turning the pages so hard I ripped one out by accident and had to stick it back together with a Band-Aid when I couldn't find any tape. I wanted to go talk to Alex, but the boys had a performance that night and wouldn't be back until late. Finally, I figured I might as well just go to sleep, or try to, but when I opened the door that connected my room to the bathroom, Olivia was opening hers at the same time. We stood there for a second, stared at each other with contempt.

"You can have it," I said finally, shrugging in a way I hoped looked careless. "I can wait."

"No, go ahead," Olivia said, her voice high and brittle. "I mean, you'll probably butt in and take it anyway, so."

"Oh, shut *up*, Olivia." I shook my head, stung. "Jesus Christ, stop being such a princess about everything. You didn't actually get cut, in case you somehow haven't noticed. You're still here."

"No thanks to you," Olivia replied nastily. Her hair was pulled back in a ponytail so tight it had to have been uncomfortable; I could see a tendon sticking out in her neck. "You've been sabotaging everybody else since you got here."

"*Sabotaging* you?" I gaped at her. "What is this, a Lifetime movie? You're being ridiculous."

"And you're being a backstabbing bitch!"

I blanched at that. Olivia and I had never name-called, not ever; it wasn't something we'd needed to do, until now. "*I'm* a bitch?" I repeated, shaking my head slightly. I hated her in that moment. I blamed her for everything that had gone wrong. I wanted to slap her, and I actually might have if Charla hadn't come into the room.

"What the hell is going on in here?" she demanded, looking at us like we'd lost our minds entirely. "They can probably hear you down in the parking lot. You sound like infants, both of you."

"Ask her," we both said in unison, like a couple of idiots. I huffed a furious breath out, shook my head. "Just stay the hell away from me," I told Olivia, then spun around and slammed the bathroom door.

I heard the shower go on a moment later, then the sound of Charla knocking on my bedroom door. "Dana," she began, easing it open, but I held my hand out to stop her.

"I know," I said, sitting up on my bed. "I'm being an infant. There's nothing to be upset about, this is the opportunity of a lifetime, I could have gotten sent home like Ash and Kristin, so who cares if my best friend hates me and everyone here is full of shit?" I glared at her. "Does that about cover it?"

I was expecting blowback, but Charla just looked at me calmly for a moment. "No, actually. That's not what I was going to say at all."

I raised my eyebrows. "No?"

"No." Charla stuck her hands into her back pockets, put one knee up on the edge of the empty bed. "Look," she said, "I know you're upset with me. I know I have to earn your trust back. And I know that whatever is happening between you and Olivia is mostly our fault, and I'm sorry for that. But already this is working better as a solo project, don't you think so? Don't you feel that at rehearsal?"

I hadn't been feeling much of anything at rehearsal besides numb, actually. I shrugged. "Maybe," I said, unconvinced.

Charla pushed forward. "Guy knows what he's doing, Dana. If you don't believe anything else I say, believe that. If you work with him, and Juliet, and Lucas, and me—this could be bigger than anything you ever thought."

"Maybe," I said again, watching an empty bag of chips skitter across the concrete below us. Then I looked up at her. "But what's it going to cost?"

I was expecting some bullshit answer, but Charla held my gaze. "Well, that's up to you, isn't it?"

I nodded. "Yeah," I said slowly. "I guess it is."

"You want some ice cream?" she asked then, holding her hand out to pull me off the bed and to my feet. "Would that cheer you up?"

I knew she was trying to distract me or buy me back again, on top of which it was probably fat-free frozen yogurt as opposed to anything I actually wanted to eat. But I was tired, and I didn't want to fight anymore. I just wanted someone to tell me what to do. "What flavor?" I asked eventually, raising my eyebrows.

Charla grinned.

TWENTY-FIVE

Sitting on the kitchen counter in the apartment and clutching the receiver in my sweaty hand, I finally scraped together the courage to call Ashley at home in her ritzy Chicago suburb. I don't know why exactly I felt compelled to do it—it wasn't exactly like we'd been friends while she was here—but it bothered me, the way she and Kristin had gotten dropped so quick and so dirty. I felt like it had been partly my fault.

I was expecting an attitude, but instead Ash sounded happily surprised to hear from me. "It's fine," she said when I was finished apologizing. "It is what it is, you know? I wanted it, but it's my senior year. Everybody's really happy I'm back. I'm probably going to be homecoming queen come fall."

I laughed at that. "You definitely will be," I said, picturing her waving from the top of a crepe-paper float. "Take pictures, okay?"

"You too," Ashley instructed. "How is it there?"

I hesitated. "It's okay," I said carefully. I didn't feel like I could tell her how much I missed Olivia, how weird and lonely this new setup felt. "It's good."

"Good," Ash said, and it sounded like she meant it. "I'll listen for you on the radio," she promised as we were saying good-bye, and I swallowed something that felt bizarrely like tears at the back of my throat.

"Bye, Ash," I said.

After that I called Kristin, who hung up on me so hard I could actually feel it in my eardrum. I put the receiver back in its cradle, leaning my head against the wall.

"No rehearsal today," Charla said two mornings later, when I came out into the living room; Olivia was already sitting at the table, a bowl of oatmeal pushed to the side. "The two of you have got media training this morning."

I frowned. "What's media training?" I asked.

Media training, as it turned out, was Olivia and I sitting side by side in Guy's office while a middle-aged blond woman named Gayle taught us how to answer interview questions without embarrassing ourselves or our coaches. Gayle rubbed me the wrong way immediately, her red lipstick and carefully shellacked hair like the women who worked at the fancy department stores in Atlanta, her mouth drawn up tight like a square knot in the middle of her face.

I only half listened as she droned on through her list of dos and don'ts, looking over at Olivia out of the corner of my eye. Her attention was rapt, of course, head tilted slightly to the side as she took in everything Gayle was saying; she'd be great on TV, I knew, same as she was great in performance: poised and disciplined and confident, nothing ugly ever seeping through the cracks. I frowned and looked away, picking at a loose thread on my shorts. I kept waiting for the moment when sitting near her or hearing her talk didn't make me want to scream or punch her or burst into tears, but it hadn't happened yet. *We're a team*, I wanted to shout; I wanted to shake her. *What the hell happened to the two of us being a team?*

"People will know what you tell them," Gayle explained. "Be pleasant, but not boring. Stay on message. And for Pete's sake, *smile.* We're building a brand here. We're selling a product," she continued, "and the product is you."

There was that word again. I got an unpleasant creeping feeling every time anyone said it, like Olivia and I were a pair of dolls in boxes on a shelf. I crossed my arms and leaned back in my chair, frowning. Gayle glanced at me with open disapproval.

"Now," she said, "a word about body language . . ."

We had our first live performances that weekend, opening for Hurricane State at a festival at a big public park in Orlando. We were scheduled to go on right after the pie-eating contest, which is about the only way we convinced Mikey not to enter. "I could take this!" he protested, looking longingly over his shoulder at the racks of blueberry and rhubarb. "You're keeping me from my true calling!"

It was even hotter than usual; volunteers were handing out little bottles of water, and spritzing stations were set up so that people wouldn't pass out from heat exhaustion. Juliet sprayed our faces with Aqua Net to keep our makeup from melting down our cheeks. "You're up first," she told me, reaching up and tucking a stray piece of my hair back. I glanced at Olivia, who was looking away.

I'd spent the whole morning anxious out of my brain, reliving the disaster of our rehearsals in front of Guy on a never-ending loop. Why had I thought I wanted this again? As I watched the crowd gather in front of the makeshift stage, red-faced and restless, it was hard to remember.

The DJ from a local radio station introduced us over the microphone, feedback squealing out into the throng. The crowd clapped politely down in the grass. The recording Lucas and the other backup musicians had made of our tracks blared from the speakers and out across the park, and then it was just . . . happening.

"Hi, guys!" I heard myself say, my voice as clear and

steady as if it belonged to somebody else entirely. "I'm Dana Cartwright!"

I'd spent the last few days steeling myself for the possibility of disaster, expecting my nerves to swallow me like some kind of tsunami, but instead I felt calmer than I ever had. I felt . . . ready. Right away I felt muscle memory take over, like all these weeks of practicing had actually *meant* something. Like every once in a while, hard work paid off. I remembered every lyric, knew every step and combination. And when I hit my most difficult note, it took every ounce of self-restraint I had not to stop in the middle of the song and fist-pump. *Suck it, Lucas*, I thought.

Take that, Liv.

The best part, though—the absolute best, most surprising, most unbelievable part—was how much the crowd was enjoying it. They were dancing and clapping and singing along with me, and when I got to the part in "Heat Wave" where I asked everybody to throw their arms in the air, everybody did. I spotted Alex off to the side just then, watching, and the proud, happy grin on his face told me everything I needed to know.

I felt like I was magic, like I could bend the entire universe to my will as long as I was up there. I felt confident and powerful and true. *I could love this,* I realized as I headed into my last song, building to the finale. More than that: I kind of already did.

"Oh my God," I said when it was over, still smiling and

waving at the slowly dispersing crowd. "Oh my God, that was *awesome.*" I felt light-headed with adrenaline as I jumped down the last two steps off the stage, my legs going a little rubbery as I landed and a dazed, fizzy buzzing at the back of my brain. I could have turned around and done it again, ten more times.

I reached out to high-five Charla, who was waiting on the grass off to the side, but she grabbed my hand and pulled me back to her, wrapping me in a tight hug even though I was hugely, grossly sweaty. "Do you see?" she said in my ear, quiet enough so Olivia couldn't hear. "Do you see what you can do when you really try?"

"I do," I promised, and for the first time I actually meant it. "I see."

Afterward, Alex and I walked the fairgrounds for a little while, watching the rickety Ferris wheel complete its revolutions and little kids shoot down the giant yellow plastic slide on burlap sacks. I was getting my change from the fried-dough vendor when someone tapped me on the shoulder; I turned to face a rail-thin girl with long, straight blond hair who couldn't have been more than nine or ten, a hot pink marker in her skinny hand.

"Can I have your autograph?" she asked, blue eyes wide.

I laughed out loud, surprised and cackling. Somehow I hadn't imagined this. I *definitely* hadn't imagined how crazy and exciting and unbelievable it would feel, the idea that I meant enough to a total stranger for her to want a piece of paper with my name on it. For that to be something that was valuable to her. My face actually ached from smiling. "Of course," I said, signing with a flourish and drawing a heart next to it, grinning at Alex as I passed the pen back. "Anytime."

"Check you out," Alex said once the girl was gone, her ponytail bouncing as she joined her group of giggling friends next to the Fun Slide.

"Okay, I liked that," I admitted as we brought the fried dough over to a picnic table, kicking up clouds of hot, sandy dust as we walked. My fingers were sticky with melting powdered sugar. "That felt awesome."

"I can tell." Alex grinned. "You're gonna be doing a lot more of it, I can tell that, too."

"Oh, you can, huh?" I laughed.

"I can. All over the place." Alex raised his eyebrows and tore off a piece of fried dough. "They're talking about Europe after the national tour, did you hear that? Maybe even Asia."

"What?" I gaped at him. "Seriously? And you guys would get to go?"

"So would you," Alex pointed out.

"Or Olivia," I said.

"Or you," he said again.

I let myself imagine it for a moment: the notion was glittering and white hot, like it would burn my hand if I reached for it. Europe and Asia, a fall and winter spent globetrotting with Alex. The whole world—suddenly, *literally*—within my reach. "Have you ever been?" I asked instead. "Out of the country?"

"Just to Mexico," he said around a bite of dough. "It sounds amazing, though, doesn't it? I'd love to see that stuff with you. Eat croissants in Paris, that kind of thing."

That kind of thing. I couldn't keep myself from smiling. Two months ago, if anyone had told me there was a chance in hell I'd see Europe in my lifetime, I would have laughed out loud. It was dangerous, I knew, to let myself picture it. It could mean I was setting myself up for a disappointment that would grind my bones to dust. But when I looked at Alex, I could tell he believed I could get there. And just for a moment, I believed I could, too.

"Come on," I said, finishing the last of the fried dough and licking my sticky fingers, nodding my head at the spinning Ferris wheel. "Let's go get stuck at the top."

TWENTY-SIX

The thrill of performing live struck some magical match inside me. I rehearsed in the shower, in the car on the way to the studio, before I went to bed every night. Once I woke up in the dark with the sheets tangled all around my ankles, and I realized I'd been practicing my routines in my sleep. I gulped every gross green smoothie Charla handed me. I worked harder than I ever had. I wanted to be the best. More than that: I wanted everyone to *see me* be the best.

Especially Olivia.

It was stupid, maybe, but hers was the face I saw every time I missed a dance step in rehearsal; hers was the voice I heard taunting me in my head. I wanted to get up earlier than she did, to hit notes that were higher and get crowds to scream louder. I wanted her to admit that she'd been wrong. I wanted Olivia to know she'd misjudged and betrayed me, but the more I tried to get her attention, the more indifferent she seemed. As hard as I was working, it was like she was working even harder not to notice me at all.

Guy noticed, though. "Come in here," he said one day after rehearsal, motioning me into his office. I felt myself tense as he shut the door behind me, but all he did was thump me on the back, dad-like. "Nice job, kid," he said, sitting down in his big leather chair across from me. "You're really showing up now, huh?"

"Thanks," I said, feeling surprisingly proud, my face flushing with the unexpected pleasure of it. It was nice to feel like everything was paying off.

I expected that to be the end of it, and I took a step toward the door, but Guy held a hand to stop me. "You doing all right?" he asked.

"Me?" I said. "Yeah, I'm great."

"You sure?" he asked, looking at me closely. "You happy?"

I stopped, surprised. Guy was the last person I ever expected to care about something like that. "Of course," I assured him now, which was a lie. I wasn't happy, not exactly; I missed Olivia, and I felt unsure more often than not. But the longer I did this, the more there was a charge in it for me, something about it that made me want to get better; I liked being special, liked the different way Lucas and the other coaches looked at me when I came into the studio. And more than I'd ever thought I would or was capable of, I liked the feeling of working toward a goal. "I am."

It felt good to do what you were good at, I realized. And I was getting really good.

Guy nodded. "Not everybody has what it takes to do this," he told me. "Lot of girls flame out, crack under the pressure. But you're not like that, I can tell. We're gonna go all the way."

I found myself grinning at him. "Yeah," I promised, nodding in agreement. "We are."

We had another performance with the boys later that week in New Orleans; it was the first time we'd gone anywhere far enough from Orlando that we needed to fly there, and I gripped the armrests like I could hold myself up in the sky. "This your first time on a plane?" Alex asked, sitting down beside me—Mikey had been assigned to the seat, but Austin had dared him to go up to the flight attendant and ask for one of those little plastic pins shaped like wings.

"Nope," I lied.

"Really?" he asked, raising his eyebrows. "It's my first time."

"Really?"

"No." Alex grinned when I scowled at him. "Relax, though," he said, peeling my fingers off the armrest and taking my hand. "Planes hardly ever crash in real life. You're, like, a hundred times more likely to die in a car wreck."

"Gee, thanks," I said, but I was laughing now, distracted. It occurred to me that that might have been the point all along.

That night's performance was a good one, bright lights and my first time with a full backup band, an electric kind of energy in the audience. I took my bow and waved and came offstage looking for Alex—I'd tried something different in "Only for You," a little run of notes toward the end of the bridge, and I wanted to hear what he'd thought about it. I was expecting him to be waiting in the wings, like I had for Hurricane State's performance earlier, but I didn't spot him in the crowd of assistants and techs. "Have you seen the boys?" I asked Juliet, who was deep in conversation on a cell phone, the long antenna poking up into the air.

"Follow the food," she suggested, putting her hand over the mouthpiece. "Try the green room."

The green room was actually a large white tent set up behind the stage, air-conditioned by a huge whirring generator and outfitted with food tables and plenty of booze, no one checking if we were of age. I saw Alex almost immediately, along with the rest of Hurricane State, an R&B trio called Star Signs who were headlining the festival—and half a dozen girls with radio station contest winner badges around their necks. One of them, a leggy brunette in artfully tattered denim shorts, had her fingers curled around his upper arm as she leaned in and said something close to his ear.

Alex stood up as soon as he saw me, trotted over, and took both my hands. "You're back," he said, sounding surprised and happy and then worried. "Did I miss it?"

"You missed it," I said, and Alex frowned.

"Shoot," he said, "I'm sorry. How was it, how did it go?"

"It was good," I said, squirming away as he moved to put an arm around me. I wasn't a jealous person, generally, but seeing him with those girls unsettled me. Our connection felt tenuous all of a sudden, a thread that could easily be snapped.

"What's wrong?" Alex asked. Then, following my gaze to the brunette, who was currently giving me stink-eye: "Oh," he said, looking at me sheepishly. "That wasn't—they didn't mean anything by it."

"I don't blame them," I said pointedly.

Alex nodded like, *message received.* "I didn't mean anything by it, either," he promised, leading me over to a quiet corner near a long buffet of food. "Really. I know that looked questionable. Guy likes us to do that kind of thing, you know? Talk to the contest winners and stuff. He thinks it's good for sales."

"Flirting with girls is good for your sales?" I asked skeptically.

"No," Alex said immediately. Then: "Well—"

"Stop," I interrupted, holding my hands up. "That's not even . . ." I trailed off, trying to articulate what was bothering me about it, trying to understand it myself. It wasn't about him missing my performance. And it wasn't about him talking to some random girl. It was bigger than that. "It's just, today I'm here, you know? So of course nothing was going to happen. But what if I hadn't been?" I shrugged, and then I said it. "What's going to happen to us if I get cut?"

Alex shook his head. "That's not going to happen."

I frowned—that was his automatic response to everything, and I was tired of it. "What if it *does*, Alex?"

"It's not," Alex said again, putting a hand on either side of my face. "But even if it did, we'd work it out, you and me. I would never do . . . anything."

"Anything." I scoffed.

"Anything," Alex reiterated, sounding hurt. "Dana. Come on, hey. It's me."

"I know," I said quietly. It wasn't like I thought Alex would cheat on me. He was right—he wasn't the type. But now that I'd said it out loud, I couldn't stop thinking about it: Alex out on the road with Hurricane State, and me back home at my mom's. What would that possibly look like? How could it possibly work?

I didn't want to talk about it anymore. I didn't even want to think. "Come on," I said, standing up abruptly and taking his hand then, pulling him through the crowded tent. "Let's get a drink."

That night I lay awake just like always, tossing and turning on the scratchy hotel sheets, headachey and out of it: I'd never slept alone in a hotel room in my life. Every time the AC kicked on or off, I startled. There wasn't anything worth watching on TV. I remembered sharing the big hotel bed with Olivia the night of our auditions in Orlando, how lucky and content I'd felt as we flipped through the channels and chattered about nothing in particular. It felt like it had happened to someone else entirely.

I thought I'd get up and rehearse until I tired myself out, maybe, but there wasn't enough floor space to do the routines. I'd seen a sign saying the hotel gym was open twenty-four hours, though, so finally I shoved my sneakers onto my feet and took the elevator down to the basement. At the very least, I could tell Charla I'd gotten a workout in. But when I got down there, Olivia was already on the treadmill in a pair of shorts and a tank top, running like she was being chased. I saw her before she saw me; when she noticed, she stumbled just the slightest bit, not quite a missed step. *Good*, I thought. I hoped she'd break her ankle, except for the part where I didn't actually hope that at all.

Probably the smart thing to do would have been to turn around and walk right back out, but instead I put my chin up, a challenge. I had just as much of a right to be here as she did, after all, even if she didn't think so. It was the first time we'd been alone together in weeks. "Hey," I said, tucking my key card into the waistband of my shorts.

Olivia looked at me for a moment. "Hey," she said. I couldn't help noticing that her collarbones and elbows looked sharper than they had a couple of weeks ago; I wasn't sure if I was imagining it, or if her eyes seemed sunken in. I tried not to worry about the fact that she was exercising in the middle of the night, about whether she was eating. She'd made it clear she didn't want my help.

I shook off the thought and walked over to the free weights, trying not to wonder what she was doing down here—if she couldn't sleep like me, if something was bothering her. What it was that had her running so fast. I tried not to think about the dozen years we'd been best friends back in Jessell, how I'd felt like I could tell her anything and it would be okay. I missed her, badly. I wanted that not to be true.

Olivia slowed just a bit as I picked up a couple of fifteen-pound free weights, trying not to wince when they were way heavier than I thought. "You know what you're doing with those?" Olivia asked.

"Yup," I said, which wasn't strictly the truth—I'd used them with Charla a few times back in Orlando, but never without her coaching me. Still, how hard could it possibly be? They were weights. You lifted them. "I'm good, thanks."

Olivia wasn't buying. "You're going to hurt yourself," she said.

"I'm fine," I assured her, heaving a weight up in either hand. Fuck, who would have thought that thirty pounds was so much to lift at once? Not that I'd ever let Olivia see me put them down. Not now. I curled them a couple of times, the muscles in my arms crying out in protest.

Olivia hit the button to stop the treadmill, slowing down to a walk. "Okay," she said, "but I just—"

"Can you not be such a know-it-all, possibly?" I asked, whirling to face her, and of course that was the moment I dropped one of the fucking free weights onto the industrial carpet and almost took my whole foot off. "Shit!" I said, dropping the other one and jumping backward, my whole face getting tight and swollen-feeling. I knew if I breathed I would cry. *You should have just stayed in Jessell*, I remembered her saying. *Why are you even here?*

For a second, neither one of us said anything; the only sounds were the *whoosh* of the air conditioner and the news on the TV mounted in one corner of the gym, a CNN anchor yammering obliviously away.

Olivia broke first. "Dana—" she started, but I cut her off.

"Enough," I said, bending down and picking the weights up, returning them to the rack with a clank. "Just go, okay, Olivia? Just leave me alone."

Olivia looked at me for a long minute, and I thought I probably imagined that she looked like she was about to cry, too. "Yeah," she said quietly, and slipped out the door without another word.

TWENTY-SEVEN

I think Guy could sense that things were getting close to boiling over, because he sent both of us home the following weekend to see our families and regroup. Olivia didn't say a word to me the entire five-hour ride, listening to tape after tape on her headphones in the back of the shiny black car Guy had arranged. I thought of the trip down here in Olivia's Toyota, how excited both of us had been, and stared out the window at the highway rushing by.

"See you Sunday," Olivia said when we got to my house—pulling her headphones off for a moment, not quite meeting my eyes.

I nodded. "See you Sunday."

Jessell in August was a different kind of hot than Orlando: browner and drier, less unrelentingly swampy. I was half expecting my mom's house to look smaller, but it was the same as it had always been: chain-link fence and aluminum screen door, stringy weeds growing up between the cracks in our front steps. I bent down and yanked a couple of them out by the roots, then dug my keys out from the very bottom of my bag and let myself inside.

The house was dark and stuffy, a still, stale smell like nobody had opened the windows since I'd left for Orlando seven weeks ago. Elvis met me in the hall. "Mom?" I called, reaching down and scratching him behind his matted ears. His fur felt sticky, like he'd been rolling around in maple syrup. "Mom! I'm home."

No answer. In the kitchen, dishes were stacked up in the sink and on the drainboard, garbage piled high in the bin; a basket full of dirty laundry sat overflowing in the middle of the hall. I frowned. Our house was never going to win any decorating awards, but it had always been pretty tidy. It occurred to me all of a sudden that maybe that was because I'd been here to clean it up.

My mom's bedroom door was cracked open; I knocked twice, loudly, then eased it open. She was lying facedown on the mattress, the sheets twisted around her legs. For one insane, terrifying, heart-stopping second, I thought it was possible she was dead. "Mom," I said, reaching out and laying a hand on her shoulder. "Mama, hey. It's me."

My mom stirred slowly at first, then woke up all at once, gasping, suddenly alert. "What are you doing here?" she demanded, eyes wide.

"I told you I was coming, remember?" I asked, taking a step backward, catching sight of myself in a baby picture on the bureau. "I've got the weekend off."

"Oh," she said, blinking, rubbing her face for a moment. Her eyes were the same blue as mine. "Yeah, of course. Hi, baby."

I smiled, heart slowing down to normal again. "How you doing, huh?"

"Fine," she said. "I thought you were coming on Friday."

"It is Friday," I said.

My mom looked irritated at that. "I don't have anything to feed you," she said, getting up and heading out of the bedroom.

"That's okay," I said as the bathroom door shut. "We can go out to lunch or something."

My mom made noises of assent, but when she got out of the bathroom she said she didn't feel well and it was too hot out, so instead we sat on the couch drinking Diet Coke and watching *People's Court*, Elvis snoring loudly between us. It felt like a different universe entirely from Orlando. I couldn't help but wonder what Alex would think if he saw this place—Elvis's kibble scattered across the linoleum in the kitchen, the pair of empty vodka bottles standing at attention on the counter next to the fridge. There were a pair of men's socks balled up on the armchair across the room, gray and dingy; I wanted to ask my mom who they belonged to, but I didn't know what to say.

In fact, I wasn't sure how to talk to her about much of anything, all of a sudden: we sat mostly in silence, commercials flickering by. I'd thought she'd be excited to hear about the routines I was working on—she'd always loved anything resembling celebrity gossip, and she'd done pageants when she was a kid—but she didn't sound particularly interested in my stories about Charla and Lucas. In fact, she sounded almost annoyed. "Is he Jewish?" she interrupted, halfway through my description of Guy's pool party, the big house and the hissing bidet.

I felt my eyebrows knit. "I don't know," I said. "What does that have to do with anything?"

My mom shrugged. "He hasn't tried anything funny with you, has he?" she asked, crossing her arms. "You're not taking off your clothes or anything like that?"

"Mom!" I said. "God! No, nothing like that. Besides, I'm with Olivia all the time."

My mom scowled. "Well, *Olivia*," she said, like that was all the explanation necessary. I didn't say anything in reply.

She hadn't been exaggerating when she'd said she had nothing to feed me; when I looked, the fridge was empty except for a thing of yellow mustard and the half-drunk two-liter bottle of Diet Coke. What had she been *eating*?

"Mom," I called. "I'm going to run out to the store for a second, okay?"

The cool, antiseptic supermarket was a relief, the neat uniformity of the products lined up along the aisles and the quiet Muzak tinkling overhead. It felt like nothing bad could happen to me here, like I'd left all my problems on the other side of the sliding doors. I took my time, trying to balance some semblance of Charla's diet with stuff my mom would actually eat; I had just tossed some iceberg lettuce into my basket when I turned around and came face-to-face with Olivia and Mrs. Maxwell, who was pushing a cart packed full of groceries.

I felt myself go as cold as the freezer section, but Mrs. Maxwell's face broke open in a grin. "There's my other famous girl!" she crowed, wrapping her arms tight around me. She was wearing capri pants and one of her Moms "R" Us blouses, a geometric pattern in purples and blues; she smelled familiar, like Olivia's house. I felt my throat tighten up unexpectedly at the endearment—I hadn't realized how much I'd missed her. "How are you, sweetheart?" Then, before I could answer: "We're just picking some stuff up for tomorrow. What do you think, should I get sausages? Or just regular hot dogs?"

"Tomorrow?" I asked dumbly, realizing even as the words came out of my mouth that I'd made a mistake.

"For the party." Mrs. Maxwell looked at Olivia, curious. "You told Dana about the party, right?"

"I—" Olivia faltered, her eyes going wide like they always did when she was caught. "I—"

"Oh, yeah, of course she did," I lied, wanting to save all of us the awkwardness. The handle of the basket was digging into my arm. "But my mom wants to spend some time with me while I'm home, so. I don't think I'll be able to make it."

"What! Just bring her," Mrs. Maxwell said. "I've got plenty."

Well, that definitely was not about to happen. "I don't know," I hedged. "I mean, you know my mom, she's . . ." I trailed off.

Mrs. Maxwell shook her head. "I mean it, Dana," she told me, and though her tone was breezy in that moment, there was something about her that reminded me, weirdly, of Guy—this overwhelming sense that she was pulling the strings here, that she knew more than she was letting on. "Come by for an hour, have a hamburger. We'll see you tomorrow, okay?"

I looked from Olivia to her mom and back again, the rock and the hard place. "Maybe for a little while," I finally said.

"That's a girl," Mrs. Maxwell said, smiling. Olivia examined the pears.

It was late afternoon by the time I made it home with the groceries; I'd planned to fix my mom something for dinner, but she was in the bathroom putting on eye shadow, getting ready to go out. "Sorry, baby," she said, shrugging like there was nothing she could do about it. "If I'd known you were coming, I wouldn't have made plans."

You did *know I was coming,* I didn't say.

"Okay," I told her instead, ignoring the sting of it. "Have fun."

I sat alone in the house for a little while. I took Elvis for a walk around the block. I called Alex and Trevor's apartment in Orlando; it rang and rang but nobody answered, and finally I hung up with a sigh. There were a million places he could be, I told myself firmly. Not picking up the phone didn't mean he was off somewhere having the time of his life without me.

This was ridiculous; *I* was being ridiculous, sitting home alone and feeling sorry for myself on my one weekend off. Finally, I combed my hair and caught the bus that went downtown, then walked the seven blocks to Burger Delight. It was Friday, after all.

There they all were, just like I'd known they would be, in our usual booths at the back: Sarah Jane and Becky and Jonah, the whole noisy crowd. "Hey," I called as the bells above the door chimed my arrival. "Got room for one more?"

Sarah Jane let out a squeal when she saw me, jumping up and flinging her arms around my neck. "What are you *doing* here?" she exclaimed. She looked honestly delighted to see me—everybody did, actually—and I felt like kind of a jerk for not keeping in better touch. Aside from a couple of quick phone calls, we hadn't talked at all since SJ and Becky and Kerry-Ann had shown up on their way to Miami.

"I missed you guys," I told them, and it was the truth.

Tim was sitting on the outside of the booth, baseball cap perched just like always on top of his head. "Here," he said quickly, scooting over to make room for me, his knobby knee bumping the underside of the table, rattling the cheap metal silverware and almost spilling a soda. "Have a seat."

He sounded so eager that I almost laughed—and Sarah Jane actually did, a full-throated bray that echoed across the restaurant. "Don't even try it, Timothy," she scolded.

"I'm just letting her sit down, SJ." Tim frowned. "Jesus."

I smiled, sliding into the tattered booth beside him. "Hi, Tim." There was a quality to him that reminded me of Mikey, but a little scruffier around the edges, and I wondered if that's what it would be like if I came back to Jessell for good: everything here reminding me of something from Orlando, nothing quite measuring up.

I caught up on everyone's headlines, filled in everyone's blanks: Kerry-Ann's sister's wedding, Jonah's mom's latest round of chemo. Becky had gotten a new job at a clinic in town and I listened eagerly as she described the doctors there, the outreach they were trying to do in the poorer parts of Jessell. For a second I remembered what I'd told Alex, how I'd thought about doing something like that when I was younger.

"So what about you, pop star?" Sarah Jane asked, pointing at me with a French fry. "How goes it with the hundred-dollar T-shirt committee?"

"Kristin and Ash?" I made a face. "They got cut, actually." I gave them the highlights of the last few weeks, leaving out the part about how Olivia and I were barely speaking. I'd been worried it would be weird, trying to explain to these guys what my life was like back in Orlando, but the reality was, aside from one or two questions, everybody seemed kind of uninterested. It wasn't something they could relate to, I realized; I might as well have been talking about my recent trip to Mars.

Sarah Jane smelled blood, though: "So it's just you and Olivia competing now, huh?" she asked when I was finished explaining, looking at me shrewdly across the table. "What's that like?"

"It's fine," I said quickly, then shoved a handful of onion rings in my mouth so I wouldn't have to say anything else about it. Sarah Jane fixed me with a gaze that let me know she thought I was full of shit, but she didn't press. She probably didn't need to, I realized: after all, the fact that Olivia wasn't here tonight said more than I ever would have.

We ordered another round of sodas; we talked about what we were watching on TV. It was easy to be with them, to fall back into our old familiar rhythms: gossiping about people we'd gone to high school with, *do you remember the time . . . ?* I even told them a little bit about Alex. I hadn't been able to talk about him to anyone since we started dating, and it felt good to say his name out loud to people who knew me—some kind of validation that he really existed, that what we had between us was real.

Still, as the night wore on I couldn't shake the constant awareness that I might be staring directly into my future. This was exactly what it would be like if Guy chose Olivia instead of me. Liv had a failsafe—worst-case scenario, she'd go off to college in September just like she'd always planned. But I'd be right back here at Burger Delight every Friday, Tim trying to slip his arm around my shoulders and the smell of fry grease sticking in my hair.

I love those guys, Olivia had said when we first got to Orlando, *but none of them are ever going to get out of Jessell.*

The truth was, I could see myself falling into the familiarity of it; I knew exactly how easy it would be to seamlessly settle back into this life, as if I'd never left at all. A month ago, I might have given myself over to it—accepted it as inevitable, surrendered without a fight. But now there was a part of me that thrashed against the idea that the world didn't hold anything for me but a thousand more nights like this one, as if I was having my head held underwater.

Sarah Jane offered to drive me home that night—it was late enough that the buses had stopped running, and she lived right around the corner from my mom's. Still, normally I'd have gotten a ride from Olivia, and SJ must have been thinking the same thing: "So where *is* Liv tonight, exactly?"

she asked as she unlocked the door of her hatchback, fixing me with a long stare over the roof of the car.

"Oh," I said vaguely, cringing a bit. I thought I'd successfully dodged that line of inquiry. I should have known better than to let my guard down where SJ was concerned. "She had family stuff to do, I think."

"I *knew* it," Sarah Jane said, sliding into the driver's seat. "I knew when we were down there that there was something weird going on with you guys."

"There's not," I insisted. It occurred to me that even now, when things were worse between us than they'd ever been before, my allegiance was to Olivia first and always. We'd never talked about each other to our other friends, not ever; just because Olivia had broken that promise with Kristin and Ashley didn't mean I was about to. "She's just busy with her mom."

"Uh-huh," Sarah Jane said, in a voice like she didn't believe me but knew she wasn't going to get anywhere by pushing it. "Whatever you say." Then she hesitated, glancing at me as we pulled out of the parking lot. "Can I ask you something, though?" she continued carefully. "Can she, like, handle it down there?"

I thought about the night after Guy's pool party. I thought of how she'd wanted this her entire life. I shrugged a little, turning and staring out the window. "I don't know," I said finally, and this time I was telling the truth.

Sarah Jane nodded at that. "Fair enough."

We drove home in companionable silence, past the high school and Waffle House, the landscape that had made up the entirety of my life until this summer. SJ hugged me again before I got out of the car. "Stay in touch, yeah?" she told me. "And, Dana—take care of yourself."

The house was dark when I got inside that night—my mom was still out, though I hadn't a clue where. Elvis was whining for a pee at the back door, urgent; I was just shooing him back inside when the phone rang. "It's you," Alex said when I picked up the receiver in the hallway, and just like that I burst into tears.

"Oh my God, I'm sorry," I said once I could talk again. "That's embarrassing." I sniffled. "Hi. Sorry. I'm tired, is all."

"It's okay. What's up, huh?" Alex asked me. "What's going on?"

I hesitated, twisting the phone cord tightly around my finger, looking through the window at the dark, weedy yard outside. Part of me wanted to tell him everything—my mom and the socks in the living room, Mrs. Maxwell in the supermarket and how badly the idea of coming back here for good scared me—but truthfully, I was embarrassed. "Just weird being back, I guess."

"I know what you mean," Alex said. "The first time I came back after I started with Hurricane State, all kinds of dumb stuff set me off. My mom had moved everything around in the kitchen cabinets and I totally lost my mind." He paused then, like he was catching himself. "But I'm gonna go out on a limb and guess that this is a different kind of thing."

I smiled at that. "Yeah," I said.

"You want to tell me about it?"

I banged my head lightly against the wall. God, me being back in Jessell just underlined everything I'd been worried about the past couple of weeks. How would we possibly stay together if I came back here? How would we ever make it work if he was on tour with Tulsa in places like Jakarta and Manchester and I was back in Jessell, slinging burgers for two-dollar tips?

We wouldn't, was the answer. Whatever we had would have to end.

"Dana?" Alex asked, his voice low and familiar in my ear. "You still there?"

"I'm here," I managed, trying to keep my voice steady. I shook my head, forced myself to pull it together. "Just talk to me, will you?" I asked him finally, dragging the phone back to my room and climbing into bed with the receiver. "Tell me what it's like there."

"Sure," Alex promised, seeming to understand that this was what I needed more than anything else—reassurance that I had a life to come back to in Orlando, that I was a part of something there. "Of course I will."

Alex talked to me for a long time, patient, filling me in on the broad strokes and small moments alike: that Mikey had overflowed the toilet at the studio, how Guy had them learning a Jackson 5 song for their encore on tour. "I can't wait till you come back here," he told me softly. His voice was the last thing I heard before I fell asleep.

TWENTY-EIGHT

I hadn't been sure what Olivia's mom had meant by *party*, but when I turned up the following afternoon, I saw that she'd gone all out: picnic tables set up in the Maxwells' backyard piled with burgers and potato salad, a Jell-O mold Olivia's grandma Grace had made. There was also a giant sheet cake from the grocery store, the same kind Mrs. Maxwell had gotten for Olivia's graduation earlier that summer—although this one, I saw with no small amount of horror, said *Congratulations Olivia & Dana* on top. I felt my cheeks burn with embarrassment. God, if Olivia didn't already hate me, her mom slapping my name on her damn cake would probably have been enough to do it. *You steal everything*, I heard her say.

I made myself as scarce as humanly possible, lurking around the edges of the backyard where I'd spent so many summers, nibbling barbecue potato chips I knew Charla wouldn't have liked me eating. The fact that none of our other friends had mentioned the party made me think they hadn't been invited, either, and as I looked around now I saw that I'd been right. Instead, I talked to Olivia's cousins Sophie and Kayley, twelve-year-old twins who wanted to hear every breathing detail about Tulsa; they didn't seem to care that I'd only met him once. Olivia ignored me, flitting from group to group across the lawn like a brightly colored hummingbird. In spite of everything that was going on, it made me happy that Olivia had all these people at home rooting for her. It made me kind of sad that I didn't have it, too.

"How you doing, honey?" Olivia's mom asked, sitting down beside me on the steps to the side door, a plastic cup of lemonade sweating in her hand. She always made the kind with actual lemons floating in it—at least one thing, she always said quietly, that southerners knew how to get right.

"I'm good," I said, hoping I sounded convincing. "Thank you for the cake."

Olivia's mom waved me off, handing me the lemonade. "This has all been a bit overwhelming, huh?"

I shrugged. "I try not to take it that seriously."

She smiled at that. "No," she said. "I know you wouldn't." Then she sighed. "Look, sweetheart, Olivia hasn't told me what's going on between you two, and I'm not dumb enough to ask. But I can tell that she's suffering. I said this to her, and I'll say it to you also: not everybody gets to have the kind of friendship that you girls have, you know?"

I glanced at Olivia across the yard, her dark hair swinging. It didn't look like she was *suffering* at all. "I do know that," I managed. "I understand."

But Mrs. Maxwell put her hand on my arm. "She needs you, Dana. She's my girl, she's my own true heart, but you're the strong one."

I stared at her for a moment. *What else do you know?* I wanted to ask. Still, I shook my head. "I don't think so."

"I do," Mrs. Maxwell said. "Look out for her for me, will you do that? Even if you girls are having problems. Just—keep an eye on her, all right?"

I thought again of the night in the bathroom after Guy's party. I thought of how I'd stolen Alex out from under her nose. I thought of how much Olivia seemed to hate me lately, how in some ways going to Orlando in the first place had been the worst thing I could possibly do. "I'll try," I finally said.

"Sylvia!" Olivia's dad called from across the yard. "Can you grab some napkins?"

This was stupid, I thought when Mrs. Maxwell had left me; it was time to get out of here and go home. I edged across the lawn and went inside to get my purse. The house was cool and dark, quiet compared to the scrum in the yard. The kitchen was a mid-party disaster, plates and cups piled on the counters, the trash overflowing in the corner. I pulled the bag out and got a fresh one from under the sink, then stuck a block of sweating cheddar cheese back into the fridge for good measure. I put a fistful of silverware into the dishwasher, then figured I might as well load the whole thing up while I was at it. There was something soothing about it, weirdly. No notes to remember, no politics to navigate. I'd grown up in this kitchen: here was the cookie sheet we used for gingerbread men every December; here was the Dalmatian-shaped pepper shaker with her nose chipped off from when Olivia had smashed it on the floor. Even with things between Olivia and me like they were, I felt more at home here than I did at my mom's house.

I was scrubbing a pasta pot when Olivia appeared in the doorway. She was wearing a short denim skirt and a pink tank top with spaghetti straps, her hair brushed long over her shoulders. "Hey," she said. "What are you doing?"

I shrugged—feeling stupid all of a sudden, feeling like even more of an interloper than I had all day long. "Just . . . making myself useful."

"You don't have to do that."

"I know."

I thought she was going to tell me to cut it out, but instead she picked up a dishtowel and stood next to me, drying off the big chip bowls and the other stuff that couldn't go in the dishwasher. We hadn't talked all afternoon—we hadn't really talked in weeks—and we didn't talk now, either, working side by side in a silence that felt, if not exactly comfortable, then at least not quite hostile. We'd washed dishes like this a million times before; it was our job after dinner, every time I'd eaten here since we were little kids. We had a rhythm. That much, at least, hadn't changed.

Soon everything was put away and the kitchen was clean-ish, the dishwasher chunking away. All of a sudden, it felt totally weird again. It felt awkward just to be standing next to her, like the breach between us was too wide to be crossed.

"I'm going to go," I said finally. "Thanks for inviting me—or for not telling your mom that you hadn't invited me, or whatever. I'm sorry she put me on the cake like that."

Olivia looked at me strangely. "I told her to," she said.

That stopped me. "Oh," I said, taken totally by surprise. "You did?"

Olivia nodded. "This morning," she said. She held her hands up. "I mean. This is your thing, too, right?"

You tell me, I didn't say. "Okay. Well—thanks." I nodded.

Olivia nodded back. "Car's coming at eight," she reminded me.

"I'll be ready."

"Dana—"

I turned around. "Yeah?"

Olivia shook her head. "Nothing," she said. "See you tomorrow."

TWENTY-NINE

I found Alex as soon as I got back to Orlando Sunday night, pulled him out of the Model UN, where he was watching reruns of *The Simpsons* with Mario, and led him downstairs to the side of the building near the vending machines. One good thing about Olivia knowing about us now was that there was no reason to sneak around, not really; still, it felt like there was nowhere to be alone here, that we had to take every scrap of privacy where we could get it. I pushed him up against the side of the building, popped up onto my tiptoes, and pressed my mouth hard against his, rough and urgent. I felt like I needed him to ground me, to remind me what I was doing here and who I was.

"Hey," he said, both of us coming up for air after a moment, Alex gasping a bit against my mouth. "Hey hey hey, hi, talk to me."

I looked at him for a moment, searching. I didn't know exactly what to say. I wanted to tell him that spending the weekend at home had terrified me more than anything, that I didn't see how he and I would ever last if I got sent back. That until I'd made the trip to Orlando I'd never realized how little I had. I wanted to tell him that I could physically feel my life changing and that he was the reason, that I was scared I was falling in love with him and was pretty sure it was all going to end in heartbreak and disaster, but when I opened my mouth to explain all that, the only thing that came out was "I missed you." I huffed out a laugh at how lame it sounded, how completely I was failing to explain. "Shit, Alex. I missed you really bad."

"I missed you, too," Alex said, cupping my face with both hands and kissing me again, desperate. My shoulder blades scraped against the rough outside wall. "Trevor's got a date with the frozen yogurt girl," he murmured breathlessly, his fingertips skating along the hem of my tank top. "There's nobody upstairs."

"Seriously?" I said, pulling back and looking at him, the possibilities zinging through my brain and my body. "Why are you just telling me this now?"

"I don't know," Alex said, laughing a little, nervous or hopeful or both. "I got distracted."

"Yeah, no kidding." I smiled at him, knocked our foreheads together one more time. "Do you want to go upstairs?"

"I—*yeah*," Alex said. "Of course. Yeah, I do."

"Okay," I said, looking at him and making a decision. "So let's go upstairs."

Trevor and Alex's apartment had the same layout as ours did, though you could definitely tell two boys were living there with no actual adult to be found. Half-empty bags of chips gaped open on the counter in the kitchen; a pile of jumbled, unlaced sneakers sprawled near the door. Something had spilled on the coffee table and been wiped up only hastily, a film of something sticky-looking still coating the fake-wood surface.

Alex's room was neat-ish, though—neater than mine, at least, which was perpetually strewn with clothes and magazines and hair supplies—but a little stale smelling, too, air conditioner and boy. The bedsheets were rumpled, and Alex reached forward and smoothed them out. We looked at each other in the half dark, neither one of us saying anything. All the noise and uncertainty of the outside world had evaporated into the air, but at the same time it felt like everything was changing at once, like at any second the earth might start moving underneath our feet. It was as if we were in a vacuum somehow, the only two people for miles or years.

"Have you ever?" I asked him, one knee up on the mattress. I didn't *think* he had, but for everything else we'd told each other, we'd somehow never talked about it before now.

"No." Alex shook his head. "Have you?"

"No," I said, and Alex looked so openly relieved that I cracked up. "You thought I was going to say yes!" I accused, shoving him in the arm, everything feeling lighter all of a sudden, less serious, the tension breaking like an egg. "You jerk. You thought I was going to be like, *oh, yeah, with like fifty guys*."

"That's not what I thought!" Alex protested, the tips of his ears turning pink like they always did when I'd caught him at something.

"Uh-huh." I reached out and shoved him down onto the mattress, swung one knee across his lap. "You totally did."

"I didn't," Alex said breathlessly, tilting his face up to kiss me. "I just—feel like you know stuff. It's a compliment," he said when I raised my eyebrows. "I mean it as a compliment. I mean you're smarter than me, I mean you're not afraid of anything."

"That what you think?" I asked him in between kisses, working his T-shirt up over his head. "I'm afraid of stuff." I took a breath. "I'm afraid of having to leave you."

"Hey." Alex pushed my hair out of my face, looking at me seriously. "It's not gonna happen," he promised. "No matter what, it's not gonna happen."

He sounded so sure in that moment that it was impossible even for me not to believe him. It felt like all I had to do was hold on.

We kissed for a long time on top of the covers, Alex's soft tongue and his pulse thudding away beneath the vellum skin at his throat. He smelled like soap and a little bit like sweat. "Do you have . . . ?" I started, then trailed off.

"In the dresser," he told me, his voice a little ragged, and we didn't talk a whole lot more after that. My bra hit the floor, then Alex's boxers; after that he stopped, though, his breathing gone heavy and his expression concerned. I could feel him trying not to push himself against my hip.

"I'm scared I'm going to hurt you," he said, tucking my hair behind my ear.

"You're not going to hurt me," I promised, panting a little myself. Every single part of me felt almost unbearably tightly coiled, like I was a gun about to go off. "It's okay, I promise. You won't."

That wasn't entirely true—when it happened it did hurt, a little, a fast sharp pain and then something closer to an ache. Alex propped himself up on his elbows as he moved. *"Dana,"* he said quietly, his voice a desperate gasp in my ear.

It was over pretty fast: "Oh my God," Alex said again, his sweaty forehead buried in the crook of my neck. "Oh my God, Dana, please." I tangled my fingers in his hair and hung on. When he was finished, Alex reached down between us and rubbed until I felt like I was bursting into a thousand pieces, as if I were an exploding star.

"Hi," I said when I came back to myself, turning my face against his warm, soft shoulder. There were a handful of freckles scattered there, like somebody had thrown a fistful of glitter.

"Hi." Alex smiled, looking at me with a mixture of love and shell shock. "You okay?"

"Mm-hmm." I peered up at him from underneath my eyelashes. "Are *you*?"

That made him laugh. "Yeah, Dana, I'm good."

I felt wrung out and sleepy; all I wanted to do was pass out with the sound of Alex's heart in my ear. I was dangerously close to doing just that when I heard it: the sound of a key in the front door lock.

"Shit," Alex said, eyes widening as my heart swooped unpleasantly inside my chest. "Trevor."

We scrambled back into our clothes, both of us laughing a little. We smoothed the bed out as best we could manage; I ran a hand through my messy hair. He walked me to the door, and I waved a sheepish good night to Trevor, who'd made a beeline for the refrigerator and didn't seem to notice anything one way or the other.

"I'll see you tomorrow," Alex told me out on the catwalk. I didn't want to let go of his hand. But I nodded, kissed him good night, and headed home to our apartment. I looked back at him and grinned one more time before I went.

THIRTY

"You're gonna like this week," Guy promised us on Monday morning—he'd called us into his office first thing, was sitting back in his desk chair looking pleased with himself. "We're gonna get you into the studio to record."

"We're doing albums?" Olivia asked, her eyes gone wide and hopeful.

Guy shook his head. "Just singles for now," he said, and Olivia and I glanced at each other warily. Though he didn't say it, it was obvious that this was another hurdle for us to leap over. "We'll see about the rest."

The recording studio was tucked away on a side street off a commercial boulevard in downtown Orlando. It was smaller than I'd pictured it and a little grimier inside, the faint smell of cigarette smoke and what looked like coffee stains on the industrial carpet in the lobby. I liked the technician right away, though, a guy named Jerry with a patient way about him and a wide, easy smile. "Take your time," he advised me whenever I messed up and needed to start over, though I could tell Lucas and Guy were getting restless. "You can't rush these things."

Turned out you *could* rush them, actually: Olivia and I both recorded our singles in less than twenty-four hours total—the two of us in tandem, her shuffling out of the studio just as I shuffled in. I looked carefully away as we passed each other in the hallway, telling myself I wasn't aching to talk to her—about what had happened last night with Alex, about what was happening now.

It was nearly sunrise by the time Charla drove me back to the complex; I was dead on my feet in my flip-flops, my voice gone hoarse from take after take. "Hey, you," Charla said, slinging an arm around my shoulders as we crossed the parking lot toward the apartments, smiling at me in the early-morning light. "You did good tonight."

I let myself lean for a moment, exhaustion and something else, maybe, the feeling of having earned this.

"I did," I agreed happily, and yawned.

Guy hired a team of producers to mix the singles out in Los Angeles; while they did that, Charla and Juliet wanted to do what they called image work.

"What's wrong with our image?" I asked, glancing from

where Olivia was standing in our shared bathroom to my own reflection in the mirror, frowning a little.

"Nothing's *wrong* with it, exactly," Charla told me, though Juliet was peering into my closet in a way that suggested that wasn't exactly the case.

I glanced over at Olivia again, at her smooth dark hair and neat black tank top, her arms gone a deep, even tan from being in the Florida sun all summer and her eyebrows two perfect arches. She already looked like a pop star.

Me? Not so much.

"Fine," I said, huffing a little, turning away from my messy ponytail and naked face in the mirror. "Let's go get fancy."

We started at a salon in the nicest part of Orlando: all white and huge and spare, no wrinkly old *People*s stacked in the waiting area or waterlogged lookbooks with wedge hairdos from 1991—nothing like the Cuttery back home. It smelled like flowers and chemicals, weirdly appealing. An Asian girl with French-braid pigtails sat me in a big leather swivel chair, then set about wrapping strands of my hair in tinfoil. "So what do you girls do?" she asked me, nodding her head toward Olivia, who was having her hair washed a few chairs down. "Are you in school?"

I shook my head. "We're singers, actually," I said. It was the first time I'd said it out loud, and I felt kind of stupid. The craziest part was how I guessed it was true. "We might be opening for Tulsa MacCreadie at the end of the summer."

"Seriously? Tulsa MacCreadie?" The girl's eyes widened. "I've never styled a celebrity before."

"I'm not a celebrity," I assured her, leaving out the part where only one of us was going to get to go on tour.

"Maybe not yet," the stylist replied. "Shoot, I hope I don't mess this up. Not that I usually mess this up? But I'm just saying."

I was making her nervous, I realized with no small amount of wonder. That was the first time anything like that had ever happened. The coaches weren't the only ones looking at me differently lately. Soon the rest of the world might, too.

The foil had to stay on my hair for a while, so the stylist sat me on a white leather couch to wait. "How you doing?" Charla asked, coming over with a paper cup of lemon water for me to drink. Olivia, who was beside her, already had one in her hand.

"I feel like *Pretty Woman*," I said.

"Like a hooker?" Olivia asked sweetly.

I scowled, stung. "Jesus Christ, Liv."

Charla rolled her eyes at both of us, which felt patently unfair. "Can you not?"

The stylist brought me back to the chair to finish my haircut, turning me away from the mirror so I couldn't see while she dried it with a big round brush. When she finally spun me back around, though, my eyes widened. I was *blond*. Not a garish platinum but a soft honey color, with darker streaks showing through.

"I look *hot,*" I blurted before I could stop myself.

The stylist laughed. "Yeah, you do," she said, hugging me good-bye before I went. "Go be famous," she instructed, and I grinned.

We did costume fittings next, back at the studio—separately this time, Olivia working on vocals with Lucas while Charla and Juliet steered me into the dance room. "We thought we'd spend some solo time with each of you," Juliet explained.

I nodded. It wasn't lost on me that this was almost exactly what I'd been picturing when the two of us were first chosen for Daisy Chain. Here we were—new hair, new clothes, the whole celebrity treatment—and we were doing it apart.

Whenever I'd pictured what I'd wear on tour with Tulsa, I'd imagined Madonna's black catsuit or Whitney Houston's sparkly dresses, but what Juliet and Charla had in mind for me was mostly just jeans and T-shirts that showed off my midsection. I stood in the studio in my underwear as Juliet pulled outfit after outfit out of clear plastic dry-cleaning bags.

"How much did all this cost?" I asked, looking at the labels, which were stitched with names I'd only ever heard in movies. The bill for my haircut had been over two hundred dollars; I'd seen the receipt when Juliet signed it. "These are, like, really fancy designers."

"Don't worry about it," Juliet told me. "They're comped."

"Comped?" I repeated, not sure if that meant what I thought it meant. "Like, they just sent the clothes for free?"

"You're going to have your picture taken," Juliet explained, "a lot. They want you in their stuff."

The idea of anybody thinking I was the kind of girl they wanted advertising their fancy clothes was hilarious to me, but I just nodded, gazing at myself in the mirror. I looked the part more than I had when I came here: my stomach was flatter than it had ever been, my hip bones jutting out the top of my low-slung jeans.

Juliet wasn't impressed. "It wouldn't hurt to tighten her up a little more there," she said to Charla, nodding at me with her chin.

I frowned. "Tighten me up?"

"Add a few workouts, that sort of thing," Juliet explained. Then she looked at Charla. "We'd need to be careful, though. We can't have—" She raised her eyebrows. "You know?"

"What?" I peered back and forth between them. "What?"

Charla was nodding. "Juliet just means that if we changed your diet or workout program, it would need to stay between us," she told me. "So we wouldn't want Olivia to know."

I looked at them blankly. "Why's that?"

"Well," Juliet said, "we wouldn't want it to look like preferential treatment."

I didn't understand. "How is it preferential treatment if

I'm the one who has to go on a diet?"

"It's not so much preferential treatment," Charla said delicately. "It's more that we don't want Olivia to feel like she needs to do those things to succeed."

But I did? I shook my head, staring at them dubiously in the moment before it finally clicked. "You know about Olivia?" I demanded. "Since when?"

Charla and Juliet looked at each other again, neither one of them saying anything.

"Just tell me," I snapped. "She's my best friend."

"There was an incident early on," Juliet said finally, "that concerned us. But Olivia assured us that she was handling it on her own." She held out a slinky tank top with skinny rhinestone straps. "Here," she said. "Try this."

"What kind of incident?" I demanded, but nobody answered. "And you just took her at her word?" Even as I said it I felt like a giant hypocrite; after all, wasn't that exactly what I'd done the night after Guy's party? I thought of Mrs. Maxwell asking me to look out for her. I felt about two inches tall.

Juliet, clearly, didn't want to be talking about this. "Here," she said again, still holding out the tank top, shaking it a little. Then, off my dubious expression: "It's not your job to worry about Olivia."

"I know," I said before I could stop myself. "It's yours."

Juliet raised her eyebrows.

"Dana," Charla said, "watch it."

Or you'll cut me, too? I wanted to say, but didn't. I looked around the room at the clothes I hadn't tried on yet, at myself in the mirror. My newly dyed hair shone in the overhead lights. It wasn't true, what I'd said just now: it *was* my job to worry about Olivia. It had always been my job, and I was failing. Abruptly, I wasn't having fun anymore.

"Give me that," I said, holding out my hand for the tank top. "I'll get changed."

THIRTY-ONE

Guy booked us all a spot on a morning radio show out of Orlando that week, which he was downright giddy over. "Right in the middle of drive time!" he crowed when he announced it to all of us at the end of rehearsal. "If we do it right, the affiliates will pick it up, and we'll get you on the radio in New York and California before the singles even drop." He turned and looked at me across the studio, thick eyebrows arching. "So don't screw it up."

Don't screw it up felt like a tall order: I was feeling pretty confident onstage lately, but the station wanted stripped-down acoustic performances, right in their studio. There'd be no dancing, obviously—just my voice on the airwaves for thousands of people to hear and judge. I could only imagine all the different ways it could turn into a train wreck. "Are you sure this is a good idea?" I asked Charla on the way home that afternoon.

"Guy says so," she replied, shrugging at me in the rear-view mirror.

Olivia coughed in the front seat—she was getting a cold, had been sniffling all day—and tossed her hair a bit. "I think it sounds amazing," she said, and I grimaced. Of course she did. Even if she didn't, she'd never let on, not to me; there had been a time when we told each other everything, but that was over now.

"Can't wait," I said, to no one in particular. I looked out the window, squinted up into the sun.

We had to get up at four-thirty to make it to the radio station on time, the sun coming up red and bloody to the east of the highway and everybody a little bleary-eyed. Olivia looked especially tired, her skin gone waxy and pale. The cough she'd had yesterday had turned into a full-on hack now, her eyes dull and nose red. She clutched a travel mug of Charla's mossy green tea in one hand.

"You okay?" I asked as we headed downstairs to the parking lot.

"Yup," Olivia said shortly, tucking her mug in the crook of her elbow as she blew her nose. She didn't look at me. "I'm fine."

The DJ at the radio station was a short white guy in his

forties, a baseball cap over his greasy hair and a generally gone-to-seed quality about him, right down to his crinkled plaid shirt. "We've got something for the kiddies this morning," he said as he introduced Hurricane State, who were performing first. I saw Mikey and Austin roll their eyes; Trevor made a face at me like, *can you believe this guy?*, but Alex wasn't giving anything away.

"Thanks for having us," he said graciously, leaning over the microphone and smiling in a way you could hear in his voice. He didn't sound nervous at all. "I'm Alex Harrison, and we're Hurricane State."

The boys did two songs, "Express Train" and their cover of "Signed, Sealed, Delivered," Alex taking lead on both. Olivia had curled up on a fake-leather couch in the lobby with her eyes closed, but I perched in a rolling chair in the booth with everyone else, trying not to smile too goofily. My own nerves were momentarily forgotten as I watched and I listened: Alex was the kind of pure, natural performer you only come across once in a lifetime, clear-voiced and unflappable and so, so good. Watching him made me want to be better. Hearing him made me want to work hard. Even the rude, scruffy DJ sat up and took notice, pulling his baseball cap off in surprise.

Halfway through the second song, Alex caught me looking, his gaze hooking mine and holding it there, smiling a slow, easy smile. It felt private, even though we were in a studio full of people and he was being listened to by who knew how many more on the radio. It felt like his heart was saying something to mine.

I love you, I wanted to tell him. I pushed the thought away.

Hurricane State's performance was over before I knew it, the DJ and his producer clapping and pushing the button to go to commercials. "Nice job," the DJ said, slapping a hand on Alex's back. "You're a talented kid." He nodded at all the rest of them. "All of you are."

My skin was still thrumming like Alex had touched me. I wanted to jump up and throw my arms around him, show everyone how proud I was, but there wasn't any time for that: thirty seconds later, we were back from commercial and the DJ was saying my name into the mic. I didn't have the brainpower to be nervous. Instead I just closed my eyes, clamped the headphones over my ears, and *sang*.

"That was amazing," Alex told me when I was finished. The rest of the boys had taken off, but he'd hung around, listening to me like I'd listened to him; the pride on his face now was genuine, and I knew I'd done a good job.

"*You* were amazing," I countered.

"All right, we're all amazing," Guy said, rolling his eyes at us from his seat in the corner. Then, frowning: "Is somebody getting Olivia in here?"

When Juliet brought her into the booth, Olivia looked even worse than she had earlier, her movements shuffling and her expression not entirely alert. "It'll be quick," Juliet was promising as they came through the doorway; Olivia stopped, braced her hands on her knees, and let out a long, wheezy cough. When she righted herself, her eyes were wide.

"I can't do this," she said.

Guy snorted. "A little late for that now, sweetheart. We're back from commercial in forty-five."

"I'm too sick," Olivia protested. "I'm gonna sound like total shit." Her expression was panicked, like a spooked pony. "Dana," she said, turning to me all of a sudden. "Tell him I can't."

I blanched. "Me?" I said.

"Thirty seconds," the DJ told us.

"It'll be fine," Juliet promised, but Olivia shook her head rapidly.

"Olivia," Guy said, sounding irritable, "pull it together."

"I can't," she repeated, her eyes filling with tears—she was sick and exhausted and wrung out, I could tell, starting to lose it entirely. "I'm going to sound like shit, and everybody's going to hear me. Dana," she said again, "please."

I hesitated for a moment, some small, nasty part of me fully aware that this could only be a good thing for me—my only competition, the girl who'd spent the last six weeks telling me I wasn't good enough to be here, melting down in public seconds before she was supposed to go on?

But it was Olivia.

And she needed me.

"You got this," I heard myself say quietly, reaching out and tucking her stringy hair behind her ears. Her skin was warm with fever; I wondered if she'd eaten today, if this was garden-variety sickness and nerves or something more. It unsettled me, looking at her and not being able to tell exactly what was wrong. I hated it, the not knowing. I didn't want that to be how it was anymore. "Just take a deep breath and do the best you can, okay? I've heard you sing sick before. It'll sound like you're doing it on purpose—you'll have a rasp or something. It'll be over so fast." Olivia shook her head, but I pushed on. "You can do it," I said again, looking her in the face and trying to keep my voice as steady as possible. "It's me, and I promise you can. I won't let you look dumb, remember? Do you trust me?"

Olivia nodded.

"Okay. You gotta live your life forward here, just for a minute."

That got a smile out of her, albeit a watery one. "Okay," she agreed.

She sounded fine in the end, all things considered; the cold put a bit of a break in her voice, but not anything you'd notice if you didn't hear her sing every day of your life. Still, I held my breath, wanting it to go well for her in spite of myself. As soon as the red light went off she doubled over coughing again.

"That's a girl," Guy said, nodding in approval. "That's

what you gotta do in this business, just push through. Lucky your friend was here to pep-talk you, huh?"

"I didn't do anything," I protested, but Guy had already turned his attention elsewhere, glad-handing the DJ and his producer while Juliet rounded up the boys. When I turned to Olivia, she looked like she'd just run a marathon, like it was taking every last ounce of her energy just to stay upright.

"You did it," I told her, taking a step forward to hug her before I could stop myself, then freezing abruptly halfway through the motion. We looked at each other for a moment. I lowered my arms again.

Olivia nodded just once, vaguely. "Let's go" was all she said.

THIRTY-TWO

Guy gave us the rest of the day off after the radio station performance. Olivia collapsed face-first on the couch and immediately fell asleep, Charla waking her up periodically to feed her cold medicine and tea. I spent the afternoon napping, too, sprawled on Alex's bed, listening to the sound of his heartbeat tapping steadily away through his shirt. I liked how he smelled, soap and clean bedding and the faint sourness of sleep underneath it. I wished it could always be like this.

Olivia was still sleeping when I got back to the apartment. Charla and I ate dinner quietly, neither one of us wanting to wake her. I was lying on the bed listening to a tape of the songs Hurricane State had recorded when Olivia appeared in the doorway. Her color was better, though there were still dark rings under her eyes. "How you feeling?" I asked, pulling my headphones off.

"Better," she said. She was wearing her pajamas, a pair of workout shorts and her Jessell Jaguars gym shirt, which surprised me. I hadn't even realized she'd brought it. Olivia hated gym: last year she'd been late to dress so many times that Ms. Farano made her come after eighth period to do wall sits every day for a week to make up the time. "Hey," she said now, leaning against the jamb with her thin arms crossed. Her dark, glossy hair hung in a fishtail braid over one sharp shoulder. "You did amazing today," she said, not quite looking at me. "I just wanted to tell you that."

I looked up at her, surprised and also feeling like a jerk. "You did amazing, too," I said softly. "I love that song Guy has you doing, with the chorus that's like, *rise rise rise*."

Olivia shook her head. "It's almost out of my range."

"It's not," I told her earnestly. "It's perfect."

Olivia smiled. "Okay," she said. "Well. Thanks." She hovered in the doorway for another half second, and as she turned to go, a hot, briny panic rose in the back of my throat. Suddenly it felt like maybe I'd never see her again.

"I hate this," I blurted before I could think better of it. "I hate fighting with you."

Olivia stopped in the doorway, turned around. "I hate it, too," she said.

"You do?"

"Of course I do!" Olivia's eyes widened; she came back into the room then, perched on the edge of my bed. It was the closest we'd been to each other in weeks. "You're my best friend."

"You're my best friend!" I told her. "You know that. And I feel weird and crappy that me coming here is what started it. Like, if I had stayed back in Jessell obviously I'd miss you, but maybe it would be better to miss you if you were far away instead of, like, right down the hall."

"You coming here didn't start it," Olivia told me, pulling her knees up onto the mattress and settling in. "I loved having you here, are you kidding?"

"Really?"

"Yeah!" Olivia said. "What *started* it was everybody here pitting us against each other like we're on *American Gladiators* or something."

I wasn't sure if that *was* what had started it, actually; I worried it was deeper than that, some deep fissure in our friendship that dated back longer than we knew. Still, she was smiling at me, and I wanted things to be better. "Next thing you know they're going to try to make us fight each other with those giant Q-tip things," I joked.

Then, because I wanted to be honest with her, because talking to her at all felt like a gift and I didn't want to waste it: "I know I was dragging you down at the beginning," I said slowly. "You weren't wrong to be pissed at me."

"I was wrong to be a massive bitch about it, though." Olivia shook her head. "But you've come so crazy far since we got here, you know that? Guy totally knew what he was doing when he picked you. You're amazing to watch."

I grinned at that, ducking my head kind of shyly even as I wanted her to say lots more. Olivia's opinion meant more to me than anyone else's; even more than Alex, she was the person I'd wanted to impress all these weeks.

"I'm sorry about Alex," I told her, as long as we were apologizing. I'd said it before, but it was important to me that she knew I'd never meant to steal him out from under her, that our friendship was worth more to me than that and I knew I'd been wrong to do what I did. "The whole thing was fucked up of me. I should have stayed away from him to begin with, or at least talked to you about it right up front."

Olivia shook her head, twisting the end of her braid around her fingers. "I didn't even really like Alex that much, honestly. I was mostly just mad because I felt like you were keeping secrets to punish me, or pulling away on purpose, or something."

I chafed at that a little. "You were off being best friends with Kristin and Ashley!"

Olivia scoffed. "I was never going to be best friends with Kristin and Ashley," she assured me. "I tried to make them watch *Junia* with me when they were still here, did you know that?" She made a sheepish face. "Shockingly, they were not as into her as we are."

I laughed. "Well, sad but true, not everyone has impeccable taste like you and me. Did you teach them the dance?"

"I tried to, like, *explain* the dance?" Olivia shook her head. "They were not buying."

"Really?" I hopped up off the bed and struck the first pose with great drama, my arms in a big, exaggerated V over my head. "This didn't entice them?"

Olivia scrambled up and hit the same pose. "I can't imagine why."

We did the dance in goofy, overblown synchronization—both of us singing the *Junia* theme song at the top of our voices, purposefully off-key, hitting all our made-up dance moves with a verve that would have made Charla proud until we were laughing too hysterically to finish. Finally, we collapsed into a helpless pile on the bed, still giggling so hard I thought I might actually barf. I hadn't laughed like that all summer. Olivia was the only person I ever did it with.

Eventually we caught our breath again, lying side by side on the mattress, both of us quiet except for the odd hiccup. Even breathing felt better now, like there'd been a hair elastic wrapped around my lungs the last couple of weeks and it had finally snapped.

"So, you and Alex," Olivia said, still staring at the ceiling. "Have you guys . . . ?" She trailed off.

I smirked. "Have we what, exactly?"

Olivia rolled over, fixed me with a look. "You know what."

I hesitated a moment, and then I nodded. "When we got back from Jessell," I told her. "That first night."

Olivia nodded slowly. "What was it like?" she asked.

I thought about that for a moment. "Good," I told her. "You know, new, but good."

"Good," Olivia repeated. She scooted down on the mattress then, laid her head in my lap. "Can I tell you something weird?" she asked, peering up at me. Her eyes looked very bright. "It makes me kind of sad, honestly. Like, not that you guys did it, but I guess I just always assumed that as soon as one of us did it, the other one would know right away."

My heart broke a little at that, an ache in my chest I could actually feel. "I wanted to tell you," I promised her, reaching down and tugging the end of her braid, just lightly. "It's like it wasn't even real until I did."

"Oh, it was *real*," Olivia said, wiggling her eyebrows like a pervert.

That made me laugh. "Okay," I admitted, "it was real. But you know what I mean."

"I do," Olivia agreed. Then: "I missed you, jerk."

I grinned down at her. "I missed you, too." It was like I hadn't even let myself feel how much until then: like there'd been a part of me that had gone quiet since we hadn't been speaking, some vital slice of who I was. *She needs you*, Olivia's mom had told me. I needed Olivia, too. We needed each other.

I took a deep breath, cautious. "Can I ask you something without you getting mad?"

Olivia looked up at me curiously. "Uh-huh," she said. "Of course."

"What's going on with eating stuff?"

Olivia waved her hand, dismissive. "I told you," she said, "I'm handling that."

"Liv," I said. One of the things I'd realized while we weren't speaking was how dumb and naive it had been of me to think I could solve Olivia's problems on my own—by watching her eat a sandwich, by forcing French fries on her and watching to make sure her ankles didn't get too thin. The truth was, this was bigger than me. Possibly it was bigger than both of us. I hadn't been doing anybody any favors by pretending it wasn't. "Come on."

"You come on," Olivia said stubbornly.

But I shook my head. I couldn't let things go on like they had been. I owed her more than that. "Look," I said. "I know you haven't been totally honest with me about what's going on with you when it comes to that stuff. And part of that is my fault, too, because I was afraid to make it into a big deal, so I never wanted to push it. But it is a big deal, Liv."

Olivia rolled her eyes. "It's really not," she insisted.

"It really is, though. And it's freaking me out, and if it keeps happening I'm going to call your mom. No more screwing around. And maybe that means you're going to be mad at me again, and I get that, but"—I shrugged—"you're my best friend, and that's what best friends do."

Olivia was quiet for a minute. "I'm not mad at you."

"Okay," I said. Then, carefully, "So, like. We're clear? And you won't, like—keep stuff from me?"

"Yeah, Dana, we're clear." Olivia huffed out a sigh.

"Good," I said, though in the back of my head I knew it might not be that easy. "I want to help you, you know? I'm here to help you."

"Dana—" she started, but then she just kind of sagged. "I'm working on it," she promised. "Is that fair? I'm not always perfect, but I'm working on it."

I thought about that for a moment. "As long as I'm here, and we're together," I decided. "As long as we're together, it's okay."

THIRTY-THREE

"What about this one?" Olivia asked, popping out of my closet with a flowered sundress in one hand, waving it in my direction. "Too sweet?"

I squinted for a moment. We were doing a mall performance the next morning, were supposed to pick our own costumes from the cache of clothes Juliet had given us. We'd been at it for over an hour already, the radio playing on the dresser and a bowl of microwave popcorn on the bed. "Too sweet," I decided finally.

"Yeah," Olivia agreed. "I feel like we should put you in something sexier."

I snorted at that. "Because I'm such a sexy individual?"

"I mean, yes, obviously. But also for, like, brand-recognition purposes."

"Ugh," I said, sitting back on my bed and reaching for

a handful of popcorn. "I hate that word, *brand.* It makes me feel like a sanitary napkin."

"Better get used to it, pop star," Olivia said cheerfully. Then, turning back to the closet and scrutinizing its contents for a moment: "Can I tell you a secret?"

I leaned forward eagerly. "Always."

She whirled and looked at me again, this time holding the infamous forty-dollar T-shirt. "I have to say, these are actually butt-ugly."

"Oh, come on! I'm going to kill you," I told her, but I was laughing. It was hard to get worked up over it anymore, to even remember how far from her I'd felt those past weeks. "They *are* ugly, right?"

"Yes!" Olivia nodded. "I should have listened to you to begin with," she said.

"That's a good motto for you to live by all the time, really," I teased.

We listened to the nightly countdown on the Top 40 station, settled on jeans and a tank top for Olivia and a faded denim miniskirt for me. "Can I crash in here?" she asked, hovering in the doorway once we'd brushed our teeth.

"Obviously," I said. I yanked the comforter off my bed and tossed it over to her, and we settled side by side on the twin mattresses just like we had when we first came here. Of course she could have gone and gotten her own blanket. Of course she could have gone next door to go to sleep. But that wasn't the point, and both of us knew it.

Once the light was off Olivia stared up at the ceiling for a while, quiet; I thought she'd just about fallen asleep when she spoke. "What I don't understand," she said thoughtfully, rolling over to look at me, "is why Guy doesn't just keep us both. I feel like *that* would be the better business move, not cutting one of us. He could brand us differently or something, you know what I mean?"

I looked over at her, surprised. "I guess," I said.

"Because it doesn't make sense for him to be putting these kinds of resources into both of us if one of us is about to get cut," she continued. "Like, the studio time, sure, he crammed us both in there and didn't have to pay extra. But paying Lucas and Charla to coach us both, double the media training, the image stuff—that all seems like a waste to me. And Guy's not wasteful."

She had a point there, I thought—after all, Guy keeping us both up to this point meant he thought there was a chance both of us were viable. "Would you want that?" I asked cautiously. "For him to pick us both?"

Olivia looked at me like I was crazy. "Of course I would," she said. "If we could take this whole stupid competition out of the equation? That would be amazing."

"Yeah," I agreed, smiling into the darkness, feeling like I was finally back where I belonged. "It would be pretty freaking great."

I fell asleep easily, deep and dreamless. I didn't wake up once the whole night through.

Guy finally bought us all tickets to Disney one hot, humid Saturday—ostensibly to shoot some promo pictures to show how family-friendly we all were, but we also got to skip the lines for Space Mountain and the Tower of Terror, a park employee leading us around and giving all of us personalized Mouse ears for free.

"That's it," the photographer said as I tossed my hair in front of Cinderella's Castle, the camera clicking away. "America's gonna love you."

"You're a natural," Juliet said, eyeing me approvingly, and I grinned.

We stayed until it got dark and was time for the fireworks, booms so loud I could feel them vibrating in the base of my spine. "Beats watching from the parking lot, huh?" Alex asked. We'd peeled off from the others and were sitting on a bench on Main Street with our heads tipped back to watch the explosions, passing a giant Diet Coke back and forth.

I nodded. Of course it beat the parking lot, in some ways—after all, just a few weeks ago we couldn't even afford tickets to get in here, had been stuck on the outside looking in. But when I remembered how it had felt being in the car with him that night, like we were the only two people in the universe—I couldn't help but wonder if we were losing something, too. The summer was almost over, and both of us were on the precipice of something potentially incredible. What I didn't know was if we'd be able to make the jump holding hands.

God, I was being a weirdo. "It's great," I said, knocking my forehead against his lightly.

But Alex must have been able to read my mind. "Come on," he said, taking my hand with his free one and pulling me to my feet. A firework in the shape of Minnie Mouse erupted over Cinderella's Castle, and everyone cheered.

"Where are we going?" I asked, but Alex didn't answer, fingers threaded through mine as we wove through the tightly packed throngs, his wavy hair curling up in the heat. We were nearly to the edge of the Magic Kingdom before I figured it out. "Alex," I said, a slow grin spreading over my face as we pushed through the turnstiles out into the parking lot. "Are we—"

"View's better from here anyway," Alex said, grinning back at me. He held up the keys to the Suburban. I laughed out loud, grabbed his hand.

"You're something, you know that?" I asked as we climbed up on the hood—side by side, his body warm and solid next to me.

"Weird," Alex said, smiling a little. "I was just about to tell you the same thing."

"Oh, *were* you?" I said, mocking, but Alex turned serious.

I sat up, suddenly nervous. "I didn't mean—" I began, then broke off, worried I'd offended him.

"Dana, I've been singing love songs since I was five," he

told me. "But I've never really gotten it. Not like I do when I look at you." He took a breath. "I love you. Whatever else happens, will you just remember that?"

For a second I only stared at him—the stubborn set of his jaw and his hair falling forward, the resolute truth in his eyes. I felt like I was seeing him clearly for the first time all night.

"I know," Alex said, shaking his head, ducking his face as his cheeks turned faintly pink. "I'm corny. But it's true."

"That's not what I was going to say," I told him quickly. My heart was a runaway train inside my chest. "It's not corny. It's not corny at all."

A real smile at that, wide and *happy*—the pureness of the emotion on his face was shattering, like I was something he'd wanted and wanted but never dreamed he'd get. "No?"

"No," I promised, and then I finally said it. "I love you, too."

I sat there and looked at him for a moment, wanting to laugh in disbelief and wonder. Wanting to cry and not entirely sure how come. I leaned forward and kissed him. The sky exploded over our heads.

Charla took Olivia and me for manicures on Friday afternoon, the three of us sitting side by side in the chairs while a pink-haired girl who couldn't have been much older than me painted tiny stars on the nails of my ring fingers. "Looks pretty," Olivia said, peering over my shoulder on her way to the dryers, her long hair hanging down into my face.

"*You* look pretty," I crowed, and she grinned.

"Get a room, you two," Charla chided, but she was smiling. Since Olivia and I had finally made up, we were inseparable in a way we hadn't been since middle school, when we went to the bathroom together and made everyone call us Dolivia.

We stopped for sugar-free raspberry smoothies afterward, and as we pulled out of the parking lot I was flipping radio stations when I heard the first few notes of a cheery, synth-y pop song I vaguely recognized but couldn't place. At first I thought it was one of the eighties-era love anthems my mom liked, but then Charla slammed on the brakes and I turned to Olivia in shock.

"This is *you*!" we both exclaimed at the same time.

I'll never forget what Olivia's face looked like then, shock and disbelief and happiness and awe all playing across her delicate features in rapid succession. "Holy shit!" she said, mouth dropping open. Then she burst clean into tears.

"I'm happy, I'm happy," she said, laughing through her sobs as I reached into the backseat and tried to hug her, Charla making a sharp right that sent horns blaring and pulling into a parking spot in a strip mall so that we could listen properly.

Adrenaline was thrumming through my veins as Charla cranked the car stereo, rolling all the windows down so the sound spilled out into the heat. "You sound amazing!" I said, and she really did. Of course I'd heard the demo—I'd heard the finished version, too, but this was different, the thrill of it coming out of actual radio speakers on actual airwaves, where the whole world could hear it, too. My heart thrummed along with the bass line. The chords echoed deep inside my brain. Of all the stuff I'd pictured about Olivia or me possibly getting famous, somehow I'd never imagined this moment. I felt so hugely, enormously *proud.*

"Come on," I said, throwing the car door open. I scrambled out onto the pavement, pulling Olivia out alongside me with one manicured hand. We sang along at the top of our lungs to her song on the radio, snotty, happy tears still running down her face as Charla shook her head and smiled like we were a couple of overgrown kids. Maybe this was success, I thought as we spun around on the concrete, the neon brightness of Orlando blurring by, maybe this was why I'd come here: to dance on the side of a highway with my one best friend in the world.

THIRTY-FOUR

That was the week we hit the road. August was fair season in the south; it seemed like every town from South Carolina to Texas was putting on some kind of festival, and Guy had booked Olivia and me to perform at what felt like all of them. The boys did the bigger ones with us, polishing their routines for Tulsa's tour, but at some of them Olivia and I were solo, coming on before the crowning of the apple pie queen or the prize-winning Holstein cow. Still, I gave those performances everything I had, knowing that each one mattered. Even if Olivia and I wouldn't admit it to each other, neither one of us had forgotten what was at stake here. Guy would be deciding which of us to take on tour any day now. Every bow I took felt like it could be the last.

The boys headed back to Orlando before our last stop, a county fair in Alabama a couple of hours in the van from

Birmingham. It was redneck country—farmland and tiny grocery stores attached to gas stations, bars that made the dive we'd been to in Orlando look like a velvet-rope club.

The fair itself was actually kind of charming, though, or would have been—there were rides and games at one end and lines and lines of food stalls down the center, a flea market and a whole section for 4-H competitions complete with prize spaghetti squash and fat, oinking pigs. But it had rained earlier in the week and never dried out entirely, and the fields were sodden and muddy, sucking at our feet. Mosquitoes hung in dense, predatory clouds—I counted four bites on my arms and legs in the first twenty minutes we were there. It was so incredibly, sulkily hot. And there was a quality to the crowd I couldn't put my finger on exactly, a tense, edgy restlessness that set my skin humming. I had a bad feeling from the moment I got out of the van, crossing my arms as I followed Juliet across the fairgrounds, glancing uneasily at the overflowing beer tent.

"It looks like the zombie apocalypse here," I told Olivia as both of us sidestepped a glassy-eyed girl about our age dragging a screaming toddler by the hand. "I don't like it."

Juliet overheard me, rolled her eyes. "Don't be getting too big for your britches," she scolded. "We're not at Madison Square Garden yet."

We were meant to go on at seven-thirty, right after the 4-H contest winners were announced, but there was a problem with one of the generators and it was fully dark by the time Olivia hopped up onto the makeshift stage, the end of summer coming. The platform was only about two feet off the ground, no barricades set up between her and the crowd, which was a few hundred people this time—a handful of kids who'd heard Olivia and my songs on the radio and come specifically for us, sure, but mostly folks who'd been hanging around the fair all afternoon and wanted to see what the fuss was all about. It occurred to me that there probably wasn't a ton to do around here, other than this.

It was a weird, tense-feeling set, Olivia's mic shrieking feedback out into the crowd at one point, plus a cluster of drunk college-age dudes off to one side who kept howling like wolves and yelling shit, catcalling all the way through her first couple of songs. They'd obviously been drinking and baking in the sun all day, their faces gone red and their eyes slightly glazed. "Yes, gentlemen," Olivia said at one point, trying to make a joke of it, but I could tell by the expression on her face and the way she was sticking mostly to the other side of the stage that she didn't think it was funny at all. "I see you over there."

"You wanna see some more?" one of them called back, grabbing his crotch.

"What the—" I whipped my head around to look at Juliet. "Did you—?"

"She's all right," Juliet told me, laying a hand on my arm like she was worried I was going to charge out there and punch the guy in the face, which in fact was exactly what I wanted to do. "She's handling it."

I wasn't so sure. When I glanced over, I was glad to see Guy on the other side of the stage—the bulk of him reassuring, like nothing truly bad could happen as long as he was here. Still, I watched the rest of Olivia's performance uneasily, arms crossed and spoiling for a fight.

The set seemed to go on forever, though finally Olivia made it to her second-to-last song, an up-tempo number called "Rush" with a bunch of complicated turns and spins in the choreography.

I had just turned to get miked for my own set when one of the guys in the front row reached up and smacked Olivia squarely on her ass.

For a moment I wasn't entirely sure what was happening; I felt the rush of pure white terror as clearly as if it had happened to me, this tidal wave of adrenaline like my whole body was on fire. Up onstage, Olivia froze. The guy was just *grinning* at her—pleased with himself, his face tomato-red and shiny. His buddies were laughing like he'd gotten to the punch line of a particularly funny joke.

That was when Olivia bolted off the stage.

I met her almost before she made it down the steps and behind the makeshift curtain—her backing track still clanging out into the audience, sounding tinny and artificial without her voice out in front of it. Guy was making his way across the stage with security by now; they grabbed the guys roughly, hustled them quickly away. Olivia was shaking. "Are you okay?" I asked, catching her face in both hands and forcing her to look at me, to focus over the noise of the confused, rowdy crowd. "Are you hurt?"

"No," she said, and her voice sounded like she was at the bottom of the ocean. I thought maybe she was in shock. "I'm okay."

"Are you sure? I'm going to kill those guys, I can't believe they actually—I'm going to go out there and find them and rip their spines out like a video game." Then, again: "Are you sure?"

Olivia nodded slowly. "Yeah," she said. "Yeah, I was just—I'm okay."

"Olivia, sweetheart," Juliet said, coming up behind me and placing her hand on Olivia's shoulder. "I'm so sorry that just happened, that was terrible. Guy's taking care of it now, all right? They're gone."

"Okay." Olivia nodded again—compliant or just dazed, I couldn't tell. "Thank you."

"So what I need is for you to go back out there and finish your set, all right?"

Both of us whirled to stare at her. "Are you serious?" I asked. "After what just—you want her to go back *out* there?"

"It's not up to me," Juliet explained, looking sorry. "We're contracted for a six-song set from each of you. Olivia's only done five."

"Who the hell cares?"

"The promoters care, Dana," Juliet said, slightly testy now. "The same ones who have booked your last dozen performances, not to mention Tulsa's entire tour."

"I can't," Olivia said, sounding frantic. "Dana. Tell her I can't."

Tell them I can't. I thought of the radio station performance a couple of weeks ago. I thought of her audition for Daisy Chain, and last spring's talent show. Normally it was my job to convince Olivia that she had what it took to perform, that she could push past her fear and anxiety and stage fright and get the job done. But there was no way I was doing that today.

"She can't," I told Juliet flatly.

"Well, that's not a call that she gets to make."

"*Well*, she's making it," I countered. "End of discussion."

Juliet stared at me for a moment, pissed and baffled. Neither of us had ever rebelled this openly before. "Fine, Dana," she snapped eventually. "Have it your way. Go get miked, then; you're up next."

I barked out a laugh, I couldn't help it. "There's no way I'm going out there," I said.

Juliet wasn't amused. "Dana, I don't know what you think you're up to here today, but I'm not screwing around."

"No," I told her evenly. I was tired of this, tired of being bossed around and prodded. Tired of feeling like everyone else's interests were more important than ours. "Olivia's not going back out there, and neither am I."

"What is this, a mutiny?" Juliet's eyes narrowed, her gaze flicking back and forth between us. When neither one of us answered, she sighed. "All right, girls. That's fine. Let's see what happens when I bring Guy back here, how about."

"Fuck her," I muttered when Juliet was gone. "Guy can come and say it to my face if he wants." Olivia was looking at the floor now, hugging herself a bit.

"I shouldn't have been so close to the edge of the stage," she said.

"What? Bullshit," I told her. "You did everything right. That guy was an asshole. That guy was a *criminal*!" I said, loud enough that everybody around us looked over, and Olivia started laughing, and then as soon as that happened she burst into tears.

"Hey," I said, wrapping her arms around me. "Hey hey hey, Liv, you're okay. I gotcha. You're with me," I promised, holding on tight. "You're safe."

Guy took my side, surprisingly: "Take 'em home," he said to Charla, who drove us back to the hotel while he dealt with the fair runners.

"I'm right next door if you need me," she promised, hugging the both of us good night. They'd gotten us separate rooms, but I went in with Olivia, waiting on the bed while she scrubbed this whole place off in the shower. I couldn't wait to get back to Orlando.

"Are you okay?" I asked again, when she emerged in her

pajamas, her hair hanging in a long wet tail down her back. I wanted to keep asking. I wanted her to know I was here if she wasn't.

"Yeah," she said, sitting down on the bed with her legs folded up like a pretzel. She looked like she had back when we were in middle school, her face scrubbed clean and pink. "I'm fine, I just—"

"You're rattled."

She nodded.

"You want to call your parents?"

She shook her head.

"Well, okay." I grinned. "I'll just stay here and pee a circle around you, then."

That made Olivia smile. "Please do," she said, leaning back into the pillows. "And then maybe go rip somebody's spine out like a video game."

"I was worked up!" I said. "I'd still go rip somebody's spine out. That was shit, that the coaches sent you out there when it wasn't safe."

Olivia shrugged. "I don't think they could know," she said.

"It's their job to know," I shot back.

"You're sure Guy wasn't mad at us, though?" Olivia asked, sounding uncertain. "About ganging up on Juliet?"

"Nah," I reassured her. "When I talked to him he said he admired my chutzpah."

"I admire it, too," Olivia said, and yawned, and as soon

as she did it I yawned, too. Now that the adrenaline had worn off, I was physically exhausted, but both of us were still too unsettled to sleep, so we lay in bed side by side, flicking through the channels until we found a Meg Ryan movie on cable.

"I wish *Junia* was on," I said, and Olivia grinned.

"This reminds me of the night of the auditions," she said, stretching her long legs out in front of her. "Do you remember that?"

"Of course," I said, but I knew what she meant. Even though it had only been a few months ago, it felt like we'd been completely different people back then—weirdly innocent, like we had no idea what was ahead of us. We'd been friends most of our lives, but there was a part of her I'd never really known—that I couldn't have known—until this summer. It hadn't always been easy, but it felt like we were coming out closer than we'd ever been before.

"I'm sorry you didn't get to go on today," she told me.

"Are you kidding me?" I asked. "There's no way I would have gotten up there after what happened to you. You have zero things to apologize for."

"I'm really glad you were there," she said, rolling over to look at me. "I'm glad you've been here this whole time, honestly. You're probably the only reason I haven't gone totally insane yet."

"That's not true," I said. "You were built for this, you know that."

"I thought I was." Olivia shook her head again. "I don't know. I don't think I'd want to do it if you weren't here. Or like, even more than that, I'm worried I couldn't." She sighed. "I wish he'd just keep us both," she said, looping around to the thread of the conversation we'd had back in Orlando. She smelled like baby powder, same as she had since we were small.

"Yeah, but he'll never."

"Why not?" Olivia shrugged. "He changed his mind once, didn't he? Guy's not exactly what I would call a stay-the-course kind of guy." She propped herself up on one elbow, tilted her head to the side. "What if we could convince him he could make money on us both?"

"You think he'd go for that?" My voice was doubtful, but I could feel a tiny flicker of hope sparking inside my chest. Olivia knew how this stuff worked, didn't she? It was a long shot, but if she thought it was possible, then maybe it was.

"No way to find out except to try it," Olivia said, tucking her feet underneath her. "But I think we're different enough that there's room in the market for both of us, you know? Your dancing is stronger than mine, that's obvious. And the songs I'm really good at are the ballad-type ones. We're already focused on different things, really. There's no reason for it to be a zero-sum game."

I thought about it for a moment. "If we really play up what each of us are good at, eventually he's gotta see it for himself, right?"

"Honestly, I don't see how he wouldn't." Olivia nodded. "What if we make a pact?" she asked. "Either we get Guy to keep both of us, or we both walk away."

"What?" That surprised me. "You'd do that?"

Olivia's eyes narrowed just the slightest bit. "Wouldn't you?"

"Of course I would," I told her. "But you've wanted this your whole life."

"Yeah, and we've been friends for that long. I don't want to be fighting you for Guy's table scraps, you know? It isn't worth it to me."

"Me either," I promised, and as I said it out loud I realized it was the truth. I wanted this more than I'd ever wanted anything; I'd worked harder for it than I'd known I could work. But when I thought about what had happened today—when I thought about what had been happening all summer—I knew it wouldn't mean anything without Olivia beside me. I wanted her with me on this adventure, or I didn't want it at all.

And then, of course, there was also the flip side: that I worried about what would happen to Olivia if I left her on her own with Guy and Juliet.

"We're in this together, or we both walk away." Olivia looked at me, dark eyebrows raised. "Deal?"

I nodded. "Deal."

THIRTY-FIVE

The week seeped by; Tulsa's tour crept closer. The days had started getting shorter, darkness falling a minute or two earlier each night, but the heat was unrelenting, like all of Orlando was covered in a film of plastic wrap.

On Thursday, Olivia and I both had sessions with a photographer Guy worked with, the same woman who'd taken the iconic shot plastered on all of Tulsa's tour photos. A blond girl with bright-red lips and dozens of tattoos did our makeup, the tiny brush tickling as she gave me a dramatic cat-eye with one expert flick of her wrist. Juliet hung all our new clothes on rolling racks.

"Wait!" Olivia said just as we were finishing; she dashed out of the shot and grabbed my wrist, pulling me in front of the smooth white backdrop. "Take one of both of us," she said. We flung our arms around each other, grinning. We held on tight as the camera flashed.

I went down to the pool after Olivia fell asleep that night, the deck deserted except for the singing of cicadas and the quiet hum of the filters. I pulled my shirt over my head and slipped into the cool, placid water. I had a bathing suit now, an expensive one from Neiman Marcus that I'd thrown onto the pile as an afterthought a couple of weeks ago when Charla and I were out shopping. I hadn't even looked at the price tag.

I kicked up in the center of the pool and spread my arms out, floating on my back across the deep end in complete, heavy solitude. With my ears underwater and my eyes on the velvety black sky above, I felt like the only person for miles, like I could shut the whole world out. I remembered what Alex had told me at the beginning of the summer, about how performing filed all the sharp edges off everything for him, made his mind clear and focused. When I thought about it now, that day felt like forever ago, like I'd been an entirely different person. Like I hadn't known anything at all.

I didn't hear Alex turn up so much as I sensed him; I righted myself and there he was, standing on the edge of the deep end with his hands in the pockets of his dark-blue swim trunks, smiling at me. "Creep," I teased, tucking my wet hair behind my ears. "How long you been standing there?"

"While," Alex said, then shrugged. "You looked peaceful."

I smirked, raised my eyebrows. "Oh, is *that* how I looked?"

Alex tilted his head to the side, like I'd caught him. "I mean, among other things." He pulled his T-shirt off in one smooth motion, slipped into the water without making a splash.

I laughed, arms out again and floating a little bit away from him. A warm breeze rustled the fronds of the palm trees; somebody had forgotten to close one of the patio umbrellas, and it made a whipping sound. I spotted one or two stars as the clouds passed by, just faint. "How were your interviews?" I asked. The boys had a bunch of pre-tour publicity to do, chatting with reporters all up and down the coast.

"Weird," Alex said. Then, nodding at my bathing suit like he was noticing it for the first time, "That's pretty."

"Pretty?" I asked him, scrunching my nose up. "That's the best you got?"

Alex scrunched his up in return. "More than pretty."

"How much more?"

"A lot more," he said, moving in to kiss me, but I feinted away again.

"That's better," I said, moving my fingers through the cool, bleachy water. "So, wait, tell me more about the interviews."

Alex shrugged again. "They were good," he said. "They were fine. I don't know why they all cared so much about my favorite color, but I got to talk a lot about my musical influences and stuff, so that was cool."

"Nobody asks me about my musical influences!" I said, frowning.

"Who are your musical influences?"

That made me smile. "I don't know, actually," I admitted. I thought about it for a moment. "You are," I told him. "You're my musical influence."

That stopped him, surprise and then pleasure flicking across his expression, a slow grin spreading over his face like that had been the exact right thing to say. "Are you flirting with me?" he asked.

"I dunno," I said, smiling back. "Is it working?"

"It is," Alex said.

"Good. I'm serious, though," I told him. He *had* influenced me, since the very first night I'd met him: with his easygoing patience and constant encouragement, with the way he looked at me. As the weeks had gone by, without even realizing I was doing it I'd started to see myself the way Alex saw me: as someone who had something to offer. As someone whose future wasn't fixed. I'd meant it when I'd said I didn't need him to unlock my secret potential. But it was possible he'd unlocked something else just the same. "You've made me work harder. This whole summer you have. Like, technical stuff, sure, but also your attitude or whatever. How much this means to you and how you always act like it's important. I've learned a whole lot, watching you."

"You *are* flirting with me," Alex said, grin wide.

"This is, like, music nerd dirty talk for you, huh?" I teased, winding my arms around his neck, and Alex nodded.

"I'm into it, Cartwright," he told me. "I will not lie."

THIRTY-SIX

The boys invited us over to the Model UN the next night, lukewarm beers and a greasy Domino's delivery that I didn't think there was any way Olivia would actually eat. Still, when I glanced over at her, sitting cross-legged on the carpet, she held up her slice of pizza as if to say, *see?*

"We don't have to go," I'd told her earlier tonight, the two of us side by side at the mirror in the bathroom. "I don't want there to be Alex-related awkwardness, or for you to feel like—"

"It's fine," she'd assured me for the millionth time. "First of all, it's abundantly clear to me that you like him more than I ever, ever did. And second of all, even if it *was* weird, I'd better get used to it if we're both going on tour, right?"

Now I grinned at her across the room as she chatted animatedly with Austin; Olivia stuck her tongue out at me, then grinned back. Mikey flipped through the movie channels on cable; Austin and Mario lit up a joint and passed it around, the smoke sweet and heavy in the air. Trevor wanted to get a round of Flip Cup going, but the boys were out of plastic cups, so instead we played Seven Up, which I hadn't even thought about since middle school. It should have felt ridiculous—and it did, kind of, all of us with our heads down and our thumbs in the air, tiptoeing around the living room and trying to stifle our laughter—but it was also strangely fun.

I tried to relax and enjoy it—the sound of Olivia's giggles, Alex's warm arm around my waist—but the truth was, I felt edgy and out of sorts tonight, like I couldn't settle into the moment. I wanted to imagine us all on tour like this—in buses and hotel rooms, goofing our way across the world—but there was another part of me that couldn't help seeing tonight as some kind of last hurrah. I couldn't picture the future, not clearly. Whenever I tried, it reminded me of a corny, old-fashioned sitcom—the dialogue stilted, the colors too bright. Something clearly fake and invented, with no correlation to real life.

I slipped out onto the balcony when I thought nobody was looking, stared out at the boulevard feeling absurdly homesick for a place I hadn't even left yet. Over the last couple of months this dumpy complex had turned into my whole world. The idea of losing it filled me with a dark, heavy dread.

"You know," Alex said behind me, a slice of chilly air cutting through the humidity as he opened the sliding glass door, "if you wanted to be alone with me, you should have just said so."

I snorted. "Dork."

"Mikey's practicing his breakdancing inside," he said as he came to stand beside me, hands wrapped around the railing and his bare arm warm and solid against mine. "You're missing a real show."

"Oh God." I laughed at that; I couldn't help it. "Did somebody put a blanket over the TV so he doesn't put his foot through the screen?"

"Good thinking," Alex said. "We probably should have moved the lamps, too."

"Probably," I agreed. Then, unable to hold it in any longer: "Do you realize this could be the last time we do this?" I asked.

Alex grinned. "Leave the room when Mikey is putting on a one-man talent show?"

I frowned. "You know what I mean," I said. "The tour starts in two weeks. Guy's going to make his decision any minute, and then"—I waved my arms vaguely—"poof."

"Poof, what?" Alex asked, eyes narrowing. "He's going to pick you."

I shook my head. "We need to convince him to pick us both."

"Okay," Alex said slowly. "Well, then, that's what you'll do."

"And if we can't?"

"You will."

"Based on *what*?" I asked sharply, then immediately regretted it. "I'm sorry," I said, digging the heels of my hands into my eyes. "I don't mean to snap at you, I'm just—"

"You're freaking out," Alex said. "I get it. And I know you don't like when I say this—I know you think I don't understand how the real world works. But you've come too far for things to fall apart now, you know? You and I both have."

He tipped his chin down to kiss me then, fingers splayed across my backbone and his broad, solid chest against mine. I closed my eyes tightly, tried to relax. Normally the press of Alex's mouth was steadying, but my brain was spiraling out in a million different directions—Guy and Olivia and the glittering prize of a cross-country tour with Tulsa, the blankness of my life back in Jessell if I got sent home. What Alex and I had felt fragile and temporary, like it might blow away forever in a hot gust of tropical wind.

There was a part of me that wanted to end things now, I thought, even as he kissed me: to have this much, at least, be my choice instead of throwing myself on the mercy of the universe. I hated how powerless I felt all of a sudden. I'd come to Orlando in the first place to try to get some control over my future. But even after everything, my fate wasn't mine to decide.

Alex could tell I wasn't with him. "Hey," he said, pulling away and reaching for both my hands, lacing our fingers together and looking at me urgently. "It's me, remember? Don't go where I can't find you."

I shook my head, let him pull me closer again. "I'm right here," I promised, which wasn't entirely true.

"I love you," he reminded me. "Whatever else happens, that's going to stay true."

I nodded, tried to believe him. "I love you, too," I said.

Alex kissed me again and I tried to surrender to it, to what was happening in front of me right here and right now. One perfect moment—that's what I'd told him "Tangerine" was about, wasn't it? Something rare and amazing—and something that couldn't possibly last. I pushed the thought out of my head, held on tight.

THIRTY-SEVEN

The next afternoon was Saturday, and the boys were splashing around in the pool, but I took Olivia's car to the studio, wanting to spend some time rehearsing on my own. It was funny, I thought as I pulled into the parking lot—when I first got here and desperately needed the practice, the last thing I would have wanted was to come here on my day off to put extra time in. Now, though, when I was arguably as good I was going to get before Guy made his decision, I actually *wanted* to work.

I thought I'd be alone in the cool, dark space, but when I let myself inside I could hear music coming from Guy's office, the fifties and sixties rock 'n' roll he liked best. "It's Dana," I called, poking my head in on my way to the voice room. Guy was sitting at his desk with a stack of papers in one hand and a pen in the other, reading glasses perched on his nose. He always looked older when he had them on.

"Oh, good, you're here," he said, setting his papers down on the desktop instead of just waving me on like I'd expected. "Come in for a minute." He dug through the stacks in front of him and presented me with a thick three-ring binder. "Take that," he said, holding it out unceremoniously. "For you."

"What's this?" I asked, my arm sagging a bit under its unexpected heft.

"It's your tour schedule," he told me. "I was going to have Juliet drop it off later, but since you're here. Learn it, live it, love it."

"My *tour* schedule?" I gaped at him. "You mean—" I broke off.

Guy looked at me coolly. "Close your mouth, kiddo. Something's going to fly in there."

I snapped my jaw shut abruptly, only to have it fall right open again. It felt like we'd skipped a million steps here. This wasn't what I'd been expecting at all. "It's *me*?" I squeaked.

"It's you," Guy said, taking off his glasses and tossing them onto the desk, then sitting back in his chair and folding his hands on his stomach. "Come on, kiddo. You know that. It's always been you. It's been you since I picked you out of that waiting room at the beginning of the summer." He looked pleased with himself. "I told you, I don't make mistakes."

I blinked silently, speechless. I honestly didn't know what to say. I was shocked—not so much by the fact of Guy picking me but by the way it was happening, a chance encounter on a quiet afternoon. This wasn't how I'd pictured it at all. I'd thought it would be like the morning he'd cut Ashley and Kristin, a formal meeting with me and Olivia both—not just him handing down the news with no fanfare, no time for me to prepare. It threw me off my guard entirely.

I wondered if that was exactly the point.

"I think the words you're looking for are *thank you*," Guy said now, gazing at me across the desk with a dry kind of amusement. Then, when I still didn't say anything, he prompted, *"Thank you, Guy."*

"Thank you," I echoed finally, coming back to myself enough to understand what he was holding out to me, enough to picture it. For the first time I let myself imagine what it would be like in full Technicolor: traveling around the country with Alex, sleeping with my head on his shoulder on a tour bus, fields and mountains stretching out on every side. Performing at arenas that held tens of thousands of people, feeling the floor shake underneath me as they clapped their hands and stomped their feet. Never having to worry about money again. *Yes*, I almost said, my grip gone tense around the binder, my sweaty fingertips slipping on the plastic and the edges of it digging into my arms as I held it to my chest for dear life. *Yes, I want this, I've earned this, it's mine.*

Then I remembered the promise I'd made to Olivia.

"I—can I think about it?" I heard myself ask.

Guy looked surprised. "What the hell is there to think about?" he asked, thick brows crawling toward his hairline.

"A lot of things!" I blurted before I could stop myself. "This is my whole life we're talking about, I just—"

"Are you kidding me?" Guy looked at me like I'd lost my mind entirely. It was the same look he'd given me at the studios on the very first day we'd met, when I'd told him I wasn't there to audition: *I'm giving you a chance, and only an idiot wouldn't take it.* "I'd be very careful what you say next, kiddo," he told me, and his voice sounded very, very calm. "Because what it sounds like right now is that you've been wasting my time all fucking summer. And I know that's not what you're actually trying to say."

"It's not." I felt my face flame. "I haven't been," I told him, struggling to keep my spine straight, not to wither under the force of his annoyance and disbelief. "Or at least, I wasn't trying to. I want this more than anything. But Olivia and I made a deal. That it was going to be both of us, or neither."

"You and Olivia?" Guy looked at me blankly. "What, on the tour?"

I nodded meekly.

"What the hell made you think that would fly?"

"I—" I didn't have an answer for that. It seemed abruptly ridiculous now, like a plan we would have come up with when we were little girls to get Olivia's mom to agree to a sleepover on a school night. "I don't know," I had to admit. "We just thought that since you'd been training us both, and we're both good, it might make more sense to—"

"Why don't you let me worry about what makes sense, all right?" Guy interrupted. "I gotta tell you, kiddo, you're scaring me right now. Haven't you listened to a word I've said all summer? Look, if you're going to do this, you gotta want it more than anything. You gotta want it with claws and teeth. You can't be worrying about bringing your friend along for a twofer for fairness's sake." He looked at me across the desk for a moment. "So," he asked. "Do you want it or not?"

I *did* want it, was the worst part. Of course I wanted to say yes. This tour was my only real chance to get out of Jessell, for a future full of hills and valleys instead of just flat gray nothingness. It was my only chance to be with Alex for longer than just right now.

But we'd made a pact.

Olivia's friendship was the most important thing to me. It was the thread that had run through my whole life. It was what had brought me here to Orlando to begin with, the only reason I was even here. If I broke my promise now, what did that make me? It had to be both of us, or neither. A package deal.

"I can't," I told Guy finally. "I'm sorry. I can't go without her. You don't understand, we made a deal, and I—"

"Stop," Guy said, holding a hand up to silence me. "You know what, just stop it." He stood up. "I gotta tell you, kiddo, I'm disappointed. I thought I saw something in you. I thought you had what it takes."

"I *do* have what it takes," I argued. My heart was slamming against my rib cage, fear and adrenaline coursing through my veins. I was losing this, I knew it. I could feel it slipping away. "I just don't want it without her."

Guy shook his head. "I'll have Juliet book you a flight out of here tomorrow, then," he told me, sitting back down in his chair and lifting his hands like, *what can you do?* "Good luck out there, kiddo. I'll tell you, you're going to need it."

"That's it?" I asked. "After all that, you're just kicking me out?"

"Like I told you," Guy said, and just like that he was completely emotionless. "I don't make mistakes."

That was it, then. It was over.

So I handed Guy the binder back, and everything that went with it. I walked on shaking legs through the darkened studio and into the bright blinding light outside.

THIRTY-EIGHT

I drove myself back to the complex, a numb kind of buzzing in my ears like the humming of ten thousand wasps. Either that was the bravest thing I'd ever done, or the stupidest. More likely than not, it was both.

I stumbled up the stairs to the apartment, let myself in with two shaking hands: "Liv?" I called into the darkened living room. "Olivia, are you here?" I banged into her empty bedroom, heart pounding with urgency. I wanted to be the one to tell her what had happened, before Guy got to her, so that we could make a plan. I'd been caught off guard, I told myself. That was all that had happened. If we went back to him together, calm and ready, there was a chance we could still convince him to keep us both.

The apartment was empty; I paced around for a while, trying to figure out where Olivia and Charla might have gone. Girl Cat meowed at the open door, but I shooed her back outside. I looked at Olivia's empty bedroom again, the bed she made so neatly every morning, everything in its place.

Somehow, that was when I knew.

I got back in the car and drove back to the studio, stepping on the gas with a heavy foot, not stopping to turn on the AC. I was sweating by the time I turned into the lot. I didn't bother with a real parking spot, just left the keys in the ignition and threw the driver's side door open. Charla was coming out as I was walking in.

"What are you doing here?" she asked, and I knew Guy had told her.

"Where's Olivia?" I asked, and it came out more hysterical than I meant.

Charla shook her head. "I don't understand you at all, Dana," she said. "All the hard work you did all summer, the distance you covered. And you didn't even want it?"

I ignored her, headed for the studio. "I need to talk to Olivia."

"You shouldn't go in there," she called after me, but I wasn't listening. I took the concrete steps two at a time, and made it into the cool, dark hallway just in time to see Olivia walk out of Guy's office with Juliet and Lucas, the tour binder—*my* tour binder—in her hands.

My stomach lurched. I felt like I was seeing something that physically didn't make sense, like the damn Loch Ness monster rising up out of some watery depths. "Oh, no," I said uselessly, shaking my head. I turned around and walked down the hall toward the exit, slamming at the push bar so hard the door crashed into the side of the building. Olivia hurried after me, calling my name.

"Dana, *stop*," she said finally, grabbing my arm in the parking lot, but I shrugged her off hard enough that she took a step back. It was hot out here; it was too impossibly humid. I couldn't get any air in at all.

"Olivia." My voice sounded like it belonged to someone else entirely. "What the hell are you doing?"

She took a deep breath, but of course I knew even before the words came out. "I'm going on tour," she said.

"He offered it to you?" I asked, though of course I'd already known that, had known it since I'd gotten back to the empty apartment, had known since I'd turned it down. "And you're *taking* it?"

"I'm sorry," Olivia said. "I know we promised each other—"

"He offered it to me first, you know that, right?" I asked immediately. I wanted to hurt her. I wanted to be as mean as I possibly could. "You know you're taking my sloppy seconds."

"I know he did," Olivia said, very voice quavering a little. "And honestly, you're probably the better performer. But—"

"You're the one who wanted to make that stupid pact

to begin with!" A thought occurred to me then, black and terrible. "Did you set me up?" I demanded. "Is that what you were doing when you said it would be both of us or nobody?"

"No, of course not." Olivia shook her head. "It wasn't like that."

"Then what was it *like*, Olivia?" I was yelling now, making a spectacle of both of us in the middle of the parking lot; Guy and the others had stayed inside, but I could see some of the workers from the shipping place watching us with interest. *Let them watch*, I thought. *Let everybody*. This was Olivia, the person I'd loved longest out of anyone in the world. I'd thought that meant something. I'd thought we were in this together.

"Please just try to understand what it's been like for me here," Olivia said, reaching for my arm again; I jerked away. "I've wanted this since I was two."

"And I had the chance to get out of my shitty life, but I picked you!" My voice cracked at that. "I picked *you*, Olivia. We're supposed to be a team."

"We *are* a team."

"We are clearly not a fucking team!"

Olivia's eyes welled up, too. "Dana," she said, and she was pleading now. "Come on. You could be anything. You could do anything. This is the one thing I'm good at."

"And I'm not fucking good at anything, Olivia, but I made this work because it was my one chance to get the hell out of Jessell! We were supposed to make this work together!"

Olivia shook her head again. "You're stronger than me, okay? You've always been stronger than me. And that's how I know you're gonna be okay."

"You're full of shit." I couldn't believe this was happening, except for the part that I could: this had been the most important thing to Olivia since we'd gotten here, hadn't it? This had been the most important thing to her all along. I felt like an idiot. I felt like the worst kind of fool.

"Just get away from me," I told her, heading for the car—hers, I realized with a nasty little cackle. Even the car I'd driven here belonged to her. "Have a nice life."

THIRTY-NINE

"You don't have to do this," Alex told me the next afternoon. He was sitting on my bed in the room I'd shared with Olivia at the start of the summer, watching me throw balled-up socks into my duffel. It was the first thing either one of us had said in a long time.

"I mean, I do," I pointed out a little snottily, checking to make sure I hadn't left anything in the bureau. "Guy gave my ticket to Olivia."

"He'd give it back," Alex said. "If you went to him and told him you really wanted it."

I shook my head, resting one knee on the mattress beside him. "That's the thing, though. Guy was right. I didn't want it enough."

"Well," Alex said, threading his fingers through mine in

the gesture that would always make me think of him, "what *do* you want?"

We kissed for a little bit, his soft mouth and soap-sweat smell, the thrum of the pulse in his neck when I put my tongue there. I pulled my other knee up so that I was sitting in his lap; he groaned and leaned backward, trying to take me with him, but I pushed him gently away.

"I can't," I told him, bumping my forehead against his. "I gotta do this. There's a car picking me up in an hour."

"I'll be fast," Alex promised, and I snorted.

"Perv."

Alex grinned, but he let me get up and head for the closet. "When am I gonna see you again?" he asked.

That stopped me. I hesitated, sitting back down on the mattress beside him.

"I don't know," I said, not meeting his gaze. "You're going to be the one with the more complicated calendar, I think."

"Not that complicated." Alex shrugged. "The tour comes through Atlanta in a month or so. We'll see each other then. And maybe you could fly out and meet me before that, in New York or someplace cool like that."

I scoffed—I couldn't help it. "With what money, Alex?"

He looked hurt, and I felt like a jerk. "I'm sorry," I said, reaching out for his hand one more time. "I'm being an asshole. But I just—I think it's better for both of us if we're honest about what's going to happen now, you know?"

Alex's eyes narrowed at that. "And what's going to happen, exactly?"

I took a deep breath. This was the conversation I'd been dreading since yesterday—that I'd been dreading all summer—but I knew we had to have it, and we were running out of time. "I'm not an idiot," I said. "I know that once you're on tour, you're going to meet girls, and have experiences, and—"

Alex barked a laugh at that, cutting me off. *"Experiences?"* he asked. "What kind of *experiences*, exactly? You sound like somebody's mom."

"It's not funny!" I snapped. I wanted to lash out in every conceivable direction; I wanted him to see what a joke this all was. "Do you realize that until this summer I'd only ever been out of the state of Georgia one time? I'm a hick, Alex. I'm going to go home and live with my drunk mom and wait tables for the foreseeable future, and you're going on tour with Tulsa fucking MacCreadie."

"So what, Dana?" He shook his head. "Who cares?"

"I care, Alex! We're about to have completely different lives, and yours is going to involve girls throwing themselves at you every second, and mine is going to involve scraping leftover burrito off people's plates."

"You chose that," Alex reminded me. "You could have gone on tour, too. So you don't get to act like this is my fault now, okay? You don't get to act like I'm the one leaving you, or like you're going to break up with me for my own good."

His eyes widened. "Is that what you're doing?" he asked suddenly, and he sounded so afraid for a second, like the possibility had only just occurred to him. "Are you breaking up with me?"

I opened my mouth, closed it again; it felt like there were razor blades in my lungs. "I—yeah, Alex," I heard myself say. "I think maybe I am."

Alex visibly flinched, like I'd shoved him. "You're not serious," he said.

That made me mad, like he thought he knew better than I did. "I am," I insisted, though I could hardly believe I'd spoken the words out loud. Part of me thought maybe I was being unfair, taking my anger at Olivia—at the whole situation—out on him because he was here and he cared about me. But another part knew this was the only way. I'd worried from the very beginning that Alex and I were too different to last, that there was no way we could stay together if I went back to Jessell and he went out on the road. He'd be surrounded by other girls the same way he had been that night at the show in New Orleans; he'd get bored, and tired of me. Eventually, it would end. And if the choice was between hurting now or hurting later—well. I was already hurting now.

"Look," Alex said, "I get that you're upset about what happened—"

"It's not about that," I argued. "It's about you and me."

"You're doing it again, you realize. You're pissed and scared and so you're picking a fight with me—"

"This is not that."

"This is exactly that!"

"I'm being *realistic*," I countered, scrambling up off the bed as my voice broke. I knew if he saw me cry he'd want to comfort me, and if he comforted me I'd never be able to go through with this.

"So that's it?" Alex asked behind me, and I could tell he'd stood up, too. Even without turning around I could picture him so clearly—his hands in his pockets, the pain and confusion on his face. It felt like I was spreading my ribs with my own two hands. "I don't— Dana. How can that just be it?"

"I'm sorry," I said into the darkness of the closet. I wiped my wet face with my forearm. "I have to pack."

FORTY

Guy's driver picked me up at the complex that afternoon, the black car idling in the parking lot as I scanned the apartment to make sure I wasn't leaving anything behind. It was bizarre to think I'd never be here again, brushing my teeth beside Olivia in the seafoam bathroom or standing in the kitchen griping about Charla's gross smoothies. This place had become home overnight, the backdrop for every crazy thing that had happened; just as fast, all of it had changed.

"Here," Charla said, reaching for my duffel. I was leaving with only what I'd brought with me, right down to the plastic grocery bags holding the overflow. The new clothes, the makeup and designer hair products—all that belonged to Guy. "Let me help you."

"I got it," I said flatly, but I let her hold the door for me anyhow; she followed me down the concrete steps into the parking lot, mid-afternoon sun shimmering on the concrete. The cats lolled in the shade of the building, oblivious.

"Travel safe," Charla said once my bags were loaded. She reached out for a moment like she wanted to hug me, then thought better of it. "I'd drive you back myself, but—"

"But you're busy with your new star," I couldn't help snapping. "I know."

Charla sighed. "Dana—"

"It's fine," I said, holding up my hands, wanting more than anything for it to just be over. I'd lost Olivia. I'd lost Alex. I'd lost whatever my future was going to be here. What else was there to say? "Thanks for everything, Charla. Really."

Charla nodded. "Good luck, sweetheart."

I was about to get into the car when I turned around suddenly, squinting at the glare of the sun overhead. "Look out for Olivia, okay?"

Charla looked surprised at that, though I couldn't blame her: it surprised me that I'd said it, too. But Olivia was my best friend—or at least, she had been. And whatever else had happened between us, I wouldn't be here to protect her anymore. "Of course," Charla said, looking at me with focus and concentration, like she was trying to work out a tricky combination in her head. "And Dana—look out for *yourself*."

"Sure," I said, shrugging, turning back to the car. "Whatever."

"I'm serious," she insisted, reaching for my arm and turning me to face her, strong despite her delicate build. "The only person you need to worry about from now on is you, all right? Try to remember that." She hugged me then, fast and impulsive like she was worried I wasn't going to let her.

"Sure," I said again, turning my head so she wouldn't see that I was on the verge of crying. I got into the backseat and went home.

FORTY-ONE

I came back to Jessell on the hottest day of the summer, the sidewalk burning straight through my sandals, the flowers all dead where they stood. Elvis barked his head off from behind the chain-link fence, as if he'd never seen me before.

"Didn't work out, huh?" my mom asked me, legs crossed on the couch, eyeing me evenly.

"Nope," I said too loudly, with a plasticky brightness I didn't feel. "Didn't work out."

I stood in the doorway of my bedroom, fighting the urge to run. It felt like the site of some bizarre time warp, like maybe the last three months hadn't happened at all—like maybe I'd made them up entirely, some deluded fantasy I'd constructed to chase my loneliness away. The sheets hadn't been changed since I'd come home in the middle of the summer. The dress I'd worn to graduation was crumpled on the closet floor. The job applications I'd started after my audition for Guy—retail jobs, waitressing gigs—sat in a dust-filmed stack on the desk, the edges gone slightly yellow. The whole room smelled dank, like the inside of somebody's gym bag; I flung both the windows open, but that only made it harder to breathe.

This was it for me, I realized, trying to quell the acrid panic I felt rising in my chest. If not this exact room, then some other room like it. I thought of Olivia, who was off on tour with Tulsa. I thought of Alex, who'd probably already met someone new.

The worst part was that underneath my bright, shattering anger was a flabby, dull kind of fear: even though Olivia and I had spent so much of the summer fighting, we'd never actually been apart before. I didn't really know who I was without her. I wasn't sure I was ready to find out.

I flopped face-first onto the mattress. I lay there, hot and motionless, until I finally fell asleep.

I spent the next three days bouncing all over Jessell, applying to every job in the want ads: a babysitting gig that turned out to be for a guinea pig named Lester, a dishwashing shift at a seafood restaurant that reeked of rotting fish. Sure, technically I'd been on Guy's payroll all summer, but each week he'd held a slice back for expenses—rent in the complex, that expensive studio time—and now I had basically less than I'd had when I'd gone to Orlando. I thought of that flashy red bathing suit I hadn't bothered to check the price on, and cursed myself for being such a fool.

It was nearing dusk by the time I got off the bus on the third day, sun sinking behind the low-slung houses and the cicadas already screeching their desperate calls for love. My shirt was sticking to my back, hot and sweaty; the backs of my feet were puffy with blisters from my uncomfortable "hire me" shoes. I let myself in through the screen door, was heading down the hall to shower when my mom called out to me from the living room.

"Come here a second," she said, hitting the mute button on the *Law & Order* rerun she was watching and patting the couch cushion beside her. "You've been running around since you got back. I haven't hardly seen you."

That was mostly because she'd been passed out in her bedroom, but I didn't say that out loud. "I need to find a job," I reminded her, but I went anyway, sinking into our ancient floral couch and gingerly sliding my feet out of my sandals.

"You'll find something," she said. She smelled like cigarettes and the same raspberry body spray she'd worn since I was a little girl, sweet and fruity and overpowering. A glass of something icy and clear sweated on the coffee table. "I got ice cream at the store today," my mom continued, looping one slender arm around my shoulders unexpectedly. Normally she wasn't much for hugs.

"You did?" I asked, smiling a little, leaning into her a

bit. It was nice to be held for a moment, even if I was too big for it.

"I did," she said, sounding pleased. She looked so young to me all of a sudden, like she could have been in a girl group herself. "To celebrate you being back at home."

"That's nice," I said, and I meant it. "Thanks."

"I'll tell you something," my mom continued, reaching up and pushing my hair back off my forehead, her palm warm against my skin. "It never made any sense to me, what you were doing down there in Orlando."

I felt my skin prickle at that, but I tried to keep my face expressionless. "No?" I said. "Why not?"

I felt her shrug. "It just felt like they were having you put on airs the whole time you were down there, you know what I mean? Tryin' to make you into something you're not."

"I could have been, though," I said, sitting up before I could stop myself. "Guy picked me over Olivia, remember? I'm the one who decided not to do it."

"I never liked that Guy, is the other thing," my mom continued, almost as if she hadn't heard me, like she'd already made up her own version of events and that was that.

"You never met him, Mom."

"No, I know I didn't, but just the way you described him. He seemed real Big City to me. Like he thought real highly of himself."

Well, that much was true. Guy did think highly of himself.

But he'd thought highly of *me*, too. It was possible he was the first person who ever had.

"Now, Olivia, sure," my mom continued, still fussing with my hair like I was a little kid. "You always kind of knew Olivia was going to go do some cockamamie thing, didn't you? She comes from that kind of family, her mom walking around with her nose in the air all the time. I don't know." She shrugged. "Anyway, it seemed stupid to me to begin with."

I nodded wordlessly, still staring at the TV and telling myself the stinging at the back of my throat was anything but tears. The worst part was how I knew she was trying to tell me something nice—that she'd missed me, that she thought I was smart for owning up to who and what I really was. In her mind, there were a limited number of things a person could do, only a few places they fit in the world; trying to change that was embarrassing and shameful for everyone involved. I got it, truly. At the beginning of the summer, I'd felt the exact same way.

Now, though, I wasn't so sure.

Still, I thought as I sat there, it didn't really make a difference anymore, did it? Maybe I could have been something else, in an alternate universe. But in the end, here I was anyway, back in the same place I'd always been. I'd made sure of that myself.

"Anyway," my mom finished, unmuting the TV just as the twist ending was revealed, everything suddenly making sense at once. "It's good to have you back where you belong."

I met Sarah Jane for breakfast at Waffle House a couple of mornings later. "So," she said once we'd placed our orders, "how is it being back?"

"It's good," I said, trying to muster some enthusiasm. I didn't want her to think I thought I was better than her, that I was—as my mom would have said—putting on airs.

Sarah Jane snorted. "You're miserable, I can tell."

"I'm not *miserable*," I protested, though in fact that was basically the perfect word to describe it. "I'm just . . . lost, I guess? I'm back at my mom's. I have zero job prospects. And I miss Olivia, honestly, which makes me feel like a huge chump."

"You're not a chump," Sarah Jane said as the waitress set our plates down on the table. "You're human. And maybe it's a good thing you're apart, you know? I know you guys were joined at the hip and all, but it's gotta be kind of freeing, isn't it? Not to have to worry about her all the time? I mean, you could do anything now."

"I don't know about *that*," I protested. "I barely graduated, remember?"

"Oh, don't be dumb, Dana," Sarah Jane said flatly, reaching for the sticky-looking pitcher of syrup. "Grades or no grades, you were one of the only people in our whole class who knew her ass from her elbow. You never even wanted to be a pop star and you got Guy freaking Monroe to offer you a spot on tour with Tulsa MacCreadie." She shook her head. "Don't insult the rest of us by acting like you're stuck at your mom's forever. What about your cute boyfriend, where's he in all this?"

I picked at the edge of my waffle. "I broke up with him before I came back here," I admitted.

"Of course you did." Sarah Jane made a face. "And for what? So you and Tim can live miserably ever after? That was dumb."

I blew out a breath instead of answering. The truth was, I could barely sleep for thinking about Alex—trying to convince myself that I didn't still miss him, that my chest didn't ache with the loss. I'd been so sure that breaking things off with him had been my only option. But what if I'd been wrong?

"Olivia always needed you so much more than you needed her," Sarah Jane continued, shaking her head thoughtfully. "Maybe now you can put all that energy into yourself instead."

I thought about it for a moment. It was the same thing Charla had said, I realized, albeit a little more bluntly, and maybe they were right. But I didn't know how to see past how angry I was at Olivia, or how hopeless I felt at being back here. I didn't know how the hell I was supposed to move on.

"What's that dorky talk show thing you guys always used

to say to each other?" SJ asked, reaching for her coffee cup. "'Live your life forward'?"

I nodded.

"Well," she said, like it was just that obvious, "do that."

My mom went out that night, didn't say where she was going; I lay in bed and stared at the patterns of light on the ceiling, waiting for her to come home.

God, was this really going to be my entire life?

I thought of the fireworks at Disney, the colors exploding above us. I thought of laughing my head off at Guy's weird bidet. I thought of being on that airplane, terrified and exhilarated, of Alex asking me what I'd do if I wasn't doing this.

Olivia had been right, in the end: I'd never really cared about being a pop star. I'd never meant to chase after fame. But I wanted something more than this—that much was undeniable.

And I knew where I wanted to start.

I threw back the covers and I went to the phone in the hallway, dialed Alex's number, and listened to it ring two hundred miles away.

"Hi," I said, taking a deep breath when he finally answered. "It's me."

EPILOGUE

My anatomy class ran over on Tuesday, and I hurried home in the late-autumn sunshine so I could get changed before my shift at work. A cool breeze blew my bangs into my eyes as I unlocked the mailbox in front of the apartment—it finally felt like fall here, the long, baking summer over at long last—and reached inside for the usual stack of junk mail and bills. There was something else wedged in the back, though, and with some effort I pulled out a small padded manila envelope addressed to me in handwriting I didn't recognize.

I climbed the narrow staircase to the unit I shared with another girl from my program, smelled the student-apartment smells of cheap cleaning solvent and weed. I was about to open the envelope when the phone rang.

"Hey, you," Alex said when I picked up the receiver in

the kitchen, the deep, familiar sound of his voice setting something alight at the base of my spine. "How was your exam?"

"Not terrible, actually," I admitted, twisting the phone cord around my finger. "Not great or anything, but not a total disaster."

"You rocked it," Alex said, all confidence, and I smiled. I'd never met someone who was so perfectly confident in my ability to do whatever I set my mind to, whether it was soloing at Madison Square Garden or correctly identifying all the bones in the human foot on a midterm at Southeast Community College. It made me feel like I could grab the sky. "We'll celebrate this weekend."

"We will, huh?" I felt my heart tumble in anticipation. Tulsa's tour was coming through Atlanta on Friday; Alex and I would have forty-eight whole hours together, the first time we'd be in the same place since we'd gotten back together three months ago. Just thinking about seeing his face in person—imagining having his hands on me again after all this time—turned my whole body warm and prickly.

"We will," Alex promised, and I wondered again how I'd managed to get so lucky. It was work, the past few months had made that much undeniable; it was missed calls and gnawing loneliness and the beat of my own jealous heart—but it was undeniably solid, too. We were good for each other. I knew it in my bones. Together we were so, so good.

"I'm excited to see your place," Alex said now, and I

looked around the tiny, sparsely furnished apartment. It wasn't much, two cramped bedrooms and a hundred layers of shiny paint on the doorjambs, everything an industrial landlord white—but the floors were clean and wide-planked and it got bright yellow sunshine in the morning. A water glass of wildflowers sat cheerfully on the desk.

Most important of all, it wasn't my mom's house.

"Yeah," I said slowly, feeling a grin spread across my face as I imagined him coming here. A part of me had known for a long time that I couldn't stay in my old bedroom forever, that I'd shrivel up there day by day. But if this summer hadn't happened, I don't know if it ever would have occurred to me to make a change. If I'd gotten anything out of this whole crazy adventure, it was the realization that my life was mine and mine alone. There was always going to be stuff I couldn't change about my circumstances. But I got to decide. "I'm excited for you to see it, too."

"I gotta let you go," I told him after we'd talked a bit longer—about the show they'd done last night where none of their mics had been working properly; about the girl Mikey had met in Tennessee. "I'm late for work." Turned out I hadn't been wrong when I told Alex I'd be a waitress if I wasn't in Orlando—but he hadn't been wrong, either, when he'd told me that wasn't all I could do. I was taking a full load of classes, trying to get my miserable grades up. And we'd see what came next after that. "I'll see you soon."

"You will," Alex said. "I love you."

I smiled. "I love you, too."

I'd almost forgotten about the padded envelope by the time we hung up, but it caught my eye again once I'd changed into my work clothes, before I walked out the front door. I ripped it open quickly and peered inside, my heart catching at the contents: the snapshot of me and Olivia from the photo shoot, and a blank tape in a plastic jewel case. No label, no note.

I glanced at the clock on the microwave. I was cutting it close for my shift at the restaurant, but my curiosity got the best of me: I stuck the tape into the boom box in the tiny living room, hit the button for play, and listened to the soft popping sound that came with a homemade recording. When I heard the opening bars of "Tangerine" I tilted my head to the side, curious; when I heard Olivia's voice my mouth fell wide-open in surprise.

I stood in the middle of the living room for a moment, full of anger and shock and a purple kind of sadness, letting myself miss her more than I had since I walked away. I thought of all the dumb songs she'd sung to me over the years to cheer me up, the two of us lying in her yard and in her rec room and tucked into our sleeping bags side by side: *Olivia, sing "Dancing Queen." Olivia, sing "I Will Always Love You."*

Olivia, sing "Tangerine."

I hadn't talked to Olivia at all since I'd left Orlando. I didn't know if I'd ever see her again. I didn't know if the two of us could ever get back what we'd taken from each other—but for the first time it occurred to me that maybe, after everything we'd been through, we'd given each other just as much.

I looked out the window of my apartment. I closed my eyes and listened to the song.

ACKNOWLEDGMENTS

Writing is a solitary job, but anyone who says they do it alone is a liar. I have so much help:

Alessandra Balzer, my editor, and every other dreamboat at Balzer + Bray/HarperCollins. What an honor to be a part of this astonishingly sharp, talented team.

Josh Bank, Joelle Hobeika, and Sara Shandler, who tell all the best stories, along with Les Morgenstein and all the cool kids at Alloy Entertainment. I am so very lucky; I am in such very good hands.

Christa and Courtney and Julie and Corey and Natalie and Tess and Annie and Elissa and Emery and Bethany and Maria and Melissa and Dahlia and Ally and every other gorgeous writer and blogger and librarian who has sat with me at a bar or in a convention center hallway or on the internet over the last few years and taught me about writing and about life, along with the hundreds of YA authors whose beautiful, complicated work inspires me every day. What an incredible club to be a part of. I am so humbled and proud.

The Fourteenery, always.

Rachel Hutchinson, to Pluto.

Lisa Burton, Jennie Palluzzi, Sierra Rooney, and Marissa Velie, beloveds; Jackie Cotugno, most favorite; Tom Colleran, best friend and old love and wartime consigliere. Cotugnos and Collerans, who hold and keep me: you are all so completely wonderful. I love you all so much.

Read on for a sneak peek
at Katie Cotugno's *You Say It First*

ONE

Meg

"In conclusion," Meg said brightly, standing at the podium under the harsh fluorescent lights of the PTA meeting room on Wednesday evening, "it's the position of the student council that our school is already sorely behind in doing its part to combat climate change. Adding solar panels to the roof of the main building is not only the fiscally responsible and environmentally sustainable thing to do, but will help ensure we're living up to the values the Overbrook community has instilled in us all these years." She smiled her most competent smile, sweating a little bit inside her uniform blazer. "Thank you very much for your time."

When the applause had finished and the meeting was adjourned, Meg made her way through the crowd of parents and teachers milling around the room to where her friends were waiting near the table of gluten-free brownies. "That was amazing!" Emily said, blond hair bouncing as she wrapped Meg in a bear hug. Adrienne and Javi saluted her with a pair of black-and-white cookies. "You looked like freakin' AOC up there."

"Nice job, kid," said Mason, ducking his head to peck her briefly on the cheek. Meg grinned and squeezed his hand. They'd been dating for more than a year now, though more often they still hung out in a pack just like this—the five of them perpetually clustered around their usual table at the juice place near school, planning a fundraiser or a protest or world domination. By now they'd all heard her solar-panel speech about a thousand times.

"Good work, Meg," added Ms. Clemmey, her AP Government teacher, coming up behind them with a cup of watery-looking coffee, her graying hair frizzing out of its bun. "Now we'll just have to see if they bite."

"They'll bite," Javi declared, all confidence, then stuffed another brownie into his mouth.

Ms. Clemmey quirked an eyebrow. "Anything from Cornell, meanwhile?" she asked quietly.

Meg shook her head, a little bit startled. "Not yet," she said, glancing instinctively over at Emily. Rooming together at Cornell had been their plan for as long as they'd been talking about colleges, but ever since she'd submitted her application, Meg kept finding herself forgetting about it altogether for days at a stretch until somebody, usually Em, said something that reminded her. It wasn't that she wasn't excited—she was, definitely. She just had a lot of other stuff on her plate right now. "We should be hearing soon, though."

Ms. Clemmey nodded. "Well, they'll be lucky to have you."

Meg shook her head, blushing a little. "We'll see."

The five of them went to Cavelli's to celebrate, ordering a large veggie pie so Adrienne could have some and two pitchers of Coke. "To the Green New Deal of Overbrook Day," Emily said, holding up her red plastic cup. They laughed and clinked and ate their pizza, Meg sitting back in her chair and listening as the conversation wandered: from Javi's parents' new labradoodle puppy, to a bunch of idiot sophomores who'd gotten drunk and thrown up all over the skating rink during spring break, to a *New York Times* podcast Emily was obsessed with. It made Meg happy to picture what they must look like from outside the wide front window, their faces lit by the fake Tiffany lamp over the table. Most of all she felt *normal*, like she hadn't for so much of last year.

It was almost ten by the time they paid their bill and headed out, Meg following Mason across the parking lot to where his Subaru was parked right next to her Prius. It was still mostly winter in Pennsylvania, with that damp blue-green whiff of spring on the air if you breathed deep enough. Meg tugged her cashmere beanie down over her ears.

"You were really great tonight," Mason said, turning to face her as he reached his driver's-side door.

"You think so?" she asked, taking a step closer. He looked handsome in the yellow glow of the parking lot light, with his dark eyes and high cheekbones. They'd known each other since kindergarten, back when Meg's mom put her hair in French-braid pigtails every morning and he was still the only Korean kid in their grade. Twelve years later, flush with victory, she wrapped her arms around his neck and pulled him close.

Mason stiffened. "Meg," he said, his hands landing gently on her waist, then letting go again.

"Hm?" she said, tilting her face up so he'd kiss her. Neither of them were into PDA—Meg hated any kind of nonpolitical public spectacle as a general rule—but it was late, and the parking lot was mostly empty. She could make an exception just this once.

"Meg," he said again, and she frowned.

"What?"

Mason hesitated, glancing over her shoulder instead of looking directly at her. In the second before he spoke, Meg had the sudden feeling of realizing too late that she'd stepped in front of a car. "I think we should break up," he said.

She blinked, her arms dropping off his shoulders. "*What?*"

"I just, um." Mason shrugged, visibly embarrassed; he looked eleven instead of seventeen. "I don't really think this is working."

"But like." Meg stared at him for a moment, running a quick, panicky set of diagnostics inside her head. Sure, lately they'd spent more time studying for the SAT Subject Tests and making fliers for the Philly Bail Fund than, like, goofing around or staring soulfully into each other's eyes, but that just meant they were in a mature relationship, right? That just meant their priorities were the same. "We never fight."

Mason looked surprised, and it occurred to Meg a second too late that that had probably been a weird way to respond on her part. "No, I know we don't," he said, tucking his hands into his jacket pockets. The jacket was new, a blue waxed canvas situation his mom had gotten him for his birthday. It made him look, Meg thought meanly, like a postman. "But that doesn't mean—I mean, not fighting isn't a reason to stay together, is it?"

"No, I know that," Meg said quickly, swallowing down the jagged break in her voice. She thought of the gentle, distracted way he'd trace his fingertips over her wrist as they were reading. She thought of the late-night ice cream runs they'd taken while she worked on her solar-panel speech. "Of course I know that." She took a step back, her spine bumping roughly against the passenger-side door of her car. Suddenly, she was cold enough to shiver. "Okay," she said, forcing herself to take a deep, steadying breath. "Well. Okay. I'm going to go, then."

"Meg, wait." Now Mason looked really confused. "Shouldn't we, like—don't you even want to talk about this?"

"What is there to talk about?" she asked, hating how shrill

her voice sounded. "It's fine, Mason. I get it." She didn't get it at all, not really. Actually, she felt blindsided and furious and completely, utterly foolish, but the literal last thing she wanted to do was talk about it, to stand here and fight it out in public like her parents in the last doomed days of their marriage. There was no way she was going to do that. "It's fine, I hear you. Message received."

Mason shook his head. "Meg—"

"Thanks for coming to support the solar panels," she managed. "I'll see you at school, okay?"

She got into her car and slammed the door a little harder than necessary, squeezing the steering wheel as she waited for him to leave, then realizing with a quiet swear that *he* was waiting for *her* to pull out first. Meg did, driving halfway home with her hands at a perfect ten and two, NPR burbling softly away on the radio. It wasn't until Mason turned off the main road toward his neighborhood and the Subaru was safely out of sight that she pulled over onto the shoulder and let herself cry.

Emily was waiting by Meg's locker before homeroom the following morning, her French book in one hand and a massive Frappuccino in the other. "Are you okay?" she asked, holding out the coffee cup. "Here, this is yours. I had them put all the different kinds of drizzles on it. You're probably going to get diabetes, but, desperate times. How are you feeling?"

"I'm good," Meg said cheerfully, sucking a mouthful of

whipped cream through the wide green straw. There was no way she was going to be a drama queen about this—even in front of Emily, who'd basically kept her upright through her ridiculous postdivorce depression fog of junior year. People broke up all the time; that was all there was to it. It was fine. *She* was fine.

"Are you sure?" Emily looked skeptical.

"I am sure," Meg said.

"Okay," Emily said, visibly unconvinced. "Because I'm just saying, nobody's going to blame you if you're not."

"But I am."

"I hear you," Emily said patiently, taking the Frappuccino back for safekeeping as Meg opened her locker, "and that's great. But it sucks when relationships end, you know? Even relationships like—" She broke off.

Meg's eyes narrowed; she closed the locker door again, peering at Em suspiciously. "Even relationships like what?"

"What? Nothing." Emily shook her head, eyes wide. "It sucks when relationships end, full stop."

"Uh-huh," Meg said, smirking a little. "Good try. What?"

Emily wrinkled her nose. "I mean, I don't know," she said, leaning back against the locker beside Meg's and hugging her French book to her chest. "It just always seemed like maybe you weren't actually that into Mason in the first place, that's all."

"What?" Meg blinked. She had so been into Mason. She'd loved Mason. She'd lost her *virginity* to Mason, for Pete's sake.

"We were together for more than a year, Em."

"I know you were!" Emily shrugged. "And in all that time I never heard you say anything like, *Oh man, I love Mason so much, I want to be with him forever and have a hundred million of his babies, he sets my loins on fire like Captain America and Killmonger combined.*"

"Rude!" Meg said, laughing in spite of herself. "First of all, there's more to relationships than your loins constantly being on fire." At least, she'd thought there was. Sure, she and Mason hadn't exactly been generating nuclear power with the sheer force of their physical chemistry, but they'd had fun together. They made a good team. And—most important—they were nothing like her parents, who'd spent what felt like the entire duration of their marriage screaming at each other. Meg had thought that counted for something. "And second of all, who knew belonging to all the same clubs and liking all the same political candidates didn't guarantee a happily ever after?"

Emily grinned. "What does that say about you and me?" she pointed out, helping herself to a sip of the Frappuccino before handing it back. "We belong to all the same clubs and like all the same political candidates."

"We're different," Meg said, zipping up her backpack and looping her arm through Em's. See? Here she was, joking around and everything. She was totally okay. "We like all the same everything. Our happily ever after is fully assured."

"I mean, true," Emily said as they made their way down

the crowded hallway. The two of them had been best friends since second grade, and even back then Meg had been shocked by how much they had in common: They played all the same games at recess. They watched all the same shows on TV. Every year on the first day of class they showed up wearing the exact same pair of shoes, even though they never planned it, and every year they burst out laughing like it hadn't ever happened before. It was the thesis statement of their friendship—that comforting sameness, the knowledge that by the time a thought occurred to her, Emily was already thinking it, too. Sometimes Meg wondered if maybe they were actually the same person, split into two different bodies by some cosmic mistake.

"What are you doing tonight?" Em asked now, stopping outside of Meg's homeroom. "Want to come over and we can watch something stupid?"

Meg did, and badly, but she shook her head. "I have WeCount tonight," she said, though honestly that wasn't the only reason she didn't want to fall back into the easy comfort of a midweek dinner at Emily's house. She'd spent any number of borderline-catatonic nights in front of the Hurds' TV last year when everything was crashing and burning with her parents, Em heaping green beans onto her plate and ghostwriting her Progressive Overbrook agendas and making sure her homework got done. Meg didn't want to be that person anymore. She *wasn't* that person anymore. She was under control.

She was fine.

"You sure?" Em pressed gently. "I'm sure the Cause will understand if you want to take one night off because you broke up with your boyfriend." Then she frowned. "It's me, okay? You can tell me."

But Meg shook her head again. "The Cause waits for no one," she said brightly, then raised her Frappuccino in a goofy salute and headed off to face the day.

TWO

Colby

Colby knew it was a dumb idea to climb the water tower pretty much from the moment Micah said he wanted to do it, but it wasn't like there was anything more exciting going on, so on Wednesday after midnight they all met at Jordan's stepdad's house, zipped their jackets against the skin-splitting rawness of March in Alma, Ohio, and set out for the wide, overgrown field at the edge of town.

"Tell me again why we couldn't just drive?" Colby muttered, balling his chapped, chilly hands into fists in his pockets as he trailed the rest of them through the darkened parking lot of the Liquor Mart, Micah in his army-green surplus coat and Jordan in the Jack Skellington hat he always wore, his ears sticking out like bat wings beneath the brim. Jordan's twin sister, Joanna, had tagged along at the last minute, her blond hair tucked up into a beanie with a furry pom-pom on top of it. Colby had been surprised: Jo, with her key ring full of discount cards and a car that smelled like vanilla cupcakes on the inside, always felt older and less susceptible to half-baked plans than the rest of them, even though Jordan was forever making a big point of telling everyone he'd been born first. But then she'd bumped Colby's shoulder and smiled hello, her straight white teeth like a slice of winter moonlight, and he thought maybe he wasn't actually that surprised after all.

"Stealth, dude," Micah said now, leading them across the service road with the slightly sketchy confidence of one of those guides who brought people down into the Grand Canyon on donkeys. "Car would be too suspicious."

Colby frowned. "More suspicious than the four of us wandering the streets in the middle of the night like a bunch of hobos?"

Micah snorted. "Moran, if you're too much of a pussy to do this, just say so."

"Fuck you," Colby said, glancing instinctively at Joanna before he could quell the impulse. "Let's go."

Alma got a little scruffier as they got closer to the tower, the sidewalk narrowing before it disappeared completely so they had to walk single file along the grassy shoulder, low-slung houses crowding close together like teeth in a mouth that was too small. A broad, stocky pit mix paced the length of a chain link fence, winter-crisped weeds nearly brushing his belly. Colby winced at the casual cruelty of whoever had left him out here, reaching his hand out for the little dude to sniff.

"Come on," Micah said, kicking at Colby's ankle to keep him moving as the dog barked and growled in response, suspicious. "We're almost there."

"I know where we are," Colby muttered, digging the fuzzy end of a package of peanut butter crackers out of his inside pocket and slipping a couple through the chain link. "I grew up here, same as you." Alma wasn't the kind of place people left, as a general rule. Colby didn't have to try real hard to picture them all in ten years, still living with their parents and working jobs that were mostly bullshit, spending every weekend trying to outrun their own boredom just like they had since they were little kids setting stuff on fire in the parking lot outside their Cub Scout meetings at the Knights of Columbus hall. Probably the idea should have bothered him more than it actually did, Colby thought, jogging across the blacktop to catch up. But there were worse things in life than knowing exactly what to expect.